Free Digital Copy of *Project RM: Genesis*

Thank you for buying *Project Renaissance Man*. To receive a free digital copy of *Project RM: Genesis* (the first serial of the Project RM origin series), early access to new content, and bonus content, become an RM at https://projectrm.com/become-an-rm/.

PROJECT RENAISSANCE MAN

A PROJECT RM NOVEL

PETER A. SCHOEMANN

Editing by Phyllis Ungerleider and Natasha Simons

Cover design and interior design by Xavier Comas

Peter A.Schoemann
PROJECT RENAISSANCE MAN

An Eck-Schoe Productions and Publications, LLC book

To my Renaissance woman, Christine Eckstein.
Thank you for making all of our dreams come true.

Acknowledgements

I would like to express my deepest gratitude to my wife, Christine, and our children, Kate', David, Kenny, and Ava. Not only did they serve as the inspiration for many of the characters' strongest and most interesting traits, but they also provided the strength that kept me going through this fun, yet extensive, process.

I had a lot to learn about writing when the inspiration for the Project RM novels first struck me. While I look forward to continuing to learn in the future, I'd like to thank those who have helped me produce a book that I love. Patricia Eckstein has been there since my first draft and has read this book almost as many times as me. Lauren Levy comes in a close second for number of reads. I also appreciate the suggestions from David Blews, Ken Eckstein, Fred Gaines, and many others. Of great importance are the editors who have reviewed this book—from the structural, content, and other edits by Phyllis Ungerleider to the content and proof edits by Natasha Simons. I'd like to thank both editors for asking tough questions and improving both the flow of this story and my prose. I'd also like to thank Natasha for her expertise on the Project RM: Genesis serials. Thank you, as well, to the Seminole County Novel Group of Writers, a great collection of writers who helped me in so many ways, from crafting a synopsis to improving many of my favorite scenes.

Compared to the years I've spent learning how to improve my writing, the publishing piece is very new to me. Thank you to Ashley Eckstein for all the suggestions and steering me to both editors and to Jeremy Gallas. Jeremy has been a great help in formulating a cohesive plan to inform others about this book, including the website and social media. On design, thank you to Xavier Comas for such unique, exciting covers, as well as for such a professional job on interior design.

The martial arts aspects of the book mean a great deal to me. Thank you to Kwan Jang Nim (Grand Master) David Turnbull for your expert tutelage for more than a decade. Also, thank you to Steve Blanton for creating comBATON and for your permission to use this exciting, young sport and its name in Project RM.

Finally, I'd like to thank the readers. Writing this book gave life to the characters. By reading the story, you help give the characters' lives meaning.

PROLOGUE

[SATURDAY, OCTOBER 24, 2020, 2:15 P.M.]

A graveyard. Zoe Cane couldn't get the image out of her head as she watched the hundreds of people going about their daily lives across the park—children playing with their parents, friends relaxing on the ground, tourists heading into museums. She shook her head to regain her focus.

"Dad!" she yelled.

Her fingers squeezed the handle of her infant son Matthew's stroller as she pressed forward across the crunching gravel in the center of the National Mall. All the while, she searched the stretches of worn grass on either side—from the Washington Monument rising high in the west to the United States Capitol gleaming atop the edge of the Hill to the east, in front and beyond the yellow and red, baring elms running the length of either side. Her eyes scoured the mile-long park, a thin valley clearing amidst the government's normal urban landscape of glass and stone.

The crisp fall breeze penetrated her bones, her thin lab coat and blonde hair fluttering behind each step. Like her feet, Zoe's mind raced: *Where is he? How can he be offline now?*

Nearby, a song ended on someone's radio. The DJ's announcement broke through the normal everyday sounds. "All is calm after the calamity at last night's game."

She screamed, "Dad. Dad. Where are you?" Her cries captured the attention of bystanders, who stopped and stared. "Dad. Joseph."

Tears streamed down Matthew's puffy cheeks.

"Miss. Miss, what's wrong?" an elderly man asked. "Can I help?"

She stared at the stranger's sun-blotched face. There was nothing he, or even she, could do to save him or the masses. She mumbled, "No. Nothing."

She offered a slight nod and resumed her search. More and more people stared as she screamed and scrambled, stopping every few minutes to try and reach her father on his Neural—a nanocomputer implanted behind the left ear of each member of their agency. She thought, *Joseph Solomon: Urgent. Respond immediately.* As she composed and sent each message, she knew she was exhibiting the typical Neural stare. Her body frozen and her vision appearing to drift far into the distance, she would resemble one of the many statues in the city.

Suddenly, she was shaken from her trance by her friend Linda Stryker. "Zoe. Zoe, what's wrong?" Linda asked, reaching out and grabbing Zoe's arm. Her husband Dan, and their eight-year-old son Rex, looked at her wide-eyed.

Zoe stared at Linda and mumbled, "It's happening."

"What? What's happening?" Linda said.

"Code 62."

"What?" Linda shouted. She looked at her husband and back at Zoe. "Let's get inside."

Zoe pulled away. "I have to find my father. He's out here."

"I'll contact him on my Neural," Dan said.

"Don't you think I've tried?" she snapped, then softened her tone. "He's not responding."

"We've got to get inside, now," interrupted an imposing voice. Zoe turned to see her husband, Eric Cane, whose pale complexion matched those of the group. "It's here."

"What's here?" Dan asked. "And what happened to your face?"

Eric's deep-set eyes focused on the group. "We've been monitoring some kind of storm that just formed nearby." He pointed at the low, dark cloud bank that had suddenly appeared over the horizon. They watched in horror as the lightning-filled anomaly engulfed the United States Capitol and sped down the Hill toward the park.

Little Rex cried out in fear.

The Capitol's emergency sirens began to wail. The crowd's screams matched their intensity as everyone scattered, many colliding with one another.

"Let's go. Now," Eric commanded.

"Not without my father."

"There's no time." He grabbed the stroller, broke the huddle, and led the charge through the masses. Zoe sprinted after him. Dan and Linda followed, but fell behind as they dragged their petrified son.

Eric raced toward the Metro escalator, which fed down into the Smithsonian subway station—a station that hid the entrance to the secret underground government facility in which they lived.

The mob continued to clamor for safety. But as the storm engulfed the park and consumed the crowd, the deafening screams diminished.

The fog closed in on them. Eric reached the stalled Metro escalator, pulled Matthew from his stroller, and darted down into the darkness. When the group reached the bottom, Eric looked at Zoe. Sobbing, she simply grabbed their son and ran.

Eric looked back. "I'll help Dan and Linda."

Zoe raced the final fifty feet to a brown, metal door. She wrapped her hand around the biometric knob sensor and the entrance to the facility swung open. Eric followed within seconds. He pulled Rex through the door, slammed it shut, and pressed a button to seal it.

Out of breath, Zoe said, "Dan…Linda. What have you done?"

"Mom, Dad," Rex screamed, reaching for the door.

Also short of breath, Eric grabbed Rex. "I'm sorry…It's too late. It can't be opened." Rex's clenched fists pounded Eric's chest. Eric held tight and looked at his wife. "They got caught up in the melee. We barely escaped." He grabbed Rex's flailing arms. "Your parents yelled for me to get you in here. If we hadn't sealed the door, you and every last person in here would have been lost." He released his grip. "I only hope it holds."

Rex continued to shriek, tears streaming out of his rash-red eyes. He took a brief look at the Cane family in front of him and bolted down the hallway into the facility.

Eric grabbed Zoe's shoulder to prevent her pursuit. "Let him go," he said.

Both of them looked back at the door, waiting to see what would happen. Waiting to see if the storm would invade their sanctuary.

Minutes of nausea and hundreds of heart palpitations later, she sniffled and dried her cheeks with her arm. "I guess that's it. It's all over."

Eric stared at the floor for a moment, then stood up straight. "No. It's just beginning."

DELIVERY

[MONDAY, AUGUST 31, 2037, 5:55 A.M.]

Matthew lay on the satin sheets of his four-post bed, dazed by the sight before him. He blinked twice. No, he wasn't hallucinating. "Mom?" "My brave son." Her arms rose in welcome.

He leapt out of bed and embraced her, his aversion to physical contact forgotten. His tears—the first he'd cried in sixteen years—were warm as they streamed down his face. "You died. You're dead."

"There'll be time to explain later."

Matt squeezed his mother once more, then fell back onto his bed. He looked into her glistening, light-blue eyes. The thumping in his chest eased.

His mother leaned down, placed her index finger over his mouth, and sat next to him. "I don't have much time. We've risked a lot to deliver this message to you. Listen carefully." Matt nodded. "Today, your life is going to change in ways you can't imagine. By the end of the week, you will have a choice. The decision you make will affect everyone."

"What do you mean?"

She smiled. "I know you fear failing in front of the RMs. And you're afraid of having to follow in your father's footsteps to become president one day."

He turned away. "How? How could you know that?"

"That's not important. You're stronger and more capable than you realize."

"So you think I can do it. That I can be an RM and a good president."

Her hand squeezed his knee. "Of course. You would be *great*. But the path you take now is up to you."

"The path?"

"Yes. And once you choose, you won't be able to turn back. It's a matter of life and death." His chest tightened. "Trust your instincts and you'll make the right choice." A far-off buzzing interrupted their conversation. She placed her hand on his. "Remember: to reach the beginning, you must achieve the end." The buzzing grew louder. "I believe in you. We believe in you."

Matt opened his eyes to a dark room. He sat up, then dropped his face into his sweaty palms. Mother.

A little over an hour later, Matt sped down the street that bordered the National Mall. The U.S. Capitol loomed in front of him, and the Washington Monument towered behind. He flew by the glass and stone façades of the Smithsonian museums on his left, and the green fields and aged elms on his right. The scent of freshly cut grass hung in the air, as the robotic tools—all solar-powered, all green, and all silently doing their jobs—trimmed the bushes, mowed the lawns, and cleaned the walkways and streets. Every so often, a supply drone the size of a young child flew by overhead.

If there had been any bystanders, they would have thought Matt looked the picture of confidence. His shoulders stood tall and his eyes focused straight ahead—although they were accented underneath by dark circles, like everyone else in the hard-working community. Here was a young man that nothing could distract. Not the beautiful sights and fresh scents. Not the silent precision of the technology around him.

With the help of his gliders—shoes that allowed him to hover inches above the ground and worked like invisible rollerblades—he continued forward. Yet, even with his Neural's community interface turned off for privacy, he could not escape his growing fear. As he sped to the Speech, it felt as if he were gliding closer and closer to a precipice—a longstanding dread that the dream of his mother had amplified. He needed a reality check. He stopped at the RM Monument, which was one of the few structures added to the city after the Storm. It had replaced the statue of Ulysses S. Grant. Like Matthew's jet-black hair and his now-dry, chiseled cheeks, the bronze memorial gleamed in the morning sun. The statues of the RMs stared out toward the National Mall from in front of the Reflecting Pool. He read the plaque secured at the foot of the statue of his father, front and center:

Dedicated to those few who execute the RM Mission

Preserving thousands of years of progress
and billions of silenced voices.

Project Renaissance Man, est. 1962.

Matt forced himself to stare into the eyes of his statue-father, but it didn't inspire him with confidence. Today he would begin his last year of school—the last year before he would likely become a trainee in Project RM. The last year before the RMs learned the truth his dream-mother didn't know—that Matt was a fraud.

After all, each of the remaining forty-four RMs was a prodigy, and not in just one discipline. Each was a living example of Leonardo Da Vinci. Beginning in 1962 and continuing until the Storm in 2020, the United States government had chosen each of these Renaissance men and women for a secret program: Project RM. The government had tasked them with the mission of maintaining civilization in the wake of an extinction-level event, and they had done so after the Storm—exceedingly well. They had led the few hundred remaining humans in executing the mission. His maternal grandfather, the late Joseph Solomon, had founded Project RM, and after the Storm, Matt's father, now-President Eric Cane, had led the community from chaos to prosperity. Matt's pride in what they'd accomplished was equal to his current shame. Matt was smart, but not a genius. He had all of the pedigree and none of the prodigy. Everyone knew he was no Renaissance man—in fact, none of his generation were—but the RMs, and his father in particular, still had high expectations for him. Soon, they would all know what he knew. As much as he needed to please his father, he could not meet those expectations. If the mission were left in his hands, they would fail.

Matt took one last look at his father's resolute face and again sped off. He stopped at the bottom of the broad, stone steps of the Library of Congress and tried to shake the doubts from his head. He raced up toward the heavy, bronze doors, pushing them open. Realizing he had made it in time for the Speech, he relaxed, taking in the fresh aroma that pumped through all the city's air-conditioning systems. Today's scent was morning mountain air, his favorite. When he closed his eyes, he felt as if he were a thousand miles away, the soft, cool breeze skimming off his skin as he peered down on a misty valley. At least, that's what Matt imagined, never having experienced an actual mountain or valley. He released his shoulders and unclenched his jaw, which he hadn't realized had been clamped since his visit to the monument.

The grandeur of the Great Hall beyond the archway never failed to overwhelm Matt's senses, even after years of coming there. The enormous room contained ample space to hold the diminished remains of humanity, and, with Matt's arrival, it now pretty much did.

Two stories of white marble archways and columns framed the dark, marble floors. The ceiling, composed of stained-glass windows, depicted the sky—blue surrounding a yellow sun, the radiance of the real sun filtering through each window. On all sides beyond the archways, an ornate pattern of tile mosaics filled the vaulted ceilings, illustrating various advancements in civilization. In front of the archways on either side rose two ornate marble staircases. Small cherub statues adorned the rising banisters, each depicting an important feature of civilization.

Everyone in the room wore multi-weather uniforms—khaki pants, a black belt, and a collared athletic shirt. The color of the shirt varied: green for Matt and the other students, brown for the homeroom teachers, red for the members of the Intelligence Department (ID) and the RMs, and white for everyone else. A five-pointed star overlaid by the letters ID adorned the left chest of each member of that specific department's shirt. In place of the star insignia, the RMs' shirts displayed their special emblem, which resembled a censored version of Da Vinci's drawing of the Vitruvian Man—an encircled man, his arms and legs stretched out. To promote balance, the yin and yang swirl split the circle—the bottom half black and the top half white, while the colors of the person contrasted with black above the swirl and white below. Between the top of the man's head and the top of the circle sat the insignia, a reverse R and an M back to back on the stem of a capital P. Only the president's shirt displayed any other unique quality, with a thin black stripe running down each sleeve.

Matt exchanged T-salutes with each friend and neighbor he passed. The RMs had instituted the T-salute after the Storm. Instead of shaking hands or bowing to show respect, people greeted one another with their forearms raised in front of their chests, forming a lower case t—left arm horizontal, right arm vertical, and both hands curled into fists. Matt's father had explained the new gesture in his 2036 Speech:

The T stands for tradition, technology, together. Our mission focuses us on tradition. Tied closely to our hearts and held level, the left arm symbolizes our mission to preserve the traditions and achievements of billions. By maintaining the buildings, the practices, and the institutions we inherited, we can succeed in our mission. Thrust upward, the right arm symbolizes our ceaseless efforts to advance technology so that the human race may once again flourish. Our fists remind us of the strength we each hold. When we salute each other, we acknowledge that we succeed only if we work together.

Matt spotted his father speaking with the vice president. True to tradition, Eric stood halfway up the right-hand staircase. He was in position for the Speech, his annual, inspirational call for continuing commitment to the RM mission.

Eric maintained an athletic build, and Matt followed suit. But while many said Matt had inherited his grandfather Joseph Solomon's looks, over time, Eric Cane had developed a more austere appearance, accented by his deep, dark eyes and a scar above his right cheek. Much of the time, Matt saw his father more as President Eric Cane and less as his dad. Vice President Hank Silverman stood in stark contrast to President Cane. He was a short, stout man with white hair. The vice president's endless chatter was a force in and of itself, causing him to rock backwards as he spoke, his feet rebalancing themselves before he toppled over.

The Speech topped Matt's list of favorite community traditions. Each year, his father's oratory motivated Matt to want to overcome his fears and make his father proud. Judging by the crowd's loud chatter, Matt assumed the Speech did the same for everyone. He approached his father and saluted him. "Hello, sir."

"Nice of you to join us, son," Eric said. "Cutting it a little close, aren't you?" He nodded at the vice president, who saluted them and joined everyone else below.

"Sorry about that, sir. The time got away from me. Well, sir, I wanted to wish you luck on the Speech. Of course, we all know you don't need it."

"Thank you, Matthew. I'll always accept a little luck." An almost devious smile crept onto his father's face. "I'm afraid, however, you've already heard the last Speech as a student in *this* school. And it is now *I* who *wish* you luck this morning."

Confused, Matt asked, "For what, sir?"

As if on cue, Principal Aaron Franklin joined them. Like Matt and his father, the principal was a tall, thin man. Unlike them, he had a bookish appearance, accented by large square glasses that hung at the end of his long nose. Despite his haphazard look, the principal had the complete respect of all of his students. "Good morning, Matthew. How are you doing?"

Still perplexed, Matt said, "Well, sir. And you?"

"I'm doing well. I love the start of the new school year. The Speech always reenergizes everyone and reminds us of the importance of the RM mission." He turned to Eric. "Mr. President, we're ready."

Eric held his smile. "Very good." The two older men shared a look.

The principal followed Eric's signal and said, "Matthew, the president and I have agreed it's time for a change. Given that this is your last year in this school, and with the likelihood of you following in your father's footsteps after graduation, we'd like you to give the Speech this morning."

The cold breeze of the air conditioning ran through Matt, freezing him where he stood. The safety he'd felt at having one last year before being found out dissolved in an instant. In a matter of minutes, they'd all know. He noticed his father watching his reaction and feigned composure. His mind raced: *How can I give the Speech? What would I say? What would happen if I say no?* He had known this would catch up with him eventually, but today?

Principal Franklin continued, "I'm sure you'll make your father and the rest of us proud."

Eric didn't say anything at first. He held his smile, his stare focused on Matt.

Matt felt as if Eric were reading his thoughts.

After a long moment, Eric broke the silence. "Well, son? What do you say? When the opportunity presents itself—"

"Grab it," Matt mumbled. He followed with a loose T-salute to his father and took a deep breath. "I'd be honored to give the Speech." Matt then saluted the principal with a little more emphasis. "Thank you, sir."

The principal returned the gesture. "Carpe diem, Matthew."

He was doubtful he could seize anything at that moment.

The principal looked out toward the crowd. "Gentlemen, it's about that time."

Franklin transmitted instructions to Matthew via a Neural note, or N-note, as they called them. Matt followed the instructions and took his place on the stairs, midway between his father above and Principal Franklin on the midlevel landing below. He looked down to find everyone in the crowd standing in position. Another chill swept over him. The crowd formed a large square, covering the tiled picture of the sun in the center of the floor. The red of the RMs and IDs bordered the sides, the RMs at the front.

Matt knew about the surprise tests that were thrown at RM prospects. This was Matt's, clearly. How would he handle a high-pressure situation? He had only a few minutes of preliminaries to prepare an oratory that would spare him from both community-wide ridicule and his father's disappointment. Principal Franklin would lead them in the Pledge and the invocation to thank God for another successful year. He would then hand it off to the president for some introductory remarks. Then: show time.

The principal began. "Welcome to the 2037-2038 school year. We'll start with the Pledge of Allegiance." Everyone faced the large United States flag that hung from the second floor center archway across from the front doors. They placed their right hands over their hearts and recited in unison, "I pledge allegiance to the flag of the United States of America..."

Matt recited the pledge as he tried to think of what he would say. Soon, the hundreds of eyes currently focused on the flag would turn to him. And he had nothing. He clutched the banister with his left hand to keep from shaking.

He had only one choice: try to recite one of his father's past Speeches. As he began to think about which one, he spotted his friend Bobby Douglas, a bulky, young man of Matt's age and height, who held the distinction of being the world's only living African-American. Bobby pointed behind his ear to his Neural implant. Matt tried to check his messages, then remembered he had turned off the community interface. He flipped it back on and several messages from Bobby and his other friend Rich popped up. The most recent message from Bobby read: "Why aren't you responding? Rich overheard your dad. Just read this."

Quicker than expected, his father took the principal's place. Matt scanned the message. The crowd applauded as the president neared the end of his introduction. Then the cheers turned to a smattering of chuckles. Matt refocused on the room and realized no one was talking. His father reached up and nudged him, prompting him to stumble down to the landing.

In an attempt to fend off giving a Neural stare, Matt maintained a dual focus on the message and the crowd. He cleared his throat. "When I look around this Great Hall, I don't see a grandiose room built in an age long gone. You know what I see? I see my friends. No, my family. And when I look at your faces, I don't think, 'This is one good looking group of people' —although you are." Many in the crowd laughed.

Matt warmed as he absorbed the energy radiating from below. "No. When I look at your faces, I think of one word—sacrifice." He paused to let the word sink in.

"As the last remnants of humanity, each of us has had to do whatever's been asked to maintain our way of life. I'm not just talking about what each of you—RMs and non-RMs alike—has done to make this such a wonderful place to live. A place where we work together in harmony, setting the needs of the community ahead of any individual's desires. A place where thousands of years of progress by billions are kept alive by a mere few hundred.

"These sacrifices are more than anyone should be expected to handle. Led by the president," Matt said, glancing up with a smile at his father, "you've handled it with class.

"But I'm talking about a much deeper sacrifice. I'm talking about what we've all had to endure. The few hundred of us have been tasked with the responsibility of keeping billions of voices alive. Not just the seven billion who were lost on the day of the Storm, including those you

13

knew and loved. I'm also talking about those whom we've lost since." Matt paused to clear his throat as he remembered the lab accident of 2021, which had claimed the lives of his mother and Bobby's parents.

"This kind of sacrifice—keeping the memories of so many alive, while still battling forward—is one of the best things a human could ever wish to accomplish." He smiled again and scanned the crowd below. "Each of you demonstrates this achievement every day, in everything you do."

"The path to resurrecting humanity is a long one. It will take a lot of time—decades, centuries, at least—to bring our species back from the brink. Alone, any one of us would find this task overwhelming. But when I look at each of your faces, and when I see the determination there, when I think about what each of you has sacrificed in the past and what you have resolved to sacrifice in the future, I am confident of one thing. We will bring it back—bigger, stronger, better. Together, we will continue to sacrifice. Together, we will do what has to be done. Together, we will succeed."

The crowd erupted. He closed Bobby's message and glanced up once more. His father was wearing the biggest grin Matt had ever seen from their stern leader. He could almost feel his father's pride flow through him. Matt finished by saying, "I look forward to working with each of you this year and in the years to come. Thank you." The crowd cheered once more.

Matt moved up a couple of steps to allow the principal to resume his place at the landing. "Wow. That was great, Matthew. Like father, like son. This is a wonderful way to start the new school year. Now, each student should have his or her homeroom assignments. Thank you, everyone. Let's have a great year!"

Matt and his father rejoined the principal on the landing where Franklin said, "If everyone feels as inspired as I do by you, we'll do quite well this year."

Matt's eyes drifted to the audience in search of Bobby and Rich, when Eric suddenly placed an arm around his shoulder. This rare public show of affection from his father caused Matt to abandon his search. He smiled up at him.

"Well done, son," he said. "I have to get going. I'll see you tonight?"

"Yes, sir. After comBATON tryouts, which could take a few hours." ComBATON was the chosen sport of the community, a mix of martial arts, football, and basketball.

"I look forward to hearing about it," his father said, before striding down the staircase and out of the building.

"He's a busy man," Principal Franklin said.

"Yes, he is." Matt thought about how little he saw his father these days. After getting to spend a lot of time with him earlier in the summer, since mid-July he had seen his father only for an occasional meal and at comBATON practice, where his father helped Matt and his friends prepare for the upcoming season.

The principal placed a hand on Matt's shoulder, causing Matt to flinch. The principal said, "You had me worried there for a second. But you really came through. I look forward to seeing what you do in Project RM."

The color that had flooded into Matt's face during the speech now drained back out. His friends had saved him, for the moment. But how could he do it on his own every day? "Thank you, sir. Well, sir...I don't want to be late for class."

"Thank you, Matthew. Have a great day."

"You too, sir."

THE ASSISTANT

[MONDAY, AUGUST 31, 2037, 8:13 A.M.]

Matt ran to homeroom, his steps echoing on the marble floor of the south corridor. Before he rounded the corner into the stuffy Members of Congress Room, a high-ceilinged room with dark, oak paneling and two marble fireplaces, the familiar scent of roses greeted him. The source was Lori Ford, an attractive, young woman who was well rounded both academically and physically. As soon as he entered, she embraced him, stood on her toes, and planted her standard, cheerful, red-lipsticked kiss on his cheek. Her silky, blonde hair flowed over his shoulder. Despite having taught himself to not pull away or tense up at his girlfriend's touch, this time Matt retreated.

"Is everything all right?" she asked in her usual sweet, albeit quiet, voice.

"Sorry, I'm just trying to sort out what just happened."

"What's to sort?"

Matt realized she thought he meant her greeting. His face flushed as he hugged her back. "Not that. I meant the Speech."

"Oh. You did a great job. My parents are so proud of you." Her father was the director of the Department of Agriculture and a close confidant of his father's. "I bet your dad is, too." She leaned in and whispered, "See? You've got nothing to worry about."

Lori's friend, Stephanie Mendel—a taller version of Lori, who always seemed to be by her side—said, "Are you kidding? I don't think your father could have done better."

Before Matt could figure out what to say, Bobby joined the circle of praise. He wore his typical, contemplative look, his chin perched on his left hand and his left elbow resting on his right. He removed his hand from his chin and said with sincerity, "Great delivery."

The end of Bobby's speech had suggested that Matt not tell anyone who had written it. But Matt couldn't take any more praise for words that did not belong to him. He opened his mouth to credit Bobby, but a sarcastic voice chimed in from behind.

"Now, that's what I call leaving it all on the floor. Look at him, he's speechless." The voice belonged to Richard Fox, Jr., the son of the director of the ID. He was thin like Matt, but the resemblance ended there. Even though he stood several inches shorter, his reddish-blond hair and light freckles always stood out in a crowd, especially when he cackled at his corny brand of humor.

Everyone's focus turned from Rich to Matt. Bobby and Rich gave slight headshakes, which reinforced Bobby's suggestion to say nothing about how they'd just saved him.

Rich slapped Matt on the back. "Maybe you should run against your father."

Matt said, "Slow down. It was just a speech." He wanted to add, And it wasn't even mine.

Lori said, "Yeah, Rich. Don't be ridiculous. Matthew should graduate before he runs for president."

Matt started to whisper to Lori that she wasn't helping, when a tall, bony woman in her mid-forties entered the room—their homeroom teacher and Bobby's adoptive mother, Elizabeth Peterson. Her hair was the same rich brown as her shirt, as were her eyes, which now trained themselves on Matt. Whenever she did this, Matt felt as if she were peering into his innermost thoughts.

"Good morning, everyone," she said in her high-pitched, nasal tone. From anyone else, Matt might have found her voice annoying, but he did not mind it from her. She took great interest in him and her other students, always providing useful advice. "Welcome back. Because of that rousing Speech, we have an abbreviated class today. I trust each of you hasn't forgotten your seating assignment over the summer?" The room was configured in a circle of twelve dark, wooden seats, each with a matching desk in front. Mrs. Peterson sat at her larger desk, positioned in front of one of the room's fireplaces. Matt sat opposite Mrs. Peterson, between Lori and Rich.

For the past thirteen years, Mrs. Peterson had instructed eleven students—the same eleven students, with the same seating assignments. The RMs had implemented the school system after the Storm. Like almost everything else in their community, in keeping with the RM mission, the new system retained parts of the old with modifications for efficiency. Given that there were no longer any full-time teachers, several adults taught one class each and the rest of the day focused on their professions. One teacher was designated a student's homeroom teacher throughout his or her schooling. This format allowed the home-room teacher to get to know the students and vice versa, fostering a relationship of trust and openness. In Matt's case, this had worked well. He felt he could confide in Mrs. Peterson about anything, even when he would not confide in anyone else, including his father. In fact, only Lori and Mrs. Peterson—and apparently Matt's dream-mother—knew his innermost fears.

"I'm sure you're excited this is your last year of school," Mrs. Peterson said. Her gaze landed on Rich's grinning face. "Some more than others. Who can tell me rule six?"

"Peterson's rule six—planning greatly increases your chance of success," Rich recited.

"Very good, Richard. As we start, I'd like to know each of your plans for this year."

Rich and Bobby both gave the same answer: win the comBATON championship. Lori and Stephanie spoke about working on impressive projects. A couple of students talked about following in their parents' footsteps. Matt was last.

He smiled at Bobby and Rich. "Everyone knows what I want."

Together, everyone said, "The comBATON championship." The entire room laughed.

Matt restrained a shudder at the thought of his father's goal for him: to qualify as the new RM trainee. Before the Storm, the government had found as many prodigies as it could to add to the project. But after the Storm, everything changed. They didn't have sufficient resources to train as many RMs as before and they lacked a source of prodigies. But they had decided to continue the program, admitting one person per year—the best and brightest—into Project RM.

Mrs. Peterson seemed to focus on Matt when she said, "Although this will be my last year as your teacher, I want each of you to know I will always be here for you. If you need anything, just contact me." Matt observed the other students' intent faces. He did not doubt they would take her up on her offer. He knew he would.

After a short pause, Mrs. Peterson said, "Each of you should receive your schedule any moment." Like clockwork, Matt received his schedule in an N-note. Matt's read:

To: Matthew Cane
From: Elizabeth Peterson
Date: August 31, 2037
Subject: Course Schedule

Dear Matthew,

Below is your schedule. I know it's similar to your prior schedules and that your father has lofty goals for you. You did well this morning. Your delivery was inspiring. Please remember: Always be prepared for unexpected changes. You can accomplish anything if you believe and persevere. I will always be there for you.

Course Schedule: Cane, Matthew (Year 14)

Monday	Tuesday	Wednesday	Thursday	Friday
Homeroom-Peterson 7:30 A.M. to 9:00 A.M.	Homeroom-Peterson 7:30 A.M. to 9:00 A.M.	Homeroom-Peterson 7:30 A.M. to 9:00 A.M.	Homeroom-Peterson 7:30 A.M. to 9:00 A.M.	Homeroom-Peterson 7:30 A.M. to 9:00 A.M.
Science & Technology Farmer 9:15 A.M. to 11:00 A.M.	Advanced Mathematics Harrison 9:15 A.M. to 12:00 P.M.	Science & Technology Farmer 9:15 A.M. to 11:00 A.M.	Advanced Mathematics Harrison 9:15 A.M. to 12:00 P.M.	Science & Technology Farmer 9:15 A.M. to 11:00 A.M.
Lunch 11:00 A.M. to 12:00 P.M.	Lunch 12:00 P.M. to 1:00 P.M.	Lunch 11:00 A.M. to 12:00 P.M.	Lunch 12:00 P.M. to 1:00 P.M.	Lunch 11:00 A.M. to 12:00 P.M.
Government Cane 12:15 P.M. to 2:00 P.M.	Human Achievement Michaels 1:15 P.M. to 4:00 P.M.	Government Cane 12:15 P.M. to 2:00 P.M.	Human Achievement Michaels 1:15 P.M. to 4:00 P.M.	Government Cane 12:15 P.M. to 2:00 P.M.
Medicine McCurie 2:15 P.M. to 4:00 P.M.		Medicine McCurie 2:15 P.M. to 4:00 P.M.		Medicine McCurie 2:15 P.M. to 4:00 P.M.

P.S. I know you will be a great leader. All you need to do is trust yourself and rely on those whom you trust.

Matt tensed up as he looked over his schedule. He knew the purpose behind the intense course load his father had chosen for him. His father had pointed out on multiple occasions that knowledge of these subjects would be of great benefit to someone who wished to become an RM and eventually, president. He exhaled at one thought. At least two people believed he could achieve his father's goals, even if one had been a product of his imagination. He eased back into the chair and wondered if the dream had been an omen. Even if Bobby had written the speech today, Matt had stood in front of the world and delivered it on a moment's notice. This hope carried him for a minute, before a Neural reminder popped up. He had ten minutes to report to Science & Technology in the Museum of Natural History, about halfway up the Mall.

Lori smiled at him. "I've gotta run. See you at lunch?"

"Sure." He smiled back, said goodbye to Mrs. Peterson, and followed Lori out.

With no time to spare, he stepped into a classroom much different than his homeroom. The sunlight poured through the windows and onto a lab setup that included six workstations with two stools at each, with two more at the front for the teacher and his assistant.

Outside of homeroom, each specialty class held students of all ages. The RMs had found this style of teaching efficient, as long as the older students understood their duty to help the younger students and the classes remained small enough for individualized attention. During the first day of each specialty class, the teacher would select a senior to be the teacher's assistant. The assistant would help the teacher ensure each student progressed to the fullest of his or her ability and, in many cases, would help teach the class. He expected Dr. Farmer to select Rich, the senior most adept at science, although Stephanie and a couple of others had a shot.

Matt made his way to one of the stools next to Rich at a table in the middle of the room. But before he could reach the safety of that stool, Dr. Farmer called Matt to his desk. Dr. Farmer, like the principal, was more academic than athletic. His graying hair added to his image as one of the most experienced scientists. Like all of the students, he wore a white lab coat while in the classroom. Dr. Farmer's hands were fidgeting, as always. Matt had the feeling they might declare their independence from his wrists. "Congratulations, Matthew. You did a fine job today."

"Thank you, sir." Matt began to turn to claim his seat.

"Wait, I'd like to give you today's lesson plan."

Matt's stomach tightened. "Why, sir?"

"Because you're my assistant, of course."

Matt looked back at Rich and asked in a low voice, "What? Are you sure, sir?"

"Of course, Matthew."

"Sir," he whispered, leaning in, "I know my father thinks I can do this, but everyone would be better off with someone else. Rich, maybe?"

Dr. Farmer's hands stopped long enough for him to touch Matt's shoulder, which tensed him further. "It's in your blood. You'll do a great job."

Matt thought again of his late mother and grandfather, both accomplished scientists. How could he compare to them? "I'll try, sir," he mumbled.

Dr. Farmer said, "I know you will. Carpe diem, Matthew."

I know, he wanted to reply, as he received an N-note with the plan and a script for the first day. "Wait, sir," he whispered to Dr. Farmer.

"Yes?"

"You want me to teach today?"

Dr. Farmer stared at Matt, but said nothing.

Another test, Matt realized. He nodded, inhaled, and turned to face the class. He began off script. "Good morning, everyone. I can't believe it's still morning."

Everyone chuckled as they responded with a good morning of their own.

Once again, Matt absorbed the energy that emanated from his audience. He jumped right into a question and answer session. "Who can tell me some of the projects that have come out of this class?" Eddie Sanford, the sixteen-year-old son of the communications director, raised his hand. Matt nodded in his direction.

"Weren't our gliders one of the first projects to come out of this class?"

"That's right. Do you know how the gliders were invented?"

"Yes, sir. Through Dr. Farmer's innovation of splitting the students into teams, a group of students developed them as a class project."

"That's right. But did you know the gliders were developed and tested in this room?"

"No. How could they have been? The electromagnetic field in our gliders works only with the electromagnetic tracks in the streets around the Mall and Capitol Hill."

"But before the tracks were laid in the streets, test tracks were laid in this room."

"Really?"

"You don't believe me? Try it out."

"You mean the track still works?"

Matt walked over to a switch in the corner of the room and flipped it on. "Go ahead."

Eddie stood up, turned on his gliders, and began to coast around the lab stations. Everyone seemed to enjoy the strange sight of someone gliding around inside. At the slightest tilt in any direction, the gliders produced a stronger magnetic field in the opposite direction, propelling him in the direction of the tilt.

He glided around the desks, like a pre-Storm racecar driver at Le Mans. The students began to clap, and Eddie smiled at his fans. Distracted, he ran out of space and collided with Dr. Farmer's station. "Sorry, sir," Eddie said as he picked himself up off the floor.

Dr. Farmer eyed him for a moment and then burst into laughter. Everyone else followed suit, including Eddie. "How long have you known about the track, Matthew?" Dr. Farmer asked.

"My father told me about it a long time ago. Talking about the gliders reminded me of the story. He told me they were intended to create efficiency, while still providing exercise."

"That's right," Dr. Farmer said. "And there's one more piece to the story. Can anyone tell me which scientist thought of the idea for the gliders?" Matt had wanted to avoid that discussion, as he didn't want to highlight his own family member. But Dr. Farmer had no such problem.

After a few moments, it was clear no one knew. "No one? Let me ask you this. Who can tell me the RM who invented many of our technologies and made many exciting discoveries?" Several students' hands shot up. He pointed to the bright, young Albert Stephenson in the first row. "Yes, Albert?"

"Dr. Joseph Solomon, sir?"

"That's correct. Matthew's grandfather. As he put it, 'They'll keep our feet out of the puddles when it rains.'" Everyone laughed. "I worked on one of Dr. Solomon's teams before the Storm," Dr. Farmer said, smiling at the memory. "He came up with some crazy ideas. Usually, though, his ideas produced great innovations. With his leadership, Project RM advanced technologically well beyond the outside world." The doctor looked at Matt. "He was one of the greatest men I ever knew. Had he survived the Storm, he would have surpassed Da Vinci himself." Looking back at the class, he added, "This class is modeled after the way Dr. Solomon ran his teams. Can anyone tell me another innovation created by Dr. Solomon and his teams?"

Several students raised their hands. Dr. Farmer pointed to Scottie Simpson, a fourteen-year-old boy. "Our Neurals."

"That's right. He and his teams used nanotechnology to develop our tiny brain implants. And then there's the amazing technology it took to create Discs. Dr. Solomon's teams created the Disc Writer, which bakes artificial neurotransmitters onto Discs. Through consumption, the neurotransmitters deliver information to your Neural. As he put it, this technology gives you the information off the tip of your tongue. These amazing innovations allowed a few hundred people to have a real possibility of achieving the RM mission. The more you look around, the more you'll find his impact continues to be felt long after he has gone."

Dr. Farmer fell silent, staring at the students. Then, he said, "As this school year starts, think about the lasting impact one person can have on the world. I'm not suggesting we can all be a Dr. Solomon. He was the definition of a Renaissance man. What I'm trying to impress on you is: to be a good scientist, you must be creative. And then maybe, with the help of your team, you too can make a huge impact on the world." He looked back at Matt one more time. "Sorry for the interruption, Matthew. Please continue." Dr. Farmer retook his seat.

Matt wondered, as he often had when he was young, how great it would have been to work on one of his grandfather's teams, or at least to have known his grandfather. After a brief pause, Matt resumed. "No problem, sir. Thank you. That was very helpful. Okay, now we'll break into our groups, after which each group will spend the next three weeks determining your innovation projects. The only rule for the projects is the hypothesized innovation must be something that will benefit our community operations or the RM mission. One more thing: beginning on Wednesday, we'll spend the first hour and a half of each class learning science. So today will be the only day you have to spend the whole class on your projects. Don't waste it."

After organizing himself at his new workstation, he spent the remainder of class moving from station to station to discuss the students' initial thoughts on their projects.

At the end of class, the students received the lunch popup reminder on their Neurals.

To get to the café for lunch, they had to walk through Matt's favorite place in the city—the Sculpture Garden, which had as its centerpiece a large circular fountain with eight streams of water shooting into the center. Matt could sit for hours on one of the stone benches that circled the fountain. He loved to meditate to the rushing water and the breeze rustling through the surrounding trees.

Rich and Matt approached the glass-walled café, where Matt caught Rich admiring his reflection in the door. Matt snickered, "Don't worry. You're perfect."

Rich gave him a small shove. "I know."

"But seriously, thanks for this morning."

"I tried to get to you when you came in, but my father wouldn't let me leave my spot."

"No problem. You and Bobby saved my butt."

Rich glanced at Matt's backside. "I'm sorry, but there's not much to save."

"Funny. And here I was about to apologize about the assistantship."

"Don't worry about it," Rich said as they entered the sunny café.

The tables formed a sort of flattened U, with many tables on the sides and fewer tables near the entrance, behind which lay the serving counter and the open kitchen. They joined Lori and Bobby, who had already arrived from their Agriculture class and were sitting at a corner table. They overlooked the fountain in front and, out the side, the massive stone-columned edifice of the National Archives—the repository for some of the most cherished documents of freedom, including the Magna Carta, the Declaration of Independence, and the United States Constitution. Matt sat next to Lori. He said to her, "Congratulations. Bobby sent me a message you got the assistantship in Agriculture. That's great."

"Thanks, but it probably had something to do with my father being the teacher."

Bobby said, "Don't be silly. You deserve it."

"Thanks. Matthew, congratulations on the S&T assistantship. That's not even your best class. You'll probably get it in Government, too."

Matt exhaled. "One's enough. Besides, you know the rule—no more than one assistantship per student."

Rich said, "It's happened once before. Something tells me they'll change the rule for you."

Matt shook his head. "I don't think so. And it should've been you in S&T. Maybe you'll get Government."

"I already said, don't worry about it. I plan to get into the family business after school." Everyone knew Rich wanted to follow his father as head of the ID. He made no secret about how he loved to fiddle with his father's gadgets. Since he could talk, he had pestered his father with questions about his job. "I don't think I need an assistantship in Government to do that. But it might help you in following your father."

"Who says I want to?"

Rich opened his mouth to speak, but Lori cut him off. "Don't be silly. You'll make a great president. After this morning, I'm sure everyone thinks so."

Matt frowned. You wouldn't say that if you knew it was Bobby's speech.

At the end of lunch, Lori kissed Matt on the cheek and whispered in his ear, "I believe in you." He wished he had her confidence. She winked at him, turned, and left.

Matt and Rich entered the majestic Capitol Rotunda, where their Government class was held. Instead of the normal ceilings in their other classes, the Capitol dome itself topped this room. The floor of light-brown marble reflected the historical portraits hanging on the stone wall above. Like the size of the city compared to their small population, the room almost overwhelmed this class of twelve. But the president felt its significance made it the perfect place to learn about government. The dark, wooden desks formed a semicircle of four rows of three, each facing the center of the room, where two large desks faced back.

Rich sat down next to Matt in the front row. Matt's father had delegated his teaching duties to Vice President Silverman. As the other students all took their seats, the vice president rose and said, "Good afternoon, everyone."

The class responded. "Good afternoon, sir."

He then proceeded with a forty-five minute lecture about their current form of government and its origins: about how no form before the current model had been able to bridge national, racial, and religious divisions, and about how Project RM had done so. The agency tasked with avoiding another dark age had begun a new age of enlightenment. After some time, Matt began to think the vice president would not appoint an assistant. Finally, he said, "Of course, much of the government we have today is based on the genius of one man, President Eric Cane. Matthew, you certainly showed this morning that you take after him in many ways." He paused for a moment. "Now we come to the selection of my assistant. I look around the class and see several qualified candidates. Based on his speech, Matthew would have been a good choice. Unfortunately, he's already been named assistant in Science & Technology and we no longer allow one person to be the assistant in two classes."

Thank God, Matt thought.

"So, I was faced with a dilemma." The vice president paused for dramatic effect. Matt's stomach tightened. "Matthew, I spoke with the president and we've agreed to waive that rule. Congratulations. I think we all agree you're up to the challenge."

The class clapped with approval, including Rich. "All right then, Matthew, come up to my desk and let's discuss the plans. Everyone else, please review the course selection on the origins of democracy."

Matt knew what this meant: another test. But he didn't need confidence or a script to teach Government. He knew it better than any other subject. First, he explained the way government had been structured prior to the Storm. Next, he explained how the RMs had realized the size of the community after the Storm did not lend itself well to that form of government and how they had initially developed a looser format. He quizzed the class on why that hadn't worked, then described their solution—a more centralized format. The resulting efficiency allowed everyone to focus on the RM mission.

At the end of class, Matt sent each student the schedule for the remainder of the term. He received a congratulatory N-note from Lori as he exited the Capitol. *Rich must have informed her,* he thought. He responded with a thank you, then sped down the left side of the National Mall to the Space and Aeronautical Museum, which had been partially converted to a hospital after the Storm. That location had also housed a hospital during the Civil War. Matt liked the way history repeated itself.

He approached the imposing symmetry of light stone and dark glass and stumbled over a distressing thought. What if he were named assistant in Medicine, also?

He stepped into the classroom and received a student-led chorus of, "And the new assistant is, Matthew Cane!" Matt knew it—and the laughter that followed—was good-natured humor, but prayed that would not be the case. Not only would it place too much of the spotlight on him, the work would be overwhelming. Unsure whether the burning sensation came from the heat of the large, incandescent lights above or embarrassment, Matt headed for the first available desk.

Director of Medicine Kate McCurie entered with her typical, bright disposition and called the class to order. Then, she called Matt to her desk. He approached, her fire-red hair seemingly intensifying the heat. Matt held his breath as the class began to buzz.

"I just wanted to say your Speech this morning was very impressive, Matthew. As was being named assistant in two of your classes."

"Thank you, Director." Every fiber of his being resisted a third assistantship.

"So."

A collective gasp went around the room.

"So," Director McCurie continued, "given your very full plate, I'm sure you won't mind NOT being named my assistant."

Never had Matt felt more relieved about not being chosen for something. He soaked in the cool breeze of the AC, letting out an exhale that he hoped didn't sound as loud to the class as it did inside his head. "No, Director. That's gr…that's fine." As he took his seat among the rest of the class, he fought to gain control over the grin that threatened to spread across his face.

A BLAST FROM THE PAST

[MONDAY, AUGUST 31, 2037, 4:15 P.M.]

After class, Matt glided across the National Mall to retrieve his com-BATON gear for his team's first practice. The cool air and bright, blue sky reflected his more relaxed and cheerful mood. Between the Speech and the assistantships, he had spent the day bouncing from one stressful situation to another. But his battles of the nerves lay behind him. It was time to join his friends on his team, DC3, and play comBATON.

Over the summer, he, Rich, and Bobby had received considerable coaching assistance from his father, who was known as the best com-BATON player ever. Remembering how their prior season had ended prematurely at the hands of a team of ID, the Blaze, Matt could barely contain his excitement at the chance for redemption.

The other seven teams in the league were mostly composed of players with many more years of experience. Several of the teams, including the reigning champions, the Raiders, consisted of members of the ID, whose livelihood mandated extensive martial arts training. In contrast, Matt, Rich, and Bobby still spent most of their time in school. The two substitutes and five practice team members they would select to add to the three of them after this first practice would likely be classmates. But they never considered themselves at a disadvantage. Matt felt confident that his father's coaching over the summer, combined with their relentless practice schedule, would be enough for them to win the championship.

Matt's excitement grew by the second. He rushed to grab his gear from a small comBATON washroom and storage facility—the one new building the RMs had erected since the Storm, located near the café and the fields of the Mall. The white, stone building had become known as the Shed.

Matt snatched his gear from his locker and glided toward DC3's practice field in the center of the Mall. The majesty of the location inspired him each time he set foot on the field. The Washington Monument and United States Capitol rose nearby on either side. Tall elms sandwiched the field on the other two long sides. Beyond the trees on the north side lay the multi-columned, domed Museum of Natural History, and on the south side was the red-bricked Smithsonian Castle. The old merry-go-round in front of it still operated for a few hours on most Saturday mornings.

Two pleasing sights greeted him—the first practice field of the season, and many hopefuls ready to try out. The sea of freshly cut grass had never smelled sweeter or felt more comforting under his feet.

Bobby and Rich had already set up the field. Ten cones established the rectangular boundaries of the 180-feet by 90-feet field and marked off three lines—midfield and the two goal zones, which began 40 feet from each end. In the center of each goal zone, the goal—a twelve-inch hollow, metallic tube, two inches in diameter—hovered vertically at chest level with the help of the same technology as in the gliders. To score, a player had to kick the goal, while maintaining possession of the baton—a tube similar to the goal, but used like a football.

Bobby and Rich lined up the thirteen DC3 hopefuls in two rows of four and one row of five. They stood at attention, feet together, facing the Capitol. They included Kevin Turnbull, the youngest member of the ID, who stood front and center with his shoulders back and chest out. Kevin's father, David Turnbull, was the athletic director and commissioner of the comBATON League. Commissioner Turnbull had played on the legendary ten-time comBATON championship team with Matt's and Rich's fathers. Kevin, like his father, had short, curly, reddish-brown hair and all of the desired athletic traits for this sport—height, strength, and speed. Matt hoped Kevin could be the right addition to the team to help them repeat their fathers' success.

Matt traded his gliders for the better gripping comBATON shoes and put on most of his gear, which included a paper-thin, dark-blue Kevlar chest protector and arm pads. He picked up his helmet, stepped in front of everyone, and T-saluted them. The hopefuls saluted back. About to begin, he noticed eight-year-old Johnny Ford at the end of the back row. Matt frowned at Rich and Bobby and walked over to Johnny. "Aren't you a little young for this?"

Lori's little brother stood as straight as a soldier. "I know, sir. But after hearing you speak this morning, I want to do my part."

"And do you know what we're doing?"

"Of course, sir. Playing comBATON."

"Good. Do you know what it's about?"

"Yes, sir. My father taught me. It was invented thousands of years ago as a way for nations to avoid large conflicts. By having a few soldiers from each nation play, they could avoid wars and save thousands of lives. President Cane resurrected the historic sport as a way to improve teamwork in hand-to-hand combat."

Matt said, "That's very good. But we don't use it for that today. Now it's just a game."

Rich said, "It's not just a game."

Matt said, "You're right. It's the best game. Johnny, I'm glad you want to help. But you're too young. Your father wouldn't be happy if you got hurt. Not to mention your sister. Do you understand?"

Johnny lowered his head. "Yes, sir."

Matt patted him on the back. "I felt the same way at your age. I tell you what. I'll work with you outside of practice once in a while if you want."

"I'd like that, sir."

"Great. You can play today until the contact starts. Okay?"

"Yes, sir!"

Matt returned his attention to the group. "I hope you're all as eager as Johnny. Welcome to DC3's first practice of the season. Rich, Bobby, and I are the only players remaining from last year's team. We're looking for two more players to complete the team, and this year we're adding five more for a practice squad." Matt paused, then said, "We didn't finish well last year."

Bobby said, "That's an understatement."

Matt continued, "To win the championship, we need every member of the team working together, from the practice team to the substitutes to the starters. We're going to put you through your paces today. After practice, we'll decide who made the team and N-note you with the results."

Matt watched the hopefuls' reactions. Everyone's eyes remained fixed on him. "All right, let's get started. I want you to remember two things when you're out there. First, maintain your focus. It's one thing to spar, fighting only one opponent. It's another to try to work with two teammates to score a goal, while one or more of your three opponents attack. You can face one opponent and get blindsided by another. You have to be aware of where everyone is at all times. By the time league play starts in less than four weeks, you should be able to analyze your opponents, determine the best strategies for various situations, and communicate with the team without using words—or your Neural, which as you know isn't permitted during the game. All of this will take a great deal of effort and focus."

Matt paused to let the information sink in, when an unwelcome voice with a distinctive sneer interrupted. "Hey, Cane! All this talk isn't going to make you or your team better." Matt cringed without looking. Rex Stryker. Eight years Matt's senior, he was an athletic specimen—taller and faster than Matt and stronger than Bobby. Rex always had a snide comment or put-down ready for Matt. He approached with his red-clad Raiders toting packs of comBATON equipment on their backs. "Your fathers can't help you on that field."

Matt glared at him. But Rich walked over to Rex, put an arm around his shoulders, and said, "You're right. We'll just have to do the best we can on our own. Hopefully, we can be as good as you one day."

Rex stood silently for a moment. Then, he removed Rich's arm. "There's hope for you yet, Fox." He and his teammates turned and marched off to their practice field.

Matt refused to let Rex push his buttons in front of his team. He looked back at the hopefuls and said, "Bobby, Rich, and I thank you for coming out. Good luck."

Bobby started the team on their stretching exercises. Matt walked over to Rich and whispered, "Why'd you say that?"

"What are you talking about? Shouldn't we worship the ground Rex walks on?"

Matt gave his friend a quizzical look.

Rich said, "Trust me. Just give it about five-four-three-two—" Several loud cracks sprang from Rex's direction.

Matt looked over to see fireworks exploding out of Rex's pack, his equipment crashing to the ground. These were no ordinary fireworks—colorful clouds of smoke blossomed in every direction, all over Rex's practice field and into the sky above. Everyone burst into laughter. Matt high-fived Rich. "Thanks." He walked back over to the hopefuls. "This brings me to the second point: have fun today. Playing comBATON is all about having fun."

As they warmed up, Matt continued. "We plan on winning the championship. If you can't commit to doing what you've got to do to help us win, you can leave now and no one will think less of you. Otherwise, stick around and let's see what you've got. Rich, go over the rules while they finish stretching. After he does that, Bobby will explain what you're in for today, which is what you can expect on most days if you're selected to be a member of the team."

Rich took up the narrative. "The most important rule is you must have eyes in the back of your head, because the players on the other team can blindside you and knock you out before you even realize what's happening. You'll be running with the baton, seeing everything in front of you, and then someone will get you from behind and end the play." He spun and hook-kicked Bobby, connecting his back heel to Bobby's chest and sending him reeling to the ground. He turned to look back at the group. Several of them stared at Rich with their eyes frozen wide open, a few with their mouths slightly ajar. "That's how quickly a play can end...one swift kick from out of nowhere. Sorry about that, Bobby." He helped his friend up.

"No, you're not," Bobby said, then smiled and addressed the group. "Just remember that certain spots are off limits." He faked a kick to Rich's back and, instead, landed the ball of his foot on Rich's backside.

Thrust forward and off balance, Rich said, "Hey, hey. Watch the goods." Everyone laughed.

"What goods?" Everyone laughed louder.

Matt shook his head. "Okay, you two. Let's break it up. That was a sad demonstration that you can kick someone in the front of the body and on the head where they're protected, but nowhere else. Also, we'd be penalized for kicks that are too excessive, like that one. So watch it."

Bobby added, "What's excessive is in the eyes of the official."

"Okay, let's run some drills, then scrimmage. We can discuss the rules along the way, if we need to."

The drills got progressively harder. First, they practiced passing and catching the baton, which Bobby showed was much more difficult than passing and catching a ball. He threw the baton in many ways. Each time, it flew end over end or fluttered off course. Then, he showed the only ways to throw a catchable baton. Next, they practiced scoring without a defender. In the drill, the player had to catch the baton at full speed and kick the goal without slowing down. Jimmy Smith, a short, thin blond sixteen-year-old who didn't look like he was ready for League competition, could catch the baton in stride, but had to stop and ready himself to kick the goal. "That's no good," Bobby shouted. "By the time you're ready, the defender will kick you in the chest to end the play." Jimmy nodded and sprinted back into line. Kevin had no problem scoring any type of goal. He could score three points on a simple kick, four on the jump kick, and five on the spinning jump kick. Unfortunately, he was the only one at this level of ability.

They practiced running and passing plays outside the goal zone, where the style of play was like American football before the Storm—no more than one forward pass per play. In the goal zone, they practiced basketball-like maneuvers in the crowded area, as the teams worked to score on one another.

Matt blew the whistle an hour into the drills. "Okay, that's enough. Let's see how you play against each other." He broke them into four teams of three. "You'll play five-minute games, which is only one quarter of a full game. Trust me, that'll be enough for your lungs to burn...and enough for us to make our decision."

Not surprising, the games were sloppy, as none of them had played together before. The teams rarely got past the next line—whether it was midfield or a goal zone line—in the three plays they had, resulting in constant turnovers and no flow. On a positive note, Kevin was as much of an expert at kicking opponents as he was at kicking the goal. He landed quick kicks to the baton-holder's chest, ending several plays. He even managed to land a double kick to Jimmy's chest, allowing Kevin to grapple with Jimmy and effectively reducing the game to two-on-two.

The scrimmages ended. Matt felt confident in Kevin as the first substitute, but remained concerned about who would be the other substitute, the last person who would see game action. He decided to hold one more scrimmage of the starters against the best hopefuls, Kevin, Jimmy, and Sue Johnson.

The scrimmage began as expected. Matt, Rich, and Bobby began on offense. They scored in two plays.

Matt caught his breath and noticed Lori and Stephanie on the sideline. Lori smiled and winked at Matt. He smiled and waved back.

A little further down the sideline, Matt noticed Sophie Jackson. Sophie was a year younger than Matt. He didn't know much about her, except that her parents were the directors of Food Supply and Distribution. She always looked like one of the guys, standing with her arms crossed in front of her slender body. As usual, she wore a baseball cap that concealed most of her hair, other than the brunette ponytail fed out of the opening in the back. Large glasses framed her eyes. Matt wondered why she was there. Sophie never hung around with others.

The scrimmage drew his attention again. Now, it was their opponent's chance to attempt to score. With a smothering defense by DC3, Jimmy threw an errant pass, which Matt intercepted. Before the other team knew what had happened, Matt connected a perfect flying side kick with the goal. Lori cheered and Stephanie clapped. Jimmy and Sue bowed their heads, their hands on their hips. Matt smiled at Kevin, who had sprinted back in position, stood straight, and waited for his teammates to return.

The scrimmage, which was more of a drubbing than a competition, continued in a similar fashion for several more minutes. Near the end of the game, Matt held the baton and dropped back to pass to Bobby at the sideline. But someone captured his attention—a beautiful, young woman with wavy, brunette hair that flowed over her slender shoulders. Without realizing it, Matt stopped playing. He stared into her sparkling, hazel eyes and his knees buckled. A moment later, the ground rose up and struck him in the face.

Matt awoke to the pungent odor of smelling salts under his nose. Lori held his hand. "Are you all right?" Her voice quivered.

"Yeah, except for the migraine. What happened?" Matt reached up to hold his pounding head.

Rich answered, his voice low. "You stood there staring in Bobby's direction and Kevin knocked you out with a flying side kick to your head. You hit the ground pretty hard."

Bobby asked, "Why'd you stop? I was open. You've never lost your focus like that before."

Matt looked up at Lori and said, "I'm okay. Why don't you go back to the sideline? We need to finish the practice."

She glanced toward the now empty spot where the beautiful brunette had stood. Then she stared back into Matt's eyes. "Are you sure?"

He looked away. "Yeah. I'll be fine."

She nodded, pecked him on the throbbing vein protruding from his temple, and returned to her spot next to Stephanie.

"So, why'd you stop?" Bobby asked again.

"I saw someone…someone who couldn't possibly be here."

Rich ran his fingers through his hair. "What are you talking about?"

"Before she died, my mother left me a picture of a young woman. I don't know who she is or why my mother gave it to me. I know this'll sound crazy, but I just saw her on the sideline."

"What's crazy about that?" Bobby asked.

"Guys, it's been sixteen years since my mother gave me the picture, and the person standing on the sideline looked exactly the same as in the picture. She hadn't aged a day."

"I'm not sure who you're talking about," Rich said. "Maybe your eyes were playing tricks on you. The only girl in that spot was Sophie Jackson. She would've just been born around the time your mother gave you the picture."

Matt exclaimed, "That's impossible."

Bobby said, "Yeah, and kind of weird. You know how she never takes off her cap and glasses?"

"Yeah," Matt responded.

"When you got hit, I turned to see what you might be looking at—besides me being wide open—and I saw her holding them in her hands."

"Where is she?" Matt asked, scanning the sideline.

"As soon as you began to wake up, she took off running toward her parents' office."

Rich said, "You know, she's kind of cute when she's not hiding her head and face with that old cap and glasses."

Matt's day had gone from expected stress to total confusion. How could that woman be Sophie Jackson? He barely knew her, but he knew enough about her to know she had never looked like that before. It couldn't be her in the picture—maybe it was her mother or a relative.

Matt realized everyone on the field was staring at him. He willed himself to stand and took a moment to gather his balance and thoughts. "Well, everyone. I hope you learned three valuable lessons at my expense. One, Kevin throws a mean side kick. Two, never lose focus or you could end up eating turf. And three, if you can get back up, finish what you started. Let's finish this scrimmage."

Rich and Bobby exchanged looks. Bobby asked quietly, "Are you sure you want to do this?"

"Don't worry," Matt said. He stooped down and picked up his helmet. Once again, he had to steady himself when he stood. "Let's finish them off."

Kevin approached, his hands at his sides. "I'm sorry. I thought I was aiming lower, but your body dropped a little."

"Don't worry about it. It was a clean shot. Let's get back to the game."

After the scrimmage, Matt put the team and all the hopefuls through a grueling workout. Then he reminded them of what he had said while they were stretching. "So, now that you've seen how DC3 plays, is there anyone who doesn't want to join us?"

He looked at each hopeful, eager to see if any had cracked. None had. "Okay, that's it for today. We'll let you know who's in. Good work, everyone."

As the crimson sun set behind the Washington Monument, Matt, Rich, and Bobby made their choices. They agreed on Kevin as the first substitute, but haggled over the second substitute and the practice squad. Matt wanted Jimmy as the other substitute, over Rich's objections. Rich pointed out Jimmy's obvious shortcomings in size and speed, but Matt liked Jimmy's intensity and instincts. He often seemed to be in the right place at the right time. Matt won the argument. They then added Sue and four other hopefuls to the practice squad and finished their meeting. In a brief N-note, Bobby sent the new team members a copy of the playbook, rules, and practice schedule, then sent everyone else a thank you.

Their meeting over, Bobby nudged Matt and pointed to the nearby tree. Lori sat in the dark shadows at the base of the trunk. He walked over to her. "You didn't have to wait for me."

"Yes, I did. How's your head?"

"Better," Matt said, which was partially true. The throbbing had subsided, leaving a dull soreness.

"Just to make sure, let me walk you home?"

"That's not necessary. But I'll walk you home."

She smiled. "Okay."

They glided up the desolate tree-and-row-house-lined streets toward Lori's house on Capitol Hill, the lampposts lightly illuminating the otherwise dark road. Matt didn't know what to say to her. He didn't want to explain to his girlfriend that he had gotten knocked out because he was staring at Sophie Jackson. Luckily, she didn't bring it up. After an uneasy minute, Lori asked, "So, are you ready for the two assistantships?"

"I don't know. It'll be a lot of work."

"I'm sure you'll do great. Besides, I'll help."

"I knew you would offer. But I don't want you to lose focus on your own assistantship."

"You mean like you did out on the field today?"

"Touché." He hoped she wouldn't delve deeper. Fortunately, they had just reached her house. He looked at her and realized how lucky he was.

Leaning in, he kissed Lori on the lips. She grabbed him tight and held him for a minute.

Matt started to leave, but Lori held him firmly. "Feel better, Matthew."

"I will...and thank you. Goodnight."

She released him and sweetly said, "Goodnight."

Matt couldn't stop thinking about Sophie and the picture on the way home, until he had a sudden, sobering thought: *Was that just a dream this morning, or did I really speak with my mother?*

ERIC'S CLASSROOM

[MONDAY, AUGUST 31, 2037, 8:30 P.M.]

Matt neared his house and wondered whether his father would be there, and, if so, if they would eat together. After such a long day and the strange events at practice, Matt hoped this evening would involve nothing more than some studying and sleep. The dull pain in his head remained. He was sure his father already knew about the knockout and he didn't want to face his disappointment.

Matt walked up the dimly lit, rising South Lawn to the White House and noticed the West Wing lights on—a regular occurrence, as his father often worked with his staff late into the night.

A delicious aroma greeted Matt at the door and informed him tonight would be dinner with his father. On autopilot, he followed the scent to the historic Family Dining Room. His grumbling stomach provided the only sound as he walked the empty halls. He hadn't eaten anything in almost eight hours.

The simple elegance of the dining room—the white light of the crystal chandelier hanging from the vaulted ceiling above, reflecting off of the mahogany dining table below—was accented by his father's presence at the head of the table. Next to him sat Rich's dad, who looked very similar to Rich—except that Richard Sr. rarely laughed, the corners of his mouth sagging almost as much as his worn shoulders. Eric and

Richard Sr. were speaking in low, impatient voices. Unsure of whether his father planned to have a working dinner, Matt waited at the entryway for some indication as to what he should do. Matt rarely found his father in the dining room at dinner time. Typically, he was too busy to have dinner with Matt and he made sure Matt's schedule was just as busy. When they did eat together, Matt found himself digesting his father's words more than the food. After a long minute, the two men rose and Richard Sr. exited, nodding to acknowledge Matt on his way out.

Matt's father stared through him, pointed to a chair, and spoke in his typical short, authoritative voice. "Sit down."

Matt said, "Yes, sir," and took his seat.

"And how was your day?"

"Interesting, sir."

"Yes. I'm sure it was. I know you're still uncomfortable in front of groups. But hopefully today taught you what you're capable of."

Matt thought: *If you only knew how much help I had, you wouldn't think so.*

"You did well with the Speech. And you utilized your friends well."

Matt almost spit out his drink. "Sir?"

The corners of Eric's lips curled up. "You know nothing happens in this city without me knowing."

"Then why are you congratulating me for someone else's speech?"

Matt's father shook his head. "Son, a leader doesn't do everything by himself. I made sure your friend, Rich, overheard my discussion with Principal Franklin. He and Bobby were as effective at assisting you as you were at delivering the speech."

Matt did not know how to react.

"Trust me, son. Your friends follow you. That is the sign of a good leader."

"Thank you, sir. You know, I could feel the energy of the crowd as I spoke."

His father's smile broadened for a moment, then vanished. "Good. But don't let it go to your head. That admiration will be forgotten the moment the people don't get what they think they need." His father paused. "In any event, I thought it was important for our community to start viewing you as a leader. I would suggest, however, that when you're a leader, you not rely on everyone. Bobby's words were eloquent and, in a speech, it's great to encourage everyone to help and to do his or her part. But in reality, to achieve success you'll need to rely on those who know best—the RMs."

Matt stared at his plate. Even if they were not his words, he agreed with Bobby. How could he lead if he didn't understand these basic concepts? Still, his father's view differed from Bobby's, as well as Mrs. Peterson's. Considering their positions in the community, Matt knew which one worked best. But he had to ask. Paraphrasing Mrs. Peterson, he asked, "Doesn't each person have strengths that are valuable to the community? Shouldn't we encourage everyone to use their strengths to help?"

His father responded in a calm but direct manner. "Matthew, don't misunderstand me. Everyone does help. There are plenty of tasks to be performed in our community and each person helps in his or her own way. But what I'm talking about is who chooses the tasks and how they will be performed. For that, you should rely on the brightest and most well trained. That was the reason for Project RM. Think of where we'd be without the RMs. We have the opportunity to advance humanity much farther and quicker with the RMs than we ever would have done without them."

Matt sat back and, mimicking Bobby, perched his chin on his hand. Eric continued. "Let me make it simple. If we want to help everyone, the brightest of society will do the best job leading the way."

Matt nodded.

"Keep this in mind as well, son. Within the next eight months, the cloning program should be in full swing. Within five years, we'll expand to the next great city. I believe you are the logical person to lead that expansion. You see, everything I struggle for is for you, so that you can make the difference."

Matt felt nauseated. "Isn't the plan to stay here?"

Eric stared in response.

"I mean, I thought the idea was that we would stay in this community as a deterrent. Didn't you say in the 2035 Speech that staying here in this Eden focuses us on helping one another rather than on helping ourselves?"

"Yes."

"But with the cloning, I suppose we'd have to guard against overpopulation."

Eric nodded.

"The genetic program will repopulate that fast?"

"Think about it. When it's operational, we'll be able to use the genetic material of the dead left behind. Once it gets going, we'll be able to repopulate fast, without the need for gestation periods and without the risk of interbreeding in a small population. Fast enough to require a second community, if we are going to keep the same tight-knit model."

A vision of traveling somewhere else popped into Matt's head. While he feared leading the expansion, the thought of leaving their small confines intrigued him. He could not contain a smile. "What city?"

His father answered with a broad smile of his own. "Keep this to yourself—New York. That's the next logical city to repopulate. Before the Storm, it was the financial capital of the world. Expansion there will give everyone great hope for the future." His father paused once more. "You have strong leadership ability. But ability can turn into reality only if you maintain your focus. I understand you had quite a practice today."

There it was. "Yes, sir. I guess Dr. Ford told you."

"Among others. What distracted you?"

"I'm not sure."

"You know that's not good enough." Matt held his breath and hoped his father wouldn't pry further. "If you expect to beat the best this time and reach your full potential, you'll need to remain focused at all times."

"Yes, sir."

"Good. Because a leader who doesn't understand the art of war cannot be respected by the soldiers, nor can he rely on them."

"What do you mean, sir?"

"If you want to be the leader one day and if you want the IDs to respect and support you, you need to display prowess in battle situations. Do well in comBATON and you'll have their respect and loyalty. It worked for me."

Matt thought this was an interesting piece of advice and expected he'd understand it better when he wasn't so tired.

"Lori really cares about you. How do you feel about her?"

Matt shifted in his chair. "She's fine."

"That's it?"

"No. I suppose not. She's smart, pretty, and she's always there for me...and she makes me happy."

Eric grinned. "You two make quite the team. Aren't you glad Dr. Ford and I suggested you two date one another?"

"Yes, sir. Thank you."

Having finished dinner, Matt's father dismissed him. "Matthew, even with a woman at your side, I know how lonely it can be to lead. If you ever need someone to talk to, I hope you know you can come to me."

"Thanks, Dad."

Matt entered his sanctuary, a mix of mahogany and mementos. To regain his focus, he followed his nighttime ritual. He climbed onto his bed and relaxed into the goose down. He stared at the only item on his nightstand, a picture of Lori smiling at him. He smiled back and turned his attention to the large, digital portrait on the wall across the room. It contained two images. At that moment, it reflected the triumphant smiles of his father, Richard Sr., and Commissioner Turnbull, holding up their tenth and final comBATON championship trophy. After a half minute, the image transformed into a snapshot of his father's first inauguration. His father stood tall, maintaining his usual business-like demeanor, his left hand raised and his right on the bible held by the vice president.

Far from calming him down, the sight of his mother in the background produced enough adrenaline to pop him off of his comforter and over to the built-in shelves where he kept his cherished treasures, including his lucky first pair of comBATON cleats. Matt pulled from the shelf the only item his mother had left for him before she died—a worn poetry book with a frayed binding. Inside the book was a tattered picture. The picture was of the same beautiful, young woman he had seen at practice—the same beautiful, young woman who had distracted him, then disappeared. As he had done for years, he gazed at the picture for some time, wondering. He wondered about Sophie Jackson. Had his dream-mother meant that Sophie was the drastic change? He flipped the picture over and studied the small, hand printed writing in the top-right corner: 19181201A071296. He had often thought about this sequence, but still had no clue what it meant.

After a while, Matt shook himself out of his trance. He had a lot of work to do for class and didn't want to fall behind. He slipped the picture back into the book, placed the book back onto the shelf, and got to work.

FAME TO FAILURE

[TUESDAY, SEPTEMBER 1, 2037. 6:55 A.M.]

On the second day of school, everyone returned to the routine that had been suspended for the day of the Speech—the Daily Stretch. Years earlier, the government had implemented the Daily Stretch, a combination of Yoga and Tai Chi, to benefit the community both physically and socially. Each morning from 7:00 A.M. to 7:15 A.M., Richard Fox Sr. and a few of the IDs led the stretch.

A thin cloud cover had replaced the prior day's clear, blue sky, leaving the air cool and gray. Matt glided to the middle of the National Mall, with one thought: talk to Sophie.

But upon his arrival, several elders—those who were RMs at the time of the Storm—interrupted his search for her. They gathered around Matt and asked how he felt. Confused, he answered, "Fine."

Lori found him and pulled him aside. She whispered, "Rex saw Kevin knock you out." She looked around, then continued. "He N-noted half the community a picture of you unconscious on the ground."

He surveyed the field, a mix of stares and a few smiles. Matt's face began to burn. Loud enough for many to hear, he said, "Don't worry. It's not a big deal."

They joined Bobby and Rich as Rex came bounding up. "Good morning, Cane," he said. "How are you feeling today? Is it true Turnbull knocked you out during his comBATON tryout?" Rex's boisterous voice drew a crowd of students and ID, although Kevin remained at his assigned Stretch post nearby.

Matt could feel the beads of perspiration forming on his forehead, but he stood tall. "Yeah, it's true." Without realizing it, he balled his hands into fists.

"That's pathetic," Rex said, his grin wider than Matt had ever seen. "Now everyone knows you can't take a hit. You act all big out there, but when it's time for action, you simply don't have what it takes. It seems Turnbull does, though." Rex eyed the curious onlookers. "You know, I ran into him right after he left your practice. I asked him if he wanted to join the best team in the league and he accepted."

Rich cut in. "That's right. He joined DC3."

Rex continued his pompous assault. "I said he joined the best team… which is the Raiders. And just as he accepted, he received a copy of your playbook from Douglas here." He turned to Bobby. "Thanks!"

Matt suppressed the instinct to thrust a fist into Rex's mouth. Instead, he narrowed his eyes on Kevin, who looked away. Matt said, "I guess some people have no integrity." Then he focused on Rex. "I'm not worried you've got our playbook. In the end, it's execution that matters. Whether you know our plays or not, you won't be able to stop us."

Seemingly out of nowhere, Mrs. Peterson walked up and joined the tense group. This sent Rex and his teammates to the front of the group to join Richard Sr. in leading the stretch.

At the end of the Daily Stretch, Rex confronted Matt once more, whispering in his ear, "And one more thing, Cane. We all know your father pulled strings—not only for you to give the Speech yesterday, but also to make you assistant twice. Without him, you'd be nothing."

Every muscle that he had just loosened tightened up. "Get the hell away from me."

Rex complied, taking his sneer with him.

During homeroom, another concern filled the hollowness that had followed Rex's harsh but truthful words. Stephanie's father had not checked in with her the night before. As one of the three lead geneticists on the repopulation team, he frequently spent nights in the lab where they performed their cloning experiments. The lab was off limits to almost everyone. When he had to spend the night there, her father would say goodnight via Neural. But last night she hadn't been able to reach him. Stephanie's mother had figured they were at an important juncture and he had lost track of time, as he was prone to do, but Stephanie felt certain something was wrong. Matt and Lori tried to comfort her by agreeing with her mother's assessment.

The Neural alert for the next class ended their discussion. Matt headed for the door.

But before he could escape, Mrs. Peterson asked to talk to him. She waited for everyone else to leave before asking, "How's your head?"

Matt looked toward the door. "Fine."

"You know, Rex has had it rough."

"What do you mean?" He turned to face her.

"You were too young to remember, but losing his parents in the Storm devastated him. He didn't speak for months. When he finally did, the happy boy we all knew was gone."

"That's no reason for him to hate me or attack me every chance he gets."

"I'm not sure he hates you. There's certainly a deep jealousy. His father was a close confidant of Joseph's before the Storm. He was old enough to notice. If he'd been raised with your family after the Storm, I think things could have turned out differently between you two."

"Why wasn't he?"

"I don't know. I suppose your father wanted to focus whatever available time he had on you. The point is, since he lost his parents, it hasn't been the same for him. He's had to earn everything he's gotten. Not that you haven't earned what you've gotten. You have. But it might seem otherwise to him."

"I get it. You know, it's not like I haven't missed out. I grew up without a mother." Matt eyed the wooden planks on the floor. "Although it helps having you to talk to." Out of the corner of his eye, Matt noticed a tear trickle down her cheek. He raised his head and felt the warmth in her smile.

"I enjoy talking to you, too. As for Rex, I'm not telling you to ignore his insults. I'm just giving you some perspective."

"Thank you, ma'am." He turned to leave.

"By the way, she must be some girl to cause you to take your eyes off comBATON, even for a moment."

Matt's eyes flashed wide. He offered a sheepish smile and started to walk out, then stopped himself. "Ma'am?"

"Yes."

"You have access to the students' schedules. Could you tell me what classes she has today? You know, so I can talk to her about yesterday." Matt felt the warmth rising up his neck.

Mrs. Peterson peered through him for a moment. "You both have Human Achievement this afternoon."

Matt ignored his teachers and friends throughout the morning and lunch as he thought of what to ask the girl in the picture he'd stared at thousands of times. With as little information as he had about Sophie, he came up with nothing but a headache.

The aching dissipated the moment he entered the Library of Congress for Human Achievement. Sophie, now sans her normal cap and glasses, sat in the middle of the room. She looked just like the vision burned into his brain.

He needed to speak with her privately, so he decided to wait until after class and approach her on the way out. After talking with a few of the other students, he took a seat behind Sophie and waited out what seemed like the longest class he'd ever attended. He barely heard the teacher name Kenneth Pepper as his assistant or any of the following lecture on the achievements of ancient civilizations.

At the end of class, he said goodbye to the teacher and followed Sophie. Matt knew next to nothing about her and had no idea where she was headed. He followed her down the stairs to the basement and toward the stacks, where a sizable portion of the library book collection was maintained. When he entered, he didn't see Sophie anywhere. He only saw a long, well-lit room with a low ceiling, a couple of tables nearby, and an endless series of bookshelves down either side. Narrow aisles ran in between them. Matt shook his head. In another age, this sea of books might have impressed him. With the invention of Neurals, however, who needed books? These days, anyone could access a story simply by thinking about it.

Matt stood in the doorway until he heard shuffling feet a few rows away. He crept toward the noise, expecting to see Sophie, but instead bumped into her 18-year-old brother as he turned the corner.

"Oh. Sorry about that, David."

David's hazel eyes matched his sister's, although he preferred to look at the ground rather than make eye contact. He normally avoided interaction, even in crowds, and had a strange habit of tapping random objects with his hands for no apparent reason. Before responding, he tapped a shelf. "It's okay. Why are you here?"

"I was looking for someone."

"Oh. Who?"

"Well...your sister."

"Why do you want to speak with her?"

"There's something I need to ask her."

"Okay. I'm not sure where she is at the moment, but I'll let her know."

Matt figured David must have heard her enter the room, but either he was not going to give up his sister's location or he really didn't know where she had gone.

David bent down to lift a large stack of books.

About to leave, Matt asked, "Do you need some help with those?"

David eyed Matt for a moment and looked away. "No, thank you. I can manage."

"Okay, I guess I'll see you later. Maybe at Dinner Night?"

"Yes. See you later."

Matt turned toward the door, where Sophie stood. His heart pumped fast as he approached her.

"What do you want?" she fired at Matt, then crossed her arms. "Aren't you concerned about being seen following me?"

He stopped midstride. "Why?"

"You have a girlfriend. People might get the wrong idea."

"About what?"

"Never mind."

"What? You think people might think you and I..."

"Well, yes."

"Don't be ridiculous."

"Ridiculous?"

His hand combed his hair. "It's not that you're not...it's just that people know me better than to think I would do anything."

"You mean the same people who turned on you this morning?"

"You heard?"

"Everyone did."

"Great. That's what Lori was...that's what we were afraid of."

"What's to worry about? Why do you care so much what other people think?"

"Because...because...I don't know. Everyone has this image of me. I don't want to disappoint them. What's wrong with that? "

"You should know that you can't please everyone all the time."

"Hey. You're the one who asked what others would think about us. You obviously care."

"Not to the extent you seem to. Anyway, you didn't answer my first question. Why are you here?"

"You didn't give me a chance." She stood there, arms still in their menacing position. "Because of yesterday."

"What about yesterday? It's not a big deal."

"Yes, it is. Not about getting hit. I can deal with that."

"Then what's the problem?"

He dropped his arms, which he hadn't realized had matched Sophie's. "I'm not sure I can explain it. Something strange happened yesterday at practice and I'm trying to figure it out. Why were you there? You've never been there before. Why'd you take off your cap and glasses and then leave so quickly?"

"First, let me say I think you guys are ridiculous with comBATON. Boys running around trying to prove something to one another. Second, I'll tell you when you tell me."

"Okay," Matt conceded. "But first, let's calm down. I didn't come down here to argue about comBATON."

Sophie dropped her arms, looked up at the ceiling, and shook her head. "This is all so strange."

"What is?"

"Everything. The reason I came to your practice. Even the reason I took off my cap and glasses." She exhaled and recrossed her arms. "The Speech. That's the reason I came to practice yesterday. You spoke about our need to sacrifice. All of us."

He thought, *You mean Bobby's speech? You should go see him.* "Yeah?"

"That's what got my attention. My parents told me one day I'd help someone who sees the value in everyone. It sounded reasonable, but I never knew why they made such a big deal out of it."

"What do you mean 'a big deal'?"

"They told me not to speak about it except to the person I was supposed to help, a person who believes each of us has a responsibility to humanity and the billions who were lost—a responsibility to make things better." Sophie looked Matt straight in the eye. "After the Speech, I thought that person might be you, until I went to your practice and realized you're no different than everyone else."

"So, if you feel that way, why are you telling me this now?"

"I'm not sure. I see things differently than you, but for some reason I found hope when I heard you speak. I don't mean hope in continuing down our current path. I mean hope in taking a different path that could lead to great things."

"What? What's wrong with the way things are? Wait." A chill ran through his body, making him tremble like he'd just been punched in the stomach.

"What?"

"Why'd you say path?"

"What do you mean?"

"My mother used the same word." She raised her eyebrows. "I mean, I had a dream the other night. In it, my mother said this week I'd have to choose my path. She said it was a matter of life and death."

"So? It was just a dream."

"Well, most people don't talk like that. It doesn't sound like a coincidence." He perched his chin on his hand. "Was it a dream?"

She crossed her arms again. "You don't think you actually spoke with her, do you? She's—"

"—dead. I know." Sophie eyed the ground. "Don't worry. It's okay. What I mean is, she might have planted a message in my Neural before she died, although I'm not sure how it could be so interactive."

"Actually, that would explain a lot."

"What do you mean?"

"I mean, it would also explain why I took off my cap and glasses." Matt thought through his mother's message. "How?"

"Maybe your mother…or someone else…hid a message in my Neural, too. I was standing on the sideline. You looked at me and it was like a program in my Neural commanded me to do it."

Matt found a nearby seat and sank into it. Sophie followed.

He asked, "Do you think my mother meant for us to do something together?"

"Maybe, but we need more information."

"I have it." They both leaned forward. Matt looked around the room before he spoke. "When you took them off, I saw the face of…of someone I'd seen many times before."

"There aren't many people in our community. We see each other all the time."

He shook his head. "No, I saw the exact face of someone I'd only seen in one place before, in a picture my mother gave me…before she died."

"How could your mother have given you a picture of me if she—"

"—died the year you were born?" Sophie nodded. "I know. It doesn't make sense. But look." Matt pulled out the tattered photograph and handed it to Sophie.

Sophie's face turned pale. She studied the picture, her eyes unblinking. She turned it over and saw the sequence. "It could be an ancestor," she said, offering it back.

Matt didn't take it. "I've studied that picture for years. Look at the charm she's wearing. You're wearing it now. Is it a family heirloom?"

"No, my parents said someone gave it to them for me right after I was born. They never told me anything else about it, even though I've asked them, many times." Sophie pulled the chain of the antique, gold charm from around her neck and showed it to Matt. "Look at the engraving," she said, pointing to the script letters "MS" on its face.

Matt took the charm from Sophie. He ran his fingers over the inscription and the rest of the cool, dimpled surface. "May I open it?"

"It can't be opened. I've tried for years. But go ahead. Give it a shot."

Matt pried with his fingers, but it didn't budge. "It was worth a try. Maybe we should get a tool to pry it—"

Pop. It opened.

They froze.

"How'd you do that?"

Matt didn't have an answer. They looked inside and found a circular, brown wafer marked with an S. It was a Disc, albeit smaller than usual.

Sophie spoke first. "Do you think it's for me?"

"Why? Because of the 'S'? It could be for anyone."

"True, but if that picture is of me and the charm was given to me, there's a good chance that this Disc is for me."

"Even if you're right, are you going to use the Disc without knowing who gave it to you or what's on it? Maybe we should talk to your parents about whoever gave them the charm."

"That seems like the logical thing to do…but logic hasn't played a part in any of this." Sophie took the charm and plucked the Disc out of it. "Something tells me I can trust your mother." Before Matt could stop her, she popped the Disc in her mouth.

"Are you crazy?" Even if his mother had left the picture, it was a reckless move. But now he wondered what she was seeing. Her eyes opened wide. Then, her forehead wrinkled. She looked at Matt and relaxed her expression, but didn't speak. He couldn't stand the suspense any longer. "So? What's on the Disc?"

Sophie continued to stare at him for a moment. Then, in a quiet, hurried voice, she responded, "Nothing."

"What do you mean? That didn't look like nothing."

"I thought it was something at first, but it ended up just being some useless pictures."

Matt stood there, not sure what to say.

"Listen, I need to get to my parents' office, and I'm sure you've got another practice. I'll see you later." She turned and fled the stacks.

"Wait," he yelled after her. As he began to follow, a Neural reminder popped up. He didn't believe her about the Disc, but she was right. He only had five minutes to get to practice.

Matt arrived just in time. Out of breath after running out of the building and gliding to the field so fast, he said a quick hello to Lori, then joined the team.

Rich greeted him. "Hey Matty. We were beginning to worry our fearless leader was going to be late."

"Have the team run some laps." He still needed to change.

On his way over to the Shed, he took the time to think about the weird conversation with Sophie. His mother had left him a picture of some unknown woman who had turned out to be Sophie Jackson. The charm she wore in the picture had been given to Sophie by an unknown person when she was an infant. It opened at his touch and contained a Disc that supposedly contained nothing. It seemed like his mother had intended for them to do something together. But what? His mother couldn't have known Sophie, let alone have had a future picture of her. Deciding he could not dwell on what he couldn't figure out at that moment, he compartmentalized everything he had just learned and returned his focus to practice.

A NEW TEAM

[WEDNESDAY, SEPTEMBER 2, 2037, 7:30 A.M.]

The next morning, Matt awoke with a lot on his mind. The clarity of the crisp, blue sky contrasted with his clouded head. He ate breakfast alone and glided to the Daily Stretch and then to school, taking time to plan his day. His primary focus was to talk to Sophie again. Their conversation had ended abruptly, leaving him riddled with questions. He didn't think he could concentrate on his other tasks until he got some answers.

But all Matt's planning ended when he entered homeroom that morning. Mrs. Peterson was hugging a moaning Lori, tears streaming down both of their cheeks. Students huddled in small groups were speaking in hushed tones; a few were sniffling and others were drying their faces with their arms. Matt walked up to Lori and she latched onto him. She tried to explain, but she could only utter "Steph…Steph."

Matt looked up at Mrs. Peterson, who N-noted him they'd just learned that Stephanie's father and the other two geneticists had "died in a lab explosion."

Matt thought back to the lab explosion that had killed his mother. Somehow this news felt much worse. It felt like someone had told him his mother's explosion had just happened. His face contorted and he fought off the urge to cry. One look from Mrs. Peterson made him compose himself. He tightened his hold on Lori and whispered, "It'll be all right."

When Lori finally relaxed her grasp, Matt suggested the class pray for Stephanie and the other family members whose world had changed forever.

After the prayer, they received an N-note from Principal Franklin. Class was cancelled for the remainder of the day. Mrs. Peterson offered to stay to talk with any or all of them as long as they wanted.

Matt sat and talked with Lori for a few minutes, glancing up at one point through the door's window. To his surprise, Sophie stood in the hallway. She was waving to him to join her. Matt bolted up from his chair. He focused his eyes on the ground as he told Lori he had to go.

Lori looked at Sophie, then back at him. "What's the matter?"

"Nothing."

"Wait, were you with her before practice yesterday?"

"Yes, with her and her brother. And I need to talk to her now. I'll catch up with you later and explain."

"You're leaving with her now?"

"Yes. I promise I'll explain. I'll meet up with you in a little bit." He turned to Rich, who was staring at him, his mouth wide open. Matt said, "Let's cancel practice. I don't think it makes sense to play today." He turned to Lori, feeling her pull on him to stay—but feeling a stronger urge to talk to Sophie. He bent over, kissed her cheek, and whispered in her ear, "Just trust me." On his way out, he N-noted Rich and Bobby to ask them to keep Lori company.

Matt clicked the door shut and asked, "So, are you ready to talk about everything now?"

She looked away. "Yes, but not here. Come with me."

"Where are we going?"

"You'll see." He followed her out of the building and around the Capitol to her parents' office at the Botanic Garden, a several-story greenhouse located near the RM Monument.

They passed through the main entrance and faced a bright hallway. A map on the wall showed the building's varied climate rooms, including desert, high altitude, and plains. Sophie led Matt through a glass door into the rainforest area, where the humid air filled his lungs. The sunlight sprinkled the sea of green, thin paths. A metal catwalk ran around the edges overhead. Sophie led him over a small bridge, then off the left side of the path behind a large evergreen. She reached down, as if to grab the moist earth. Instead she pulled up a hidden rope attached to a trap door. She motioned for Matt to climb down the ladder below the door. He did so and she followed, pulling the door shut above her.

Matt descended about one story and stepped off the ladder. His heart raced at the sight before him, a lab at one with nature. The walls were made of the same moist earth as above them, albeit much more compact. The roots of the tree that grew above them laced throughout the earthen walls. Man's presence was intermingled with nature in the form of several long tables, stools, and air-conditioning ducts. Matt expected the air to have the same artificial scent as everywhere else, which was "cool spring air" today. But this air was unscented, leaving the room smelling earthy.

Sophie's brother David sat on one of the stools. "Hi, David," Matt said, his eyes still darting around the tables—from the jars of seeds, centrifuges, test tubes, Bunsen burners, and microscopes on one table, to soldering equipment and motors on another table, to a large 3-D printer in the corner, to various electronics strewn across the remaining tables.

"Hi Matt. Are you doing okay?"

Redirecting his attention to David, Matt replied, "About as well as everyone else, I expect. How about you?"

"The same."

"I'm sorry, Sophie, I didn't even ask how you were feeling."

"I'm sad, like you...and concerned."

"Why?"

"You know how I told you there was no information on the Disc?" Matt nodded. "Well, I lied."

Even though he had suspected as much, his jaw tightened. "Is that right?"

She rubbed one arm with the other hand. "Yes. The Disc did contain information, but we haven't been able to figure it out yet."

"We? You mean you and David?" She nodded. "You discussed this with David, but not me? Why? Didn't you think the picture, not to mention the fact that I opened the charm, meant I should be included?"

"I'm sorry. I'm really sorry," Sophie replied. "I didn't trust you. I don't really know you. The Speech was a strong indication of what you could be capable of." Placing a hand on David's shoulder, she said, "And you accepted my brother, autism and all. You don't look at him as being different. You accept and respect him for the person he is. Others ignore him, not understanding—or even trying to understand—him." David's eyes were focused on the ground. Sophie stared at Matt and added, "But most of your life has been spent in service of the system created by your father."

"I'm confused. What does that have to do with trust? His system saved humanity."

She crossed her arms, as she had in the stacks. "I'm sure you think that. And it's because you're so close to him that I was concerned about revealing what I saw." Sophie continued to stare at Matt.

Matt's disappointment and confusion turned to anger. He matched her stare. "What do you think he's done? I'm shocked anyone would think he's done anything but what had to be done. Everyone in our community supports him, including your parents."

"That brings us back to why we're here. I think we are being included in a mission that may be against the president's wishes."

"Why would you say that?"

"The contents of the Disc. They'll answer that question and raise many more."

Matt stepped toward her, intrigued. She continued, "The first information I downloaded was the same sequence as on the back of your picture."

"I knew they were related. Did you figure out the meaning of the sequence?"

"David and I discussed that, but couldn't come up with anything. We'll figure it out. For now, let me tell you what else I learned."

Matt took another step closer. After years of studying the picture, he was going to know why his mother had left it with him.

"Second, there was a message in all caps: THE CHARM AND ITS CONTENTS MUST NOT BE DISCUSSED WITH ANYONE OTHER THAN THOSE FOR WHOM THIS MISSION IS INTENDED."

"What mission?" asked Matt.

David offered a sheepish gaze. "We don't know...but we'll figure it out."

"No offense, David, but that message said that we're not supposed to discuss this with anyone outside the mission. Why are you saying we?"

Sophie said, "That brings me to the third and final clue."

Matt's heart began to race. Sophie waited, as if to mark the importance of the moment. "What?" he finally blurted out.

"An image."

"Of what?"

"Of us. All three of us," she added, patting her brother on the back. "All three of us are touching the charm at the same time. David and I are each holding the charm up with a thumb and index finger and you're touching it with your left index finger."

"All three of us?"

"Yes."

Matt considered this for a moment. "So you want to see what happens if we do the pose that's in the image?"

"Yes."

Matt had no idea what would happen next. He sighed. "Fine, let's try."

Sophie pulled the charm from around her neck. She and David held it as she had seen in the image on the Disc. Then Matt touched the charm. After a minute, it opened as it had the previous day. To his astonishment, there were now three Discs. One labeled S, one labeled

D, and one labeled M. Matt and Sophie stared at each other mouths partially open.

David blurted, "That's not just a charm. It's a Disc Writer. I've never seen one that small. That little charm can store information, like on a flash drive, and record it onto new Discs."

Matt said, "That makes sense. Impressive, David." Smiling, David quickly averted eye contact, turning his blushing face toward the ground.

One by one, each reached in and grabbed his or her Disc. Before any of them could do anything, Matt raised his empty hand to stop them. "This time, no secrets. Agreed?" Sophie and David nodded in agreement. Almost in unison, they placed the Discs in their mouths.

Matt had hoped for a significant revelation. First, he saw the number sequence, as if the Disc confirmed the charm and the picture were linked. Then he saw the message: TRUST THOSE, AND ONLY THOSE, FOR WHOM THE CHARM IS INTENDED. If the other Discs were intended for Sophie and David, he supposed he had that one figured out. The message was followed by another: "To achieve the mission, you must look beyond the veil of ignorance." A dark circle hovered above this last statement. He had no idea what that was supposed to mean.

Matt refocused on Sophie and David, both of whom remained engrossed in their downloads.

Assuming the others' Discs did not contain the same information, Matt spoke first, repeating everything he had seen on his Disc. "So, any guesses as to what the veil of ignorance is?"

Sophie said, "I think it's in the circle. But I've got no idea what it would be."

Matt said, "I guess the three of us will have to try to figure it out."

"Actually, I think it's the five of us," Sophie said.

"Five?" Matt asked.

Sophie explained her Disc, once again, had begun with the sequence. This time, two images followed. The first image was of two people holding the charm up for Matt to touch it. He sat into one of the stools to hear the retelling of the clue she had seen the day before.

Then she said, "But it wasn't David and me. This time, it was your friends Bobby and Rich."

Matt popped up off his seat with excitement. "What about Lori?"

Sophie said, "I didn't see her on my Disc. David?"

"No."

Matt's body tightened. If he followed the instructions, he'd have to keep whatever this was from her.

"What are you going to tell her?" Sophie asked.

"Nothing about the Charm, I guess."

"Well, you'll have to tell her something. She knows you went with me today."

"And she knows I was with both of you yesterday. Don't worry. I'll think of something."

"All right," she said, her voice shaky and doubtful. "Just make sure it's plausible."

"I will. Anything else on your Disc?" Matt asked.

"I saw one more image, but I don't know what it means yet. It was of a study of some sort. The room contained very old furniture and seemed to be an exhibit of some kind. There was a message across the top of the picture. 'To save the old mission, you must embark on a new mission. Begin by digging deep to rediscover the president's writing of Emancipation.' "

Matt thought for a moment. "Maybe it's President Lincoln's Emancipation Proclamation?"

Sophie nodded. "Could be. It ended slavery in the South. So, are we supposed to come to a revelation about freedom from slavery? Or are we supposed to literally dig somewhere to find the answer?"

Matt didn't like her implication about freedom from slavery, but held off on starting a debate. There was more information to discuss.

Sophie asked, "David, what'd you see?"

"All I saw was the statement 'Trust Yourself,' followed by the sequence on Matt's picture. Above the sequence was a picture of a small statue of a woman on a chariot."

Matt said, "I wonder what that means."

Sophie and David shook their heads.

Matt asked, "So, where are we? All of us received messages and, with the exception of a possible connection to the Emancipation Proclamation, we have nothing."

Sophie stood silent for a moment, then said, "Well, we know one thing. We need to include Bobby and Rich. Maybe the charm will generate more Discs for all five of us."

Matt replied, "I guess more Discs might give us some answers."

"How are you going to convince them to come here?" Sophie asked. "And more importantly, can you trust them to keep this secret?"

There were few people who Matt trusted as much as Rich and Bobby. He understood that Sophie didn't know them and was just trying to follow the warnings. Nonetheless, he could feel the heat rising in his face. He snapped, "Yes, I would trust them with my life." In a softer tone, he added, "They'll follow me if I ask them to. The trick is going to be keeping this from Lori." He felt as if a vice had tightened around his stomach. Sophie appeared ready to say something, but Matt cut her off as he came up with an idea.

"Don't worry," he said. "I've got it covered. Can we meet here right after school tomorrow?"

Sophie and David looked at each other. They quickly responded, "Yes."

"We just need to be careful not to reveal our secrets," Sophie added. "We haven't hung out with you in the past, Matt. I suggest that, for now, we not be seen in public together. We don't want to make anyone suspicious."

Matt had no problem with this. "Agreed."

"Also, I suggest we not print or N-note any of the information downloaded from the Discs onto the hard drives of our Neurals. I expect the reason the information is split up this way is that whoever constructed the charm doesn't want anyone to have all of the information in order to keep it safe from certain people." Matt opened his mouth to speak, but Sophie cut him off. "And we shouldn't do any Neural searches. Someone might catch on to what we're doing."

Matt couldn't think of who that might be, but he had to admit she was likely right. "Okay. I'll see you later." He turned, climbed the ladder, and was quickly among society again.

Matt found Lori sitting with Bobby and Rich on a park bench near the Botanic Garden. Matt approached, his pulse quickening. Bobby and Rich walked up to him, and Rich slapped him on the back. "Good luck, buddy."

Bobby just shook his head. They left Matt to deal with Lori.

Matt cast off his desire to ask his friends to stay. He sat down next to Lori and attempted to place his arm around her.

But she slid away from him, wiping tears from her face. Her best friend's father just died in an explosion. And where was I? "I'm sorry. I wouldn't have left if I didn't have to."

"Why'd you have to?"

Matt crossed his arms in an attempt to brace himself against her anger. "A secret project for my father."

"At the Botanic Garden?"

"Yes."

"And it involves Sophie Jackson?"

"And her brother, David."

She stared at him through her swollen eyes. "Just tell me there's nothing going on with her."

"What? Me and Sophie? Of course not." He smiled at her and placed his hand on hers. "Why would I do that? Trust me. I know how lucky I am. I know what I've got...Do you believe me?"

She smiled back. "Yes."

THE CIRCLE OF FIVE

[THURSDAY, SEPTEMBER 3, 2037, 7:30 A.M.]

In homeroom the next day, Mrs. Peterson announced the details for the memorial service in Arlington for the morning of the upcoming Saturday. Stephanie was home, grieving with her mother.

Likely in an attempt to distract them, Mrs. Peterson told them some interesting stories about the building of RM City. She spoke about the extraterrestrial elements embedded in the walls. The RMs had found the metallic material in the Yucatan. After extensive experimentation, they found it impervious to many extremes, including intense heat and radiation from a nuclear blast. She then explained why the Capital One Arena had been built in Chinatown—about how RM City was built under it between two lines in the underground Metro system, so that no one would question the amount of earth the builders were removing. Everyone had heard these stories before, but Mrs. Peterson offered some new details and kept them all fixated. That is, everyone except Matt.

After class, Matt remained at his desk, deep in thought. He didn't notice Bobby and Rich had stuck around. "Where were you yesterday?" Rich asked.

Matt scanned the room to make sure Lori had left.

"It must've been really important to leave so quickly," Bobby added in a rather loud, abrupt voice. The few others left in the room turned their heads to see what was happening.

Rich said, "DC3 business."

Matt had never kept a secret from his friends. But he knew he couldn't tell them here, with Mrs. Peterson and other students in earshot. Motioning them closer, he whispered, "Let's talk about this after school."

Bobby seemed surprised not to get a straight answer. In a loud whisper, he asked, "Why can't you tell us right now? You've spent a lot of time with Sophie this week. Don't forget: you have a girlfriend."

"It's not like that," Matt said. "I promise. You'll find out everything we know after school."

Bobby asked, "Who's we?"

"The three of us. Sophie, David, and me. Meet me at the front entrance to the Jacksons' office right after class. We have to get there and then to practice on time without anyone noticing. Try not to be conspicuous. If anyone asks, just tell them you're helping me with some confidential research for a Science & Technology project."

The rest of the day dragged on for an eternity. Matt kept thinking about what to say to Rich and Bobby, and how he would say it.

Finally, the time of reckoning had arrived. As soon as Human Achievement had ended, Matt and Sophie shot out of class into the blinding sunshine and glided to the Jacksons' office. He hoped they would arrive before Rich and Bobby. And he hoped Mr. and Mrs. Jackson wouldn't be there, as he wanted to minimize the number of explanations they would have to provide.

They arrived at the Botanic Garden and waited in silence at the door to the rainforest area. Matt knew they would have to be unified in their explanation to Bobby and Rich. After several minutes had passed, they looked at each other worriedly, as if to ask, Where can they be?

Suddenly, Rich popped open the door behind them. "If you two are finished gazing at each other, maybe you can come down here and explain what this is all about. I'm sure my father doesn't know about this place and I don't like keeping secrets from him."

Before they stepped onto the ladder, Sophie tugged on Matt's arm. Her eyebrows were raised, her forehead crinkled. He thought about the strange situation he'd found himself in on the way down to the lab. Not only was he lying to Lori and keeping secrets from his father, he now felt he owed it to Sophie to get his friends to join their secret society. And he was dragging Rich and Bobby into a mess of secrets, too.

Once in the lab, Bobby offered Matt a half-hearted smile. "Hi, Matt. David saw us waiting by the door and brought us down here. Is this place the secret, or is this the secret place where we find out what's going on?"

"The latter." He took a breath. "Listen, before we start, I need both of you to understand a couple of things. One, there is nothing going on between Sophie and me. And two, this is not something we can tell anyone about." Surveying Sophie's signature crossed arms and David's fidgeting hands, Matt continued, "And I mean anyone. Not about this lab, or anything else you see and hear today. Both of you." Bobby immediately nodded. Rich hesitated, but did likewise.

Sophie finally spoke. "This is serious, guys. We brought you down here for an extremely important reason. We had to meet in a place we knew wouldn't be monitored. Matt says we can trust you, and we believe him, but I can't stress enough how important it is that no one find out about this lab."

Matt thought Sophie's concern was over the top; nonetheless, the edge in her voice stressed him out even further. "Okay, well...guys, we brought you down here because of some bizarre things that have occurred this week. It'll be easiest to start from the beginning." Matt explained what had taken place since he'd been knocked out during comBATON practice: the picture, the charm, the Discs, and the information that he, Sophie, and David had shared. He saw he was swiftly gaining his friends' interest.

When he finished, Bobby asked, "So you brought us here to touch the charm and see what happens?"

David and Sophie looked at Matt. Matt placed his hands on his hips and stared into his friends' eyes. "Yes. The five of us are meant to do something and we're hoping new clues will clear things up."

"The Circle of Five," David muttered to himself.

"What is the Circle of Five?" Rich asked with mounting impatience. "Matt, we don't know what's going on with this charm. Our fathers have spent years fighting to bring humanity back from the brink. Now, you're asking me to go behind their backs and keep secrets left by... who, exactly?"

"You mean, besides my mother?" Matt asked, matching Rich's tone.

"Fine," Rich said, "but do we even know what she and whoever wants us to do—or why? No. And what about Lori? How do you plan to keep this from her?"

Sophie said, "Good question. How did you handle it?"

"I told her I was working with you and David on a secret job for my father."

"At my parents' office?"

"Yeah, she saw me coming from here yesterday. It made sense."

"It did, except her father is my parents' boss."

Matt hesitated, the heat rising in his face. "Good point. I'll make sure she doesn't ask her father any questions."

"If she hasn't already," Sophie said, her arms crossed again, eyes narrowed.

"What's done is done," Bobby said. "She probably hasn't said anything to anyone. Matt can talk to her." He smiled at Matt. "She'll do anything he asks her to do."

Wanting to change the subject, Matt asked Bobby and Rich whether they had any ideas about the clues they had heard so far.

Bobby said, "I agree the clue has to do with the Emancipation Proclamation, and I think I know where the room in Sophie's picture is." Bobby's words drew Matt, Sophie, and David closer. "Mom," he said, referring to his foster mother, Mrs. Peterson, "has always tried to teach me about my African-American heritage, and I've also been doing my own research. There's a house about five miles north of here where President Lincoln drafted the Emancipation Proclamation. It's called the Lincoln Cottage at the Soldier's Home."

The original trio smiled at him, excited by the new information.

Finally, Bobby broke the silence. "So, are we doing this or what? We don't have much time before practice." He reached out his hand to Sophie in a gesture that was clearly a request for the charm. She pulled it from around her neck and handed it to him.

Bobby walked over to Rich. Each pinched a piece of the charm and raised it toward Matt, who stepped forward and touched it.

A minute later, the charm popped open. Bobby and Rich, mouths agape, stared at each other, then at Matt. Inside, three Discs appeared. This time, the Discs were labeled R, B, and M. Sophie and David watched as each of the others took his initialed Disc.

Matt attempted to break the tension. "Here's to the truth." Matt and Bobby each consumed their Discs. Rich hesitated, then consumed his as well.

Even though Matt had just done the same thing the day before, his anticipation seemed greater now. Once again, the sequence appeared first. Then, a series of messages appeared. "FOR NOW, TRUST ONLY THOSE IN THE CIRCLE OF FIVE. YOU CAN ACCOMPLISH ANY-THING IF YOU COMBINE YOUR FRIENDS' STRENGTHS AND PERSEVERE. YOU DON'T HAVE TO ADMIT THIS TO ANYONE, YET...BUT TRUST HER, SHE'S RIGHT."

Matt repeated the first two sentences. Everyone was puzzled by the "For now" comment. Who else might they add to the group? Lori, his father, Mrs. Peterson, one of their other teachers? How had the Circle of Five ended up on the Disc, when David had just named them that for the first time? The rest of the messages seemed clear, except—persevere in doing what? Matt hoped more information would lead to clarity. He looked to his friends. "So, what was on your Discs?"

"My message, and I received only one after the sequence, may help a bit," Bobby said. "THE NEW MISSION IS THE OLD MISSION." They all agreed the old mission was the RM's mission to protect humanity and preserve its accomplishments. But Sophie and Matt disagreed about whether the old mission needed saving.

Sophie said, "Matt, you know your history. Placing all the power in one or a few people never works."

"Except here. I doubt the clues are telling us to fix what my father and the RMs have accomplished."

An argument seemed imminent, until David interrupted. "Rich, what's wrong?"

Rich was as still as a statue. His face was as white as any monument and beads of sweat had accumulated on his forehead. He shook himself out of his trance. "Nothing you need to concern yourself with."

David dropped his head.

Before Sophie could come to her brother's aid, Matt took charge. "Don't talk to David like that. You look upset. He was concerned. And I'm sure it does concern him and the rest of us. Apologize."

Rich clenched his fists and looked away, as if trying to fight himself to do the right thing. "All right. I'm sorry, David."

David's eyes remained fixed on the ground, but he nodded his acceptance.

Matt turned back to his friend. "Tell us what you saw."

Rich took a breath and copied David, eyeing the ground. "The sequence, then the message 'TRUST THEM.'" He looked up, scanned the group, and stopped on Matt. "I will trust you. I do trust you."

"That's it?" Sophie asked.

"That's it."

Matt said, "So, let's put this all together. I would guess, at least for the moment, that there are no more Discs. I would also guess that, if there are other clues, we'll find them in the room where President Lincoln wrote the Emancipation Proclamation." Everyone's eyes were fixed on him. "I'm open to suggestions, but here's what I think we need to do. Go to the Lincoln Cottage and see if Bobby's right and, if so, why we're supposed to be there. And we'll need to determine when to go, and how we can do it without being noticed."

Rich raised his hand. "I can help with that."

"Great, we'll need your expertise," Matt said. "Second, we need to put all of the clues together and figure out what they mean. Normally, we'd want to write them down or input all of them into our Neurals, but as Sophie suggested yesterday, there's probably a reason why each of us received only a few separate pieces of information. I think my mother and whoever helped her didn't want to have all of the clues in one place. So, I suggest we still tell each other everything, but no one download the others' clues to your Neural. Agreed?"

Each of the others agreed.

"Good. Finally, once we understand what the mission is and the risks of the mission, we need to decide whether to accept it."

Sophie's arms found their menacing crossed position. "What do you mean we have to decide whether to accept? Haven't we already accepted? I mean, your mother and others went to great lengths to give us this information. We've seen it and discussed it. Doesn't that mean we've accepted it?"

"I agree," Rich said.

Despite his curiosity, Matt was not convinced. He had no idea what the clues meant, let alone who or what they might need to defy. "Until we know what we're getting into and specifically why, we need to keep our minds open and consider choosing not to accept this mission. This last point is very important to me. I need to know all of you agree before we proceed."

He looked at each of them in succession. Each nodded in agreement, although Sophie only after a lengthy hesitation. "I guess we have no choice," she said. "Whatever we do, we need to do it together."

Matt knew her concession did not come easily. "I promise to take this seriously and consider everything with an open mind...once we have all of the facts."

Sophie's face softened, and Matt offered her a slight nod of apprecia-
tion. He felt a surge of energy. "Okay, everyone. Next steps. Rich, how
do we get to the Lincoln Cottage without anyone knowing?"

Everyone remained silent. From what Rich had told Matt over the
years, Rich's father had several unknown surveillance techniques. Matt
suspected that was how his father always knew what was going on.

Rich said, "The ID monitors many different places...my father says
it's to protect everyone and for deterrence. Anyway, since I hope to one
day become head of the ID, I've learned a lot from him about where
they monitor...and where they don't. There are places where we can go
that they don't watch. We'll have to do a little digging, but it will get
us to a place where we can travel undetected to the Lincoln Cottage."

Even Matt had not known some of what Rich was saying. He didn't
understand the point about protection and deterrence. He would have
liked to give it more thought, but the rest of the information was more
important for the moment. "What kind of place?" Matt asked. "A tunnel?"

"Kind of. Actually, it's a sewer that was built out of the Tiber Creek
in the late 1800s. The creek was intended to be used for commerce, but
it later carried so much waste that it caused many diseases, including
the typhoid fever that killed one of President Lincoln's children. The
government closed off the creek and used it for wastewater management. The sewer is large enough to walk in, and it runs for miles. In
fact, it runs north and south right near here. We can enter the tunnel
undetected, walk north until we're beyond the surveillance zone, exit,
and walk to the Lincoln Cottage."

Each of the others looked as if they had just seen an amazing com-
BATON play, their mouths open and eyes wide. A silent moment later,
Bobby asked, "Why doesn't the ID know about the sewers?"

David had the answer. "As you know, we have technologies today
that allow us to recycle all waste at the site at which it's produced. The
sewers aren't needed and have probably been forgotten."

"Actually, the ID hasn't forgotten about them," Rich said. "But they
believe everyone else has. So they don't bother watching them."

Everyone was caught up in the excitement. David was the only one watching the clock. "Didn't you say you have practice at 4:00?"

"We gotta go!" Matt said, heading for the exit. "Rich, Bobby, welcome to the circle. I'll talk to Lori after practice." He stopped ascending the ladder and addressed Sophie. "We'll meet here tomorrow, if that's okay."

Sophie answered, "That's fine."

"Great," Matt said. "We'll go over the final clues again. We should wait until Saturday to go to the Lincoln Cottage. We'll have more time without classes or practice."

Matt gave out assignments. "Rich, please figure out how we can access the sewer undetected. Everyone else, we know our gliders don't work outside the community. Let's think of a way to get to the cottage fast. I don't want to lose half the day walking."

And with that, Matt, Bobby, and Rich were out of the hatch. Matt inhaled the cool, clean air as he led the way to practice.

SECRETS

[THURSDAY, SEPTEMBER 3, 2037, 4:30 P.M.]

The three of them reached the practice field just in time, apologizing to the others for not being there to help set up.

Matt's body might have been on the field, but his mind was far away in the past. Especially given his knockout at the first practice, he should have had a laser focus. Instead, he couldn't stop thinking about the clues and how he was hiding what he knew from his father and Lori. With frayed nerves and growing guilt, his stomach sank further and further. As he struggled to get his head in the game, he found himself eating turf more often than not.

Rich appeared to have the same problem. He hadn't spoken much in the lab after he had consumed his Disc, after which his behavior had suddenly swung from recalcitrance to complete willingness to help. Matt didn't understand how the simple words "Trust Them" could have changed his mind so fast. The result: like Matt, Rich spent much of the practice picking himself up off the ground.

Bobby, on the other hand, played with more confidence than Matt had ever seen from him. Not only did he evade kicks, he was more vocal, chastising his teammates and suggesting that the practice squad trade places with the starting team.

After practice, the three of them helped clean up and went their separate ways. It was near dusk when Matt met up with Lori on the sideline and walked her home. He told her Rich and Bobby were now part of the project as well. His voice wavering, he explained that this group had been specifically selected by the RMs and that no one was supposed to know about their work. He asked her to keep her knowledge about the project a secret.

She cut in. "Not even my father. I won't say a word." She managed a smile.

Matt didn't know what to say.

She stopped and placed her hand on his chest. "If our relationship is going to work, we have to trust each other. I trust you. If you ask me to do something, I'll do it."

Matt exhaled and took her hand in his. He felt closer to her, yet wondered if he would have responded similarly to such a blind request.

After kissing her goodnight, Matt glided toward home. He soon realized someone was following him. Had the ID already learned what they were doing? Beads of sweat formed on his forehead. He stopped and spun around. "Rich?"

"Matt, I'm freaking out," Rich said, lowering his head. "I can't keep this to myself anymore."

"Keep what to yourself? Do you mean what we heard earlier today?"

"Not exactly. It's something, or some things, I saw."

Matt whispered, "Do you mean there was more on your Disc?"

"Yes. There were several images. I'm not ready to tell the others yet, but I've got to tell you."

Matt looked around. "We can't talk here."

"Yeah, actually we can. I have a special device on my belt. Any eavesdroppers will hear a different conversation. Right now, it's playing one of our recent comBATON strategy discussions."

With all that had happened this week, Matt just nodded at this new revelation. He asked, "What do you want to do, just walk around and talk?"

"Yes, but look down so no one will notice your mouth is out of sync with the conversation."

Matt's heart raced. "So, what is it? What did you see?"

"A monster."

"What do you mean?"

"My father's a monster. Now I understand why they call him The Hammer."

"What? I don't get it."

"You know how Stephanie's father and the other scientists died in that lab accident?"

Matt's voice quivered. "Yes."

"It wasn't an accident. My father killed them. He murdered them."

A shock ran through Matt's body. He stopped and looked up at his friend. "How? Why?"

"Keep looking down! The Disc didn't say why. But I saw images of him entering their lab when no one else was there and…and placing explosives under the equipment."

Matt shook his head. "I don't get it. Why would the Disc show you something like that?"

Rich sniffled. "Because it must be the truth. And it must be why I'm supposed to be in the Circle of Five."

Matt felt badly for his friend, but he had to know more. "Did he act alone?"

"I only saw him. I don't know if he had help or…or if he acted at anyone's direction."

"What's that supposed to mean?" Matt knew what Rich was thinking: only his father could order Richard Sr. to do something. Matt knew his father might be a stern leader, but he would never be involved in such a vicious act.

"I know, Matt. I don't really think your father had anything to do with this. I just can't imagine what would cause him to do what he did."

"We need to figure this out. Was there anything else?"

Rich hesitated. Then, he stared at Matt. "As they lay there dying, my father came back and removed the evidence."

Matt shook his head, numb.

"I can't believe I have to live with that monster. I know we don't know what our mission is yet, but we've got to take it. I need to know there's hope."

Matt wanted to help his friend, but all he could muster was, "I understand. I wish I could do more for you tonight."

"Knowing that you know helps a little."

The initial shock did not subside on the way home. Every few seconds, Matt looked over his shoulder. He felt as if his mother had lifted a curtain to reveal a different world, a world in which the people assigned to protect them might be the very ones from whom everyone needed protection. How deep did it go? If Richard had acted alone, as Matt hoped, he might be the first person since the Storm to stand trial for murder. Somehow, however, Matt expected Richard had accomplices. Were other IDs working with him? If so, why? In any event, his father would need to know—except, his mother had left strict instructions not to tell anyone outside the Circle of Five. Matt decided to listen to his mother, at least for the moment.

He tried to think about something else. What clues might be next? He hoped they would at least include Lori, because his betrayal of her trust tore at him more than anything.

Matt began to drift off to sleep, but a horrifying thought jolted him awake. His mother had died in a lab accident.

What if it hadn't been an accident? What if Richard had killed her, too?

IT'S ABOUT TIME

[FRIDAY, SEPTEMBER 4, 2037, 2:00 P.M.]

Friday crept along more slowly than any day previously that week. Matt spent much of his time reflecting on all the dramatic events. From delivering the Speech, which now seemed less important to him than he would have ever thought possible, to Sophie, to the charm and the Discs, to the Circle of Five. But the biggest surprise had been Rich's confession. His father had killed three people. How could Dr. Fox have done such a thing?

Even more puzzling was how the images had wound up on the Discs. Just like the picture of Sophie, how could the images of Richard Sr. have been placed in the charm long before the pictures were taken?

After a Government class that felt like it took longer than the Civil War, Matt left the Capitol through the old House of Representatives chamber. As he passed through Statuary Hall, the vice president called his name from the Rotunda. He turned and looked up, and suddenly saw it. A small statue of a woman in a chariot sat above the archway to the Rotunda.

It had to be the statue David saw on his Disc. He hadn't thought of it when David had relayed his clue, but Matt knew the significance of the statue from one of the vice president's boring dissertations. He stood still, feeling faint at the possible meaning behind the clue, when someone grabbed his shoulder from behind. A shock ran through Matt's body. He spun around, knocked the hand from his body, and dropped into a back stance, fists ready.

Nick Rounds, a stocky member of the ID and one of Rex's Raiders, raised his hands up, palms out. "Wow. A little jumpy, aren't we?" He stepped away from Matt and continued on to wherever he was headed.

Remembering the vice president's greeting, Matt dropped his arms and walked over to see why he'd been summoned. Fortunately, it wasn't another mystery. The vice president just wanted to discuss the lesson plan for the next class.

When classes were finally over for the week, the Circle of Five assembled again in the lab. Matt could feel the tension filling the musty air. Rich had now adopted some of David's habits, his eyes monitoring the ground, his hands tapping random objects. David had added constant eye rubbing and yawning to his routine. Sophie and Bobby stared at Matt, as if they were waiting for him to take the lead. He decided to go straight for the most disturbing news.

"Okay, before we continue where we left off, there was a little more information on one of the Discs from yesterday."

Rich cut him off. "It was mine."

Bobby and David seemed eager to hear the new information, but Sophie glared at Rich. "So you did have more information."

"Yeah. I'm sorry, but what I saw was almost unbearable," Rich replied defensively. "If I hadn't seen the images, I wouldn't have believed it. Before I could talk about it with everyone, I had to think it through."

"Fine," Sophie said. "What'd you see?"

Rich took a deep breath before he explained. "The worst sight ever. My father killing Stephanie's father and the other scientists." It felt as if the air had been sucked out of the room.

Bobby placed a hand on Rich's shoulder. "Are you sure?"

"Yes." Rich exhaled. "There were several images. My father rigged the lab to explode. I saw the three scientists getting to work, and then... then the explosion." Rich hung his head as he continued. "What's worse, there's also an image of my father removing the evidence as the others were dying."

No one said a word, or moved for that matter. Even though he'd heard the tale before, nausea mounted in Matt's stomach.

Sophie said, "Sorry, Rich. I had no idea." She waited a moment before pressing forward. "I think this demonstrates that Matt's mother, and maybe others, had real fears about our community. Whoever left these images clearly knew trouble was coming."

Bobby said, "I wish we'd known about this sooner." Matt's stomach sunk further at the realization that they might have been able to save Stephanie's father and the others. He placed a hand over his mouth.

"I agree," Rich said. "We need to go to the Lincoln Cottage right away and figure out what they want us to do."

"What about you, Matt?" Sophie asked.

"I'm still not sure what this is ultimately about and whether the entire government is involved. I'll wait for more facts, but I'm all for finding out as soon as we can."

"One thing I don't get," Bobby said, "is how those pictures of Richard were placed in the charm years ago, when he did what he did just this week."

"I've been thinking about that," Rich responded.

"So have I," Matt added, remembering the chariot. "Look at all the items we have from the past that come from now. Not only the pictures of Richard. For sixteen years, I've had a photo of Sophie looking about as old as she is now. I think I understand how it's possible. David, I think I saw the statue in your image. Did it have a winged chariot with a clock for a wheel?"

"Yes."

Matt had everyone's attention. No one even blinked. "It's in Statuary Hall in the Capitol. That chariot symbolically travels through time."

"Time travel," David said. "I've read a great deal on quantum mechanics, theoretical physics, and the theories of time travel, including a paper written by your father, Matt. He published it a year after the Storm. He was very convincing in his argument that traveling back in time is impossible."

Sophie said, "Let's get to the Lincoln Cottage and see if we can find out if he's right."

Matt said, "I agree. Do we have a plan?"

David said, "Yes. We'll use our gliders."

"But gliders work only on electromagnetic pathways," answered Matt.

"I've been thinking about the limitations of gliders for years," David said. "About how they're kind of like trains before cars were invented. I experimented with developing a device that detects the magnetic field in the ground, regardless of how weak it is, and amplifies it to make your gliders respond. Look at these. I call them Magnometers." He pulled from his pocket two small metallic discs, bent down, and placed them in small ports he had installed on the back of his shoes. He then stood and glided around the lab as easily as if he were on the Mall.

Matt said, "Perfect."

Sophie smiled. "He stayed up all night to finish them. When he focuses on something, he doesn't stop until it's done."

David blushed and looked down, the smallest grin forming on his face. "Sophie has hers. Let me see your gliders." Matt, Bobby, and Rich pulled them off and handed them to David.

In the minutes it took David to install the ports into the gliders, they discussed how time travel might work. David offered a possibility. "Time occupies the universe like space. If we can travel from one place to another, why couldn't we travel from one time to another? The question is how do you figure out a way to travel through time other than the linear course we've always traveled, forward?" David popped in the last of the discs. "Done. Try them."

Like kids with a new toy, the guys glided around the lab, eventually crashing into each other in the confined space. They lay in a tangled ball and laughed, releasing some of the tension of all the serious discussions of late.

Prying himself from the heap, Matt said, "Okay, Rich. You're up."

"I've figured out that the sewers run close to where we are right now," Rich said. "So, like the clue says, with a bit of digging, we should be able to access them from this lab." He pointed to the eastern wall. "If we have the tools, we should be able to tunnel through there and then cover the hole with those boxes."

Sophie said, "Don't worry about the tools."

"So, the only thing left," Matt said, "is to explain why we're all hanging out together these days. Not that there's anything wrong with it—it's just unusual all of a sudden. Not to mention, my excuse to Lori wasn't the best," he admitted.

Bobby raised his hand as if to indicate he had a solution. "Sophie, welcome to DC3. David, we'll find some other way to include you, but I think it'll be more believable if Sophie joins the team."

"That's fine," David responded.

Sophie asked, "But won't adding another player right now look suspicious?"

Matt answered, "Actually, there's one spot left on the team...thanks to what you started on Monday."

Considering Sophie's dislike of comBATON, Matt expected reluctance. Instead she answered, "It would make our meetings much less conspicuous."

"Do you need any help learning?" Matt offered.

"Don't worry about me." Sophie smirked. "This is just for appearances anyway."

"True, but you've got to look the part. Why don't you start on Monday? I'll send you a copy of the playbook and you can study it this weekend."

Until they fully understood what they were doing and why, they agreed they would have to do their best to go about business as usual. Rich, who had avoided his father the night before and was losing sleep, would have to find some way to live with the murderer. As for Matt, he would have to continue his clandestine activities behind Lori's back. And he would have to go home and live with Eric—and wonder if his father could be involved in whatever was happening.

FRIDAY NIGHT LIGHTS

[FRIDAY, SEPTEMBER 4, 2037, 6:30 P.M.]

Because of the weekly Dinner Night ritual, Friday afternoon's practice was always shorter than the others. Even though his focus had been off for days, Matt regained some clarity as their first week of practice came to a close. The season approached and Matt intended to be ready, regardless of what took place off the field. To prepare, he spent most of the afternoon running and rerunning offensive and defensive plays. "Repetition is the key to victory," he constantly reminded everyone.

At the end of practice, he called the team over. "Great first week of practice, everyone. But we've got a long way to go. The first game will be here before we know it. Keep practicing drills when you can. We've taken it easy on you with the playbook this week. On Monday, come ready to use every play out of every formation. Execution needs to be instinctual." Matt finished by saying, "See you at dinner."

One of the very first traditions implemented by the RMs in the wake of the Storm was Dinner Night. It helped achieve the RM mission by focusing on the arts, providing a variety of entertainment, and eating foods from many cultures. Dinner Night also offered a chance for the community to socialize after a week of hard work. While a few adults worked weekends to keep the community functioning efficiently, Friday evening marked the end of the workweek for most.

The entertainment was always of the highest caliber. On some nights, the RMs reenacted a Shakespearean tragedy. On other nights, a small band might inspire them with a selection of military music. On all nights, the children played in the nearby grass from the time they arrived until their parents dragged them home. Everyone else enjoyed the entertainment and conversation.

Dinner was held just off the western steps of the Capitol, providing a breathtaking view of the sun as it set behind the Washington Monument. After sundown, bright flood lights illuminated the Capitol grounds to liven up the celebration. The seating arrangement never changed. Eric sat at the center of a long head table that included Richard Sr., Dr. Ford, Vice President Silverman, Principal Franklin, and their spouses. Everyone else sat at circular tables all around the paved area in front of the steps. Matt sat with Lori, her little brother Johnny, Rich, Bobby, and some other friends near the head table. Sophie and David sat with their parents a couple of tables over.

Given the deaths during the week, a somber mood had settled on this affair. Matt's father had canceled the entertainment and fireworks in honor of those who had fallen. The kids—including Johnny, who could endure only a few minutes of boredom at Matt's table—still played in the grass, but everyone else simply ate and talked.

Dinner dragged on. The scraping of forks against plates drowned out the stilted conversations. While his nose was filled with the delicious smell of spices, little of the Spanish cuisine reached his mouth. Sophie hadn't even taken one bite. Next to her, however, David attacked his food as if it were his last meal—after heaping generous amounts of hot sauce on it first.

Matt always looked forward to Dinner Night, but now he longed to be with the Circle of Five. He wanted to discuss what they had learned and figure out what they were supposed to do next. He assumed everyone in the circle felt the same.

Rich suddenly broke Matt's silent reverie. He rose from his seat and turned to face Eric and Richard Sr. at the head table. "How could you?" he shouted. Everything stopped. Matt wanted to yank his friend back into his seat, but didn't want to make a bad situation worse. All eyes darted to the young man questioning the director of the ID.

Richard Sr.'s shoulders drooped more than usual. "H-How could I what, son?"

Rich stared at his father. "How could you not stop the accident?"

Eric placed his hand on Richard Sr.'s back. "Why would you think he would be able to stop that tragedy?"

"Sir, he's kept us safe for years. I thought he would be able to stop any accident, given the security measures the ID has in place."

"I know your dad is a great man, but no one is perfect."

Rich wiped the tears forming in his eyes. Matt was about to pull him back down, when Rich said, "Sorry, dad. We all feel awful and I'm having a hard time dealing with what happened. I wanted to believe the accident could have been prevented. Sorry for blaming you. I know there was nothing you could have done."

Richard Sr. looked in his son's direction for a moment. He avoided eye contact, choosing instead to talk to his plate. "No problem, son."

Eric addressed the crowd. "I think we're all trying to cope with this very difficult situation. We haven't had a tragedy like this in years. Lord willing, we won't again. Tomorrow morning, we'll have the opportunity to say goodbye and honor these patriots properly. For the rest of tonight and after the memorial tomorrow, I ask that we honor their primary mission in life…living. It will be difficult for a while, but to do anything else would dishonor their legacy."

Most of the audience nodded in agreement and, following Eric's lead, returned to their conversations.

Thankfully, the rest of the evening returned to merely slow and unbearable. After dinner, Matt had planned to ask Rich why he would risk everything with his outburst. Unfortunately, Eric had a different idea. He asked, "Matthew, why don't you come home with me?"

Matt looked up at his father's eyes and knew this was not the time to refuse. He nodded in assent, kissed Lori goodnight, and followed his father to one of the few operating vehicles. Matt sat in the passenger seat of the black, four-door sedan. The RMs had retrofitted the car to run via a battery charged by solar energy and the energy created by the car's own motion.

They pulled away and his father popped on the lights inside the car. His father's voice drowned out the low hum of the engine. "Interesting dinner tonight."

Matt looked away. "You could say that, sir. It was certainly the quietest."

"Is everything all right with young Richard? We're all saddened by the events of this week, but his accusations toward his father were out of character and out of line."

"I'm sure he feels horrible for Stephanie and..."

"Yes?"

"And...and probably frustrated his father couldn't protect everyone. I guess we're all used to feeling safe...thanks to you and Dr. Fox." At first, the ease with which he had lied surprised Matt. But the nausea that followed told him he still hated keeping secrets from his father.

His father waited until they had pulled into the circular White House driveway to respond. He parked the car, turned to face his son, and waited for Matt to look back at him. "Richard does a good job as Director of the ID, but I need to keep an eye on him at all times to make sure he does what's right."

Matt didn't know what to say, at least not without revealing what he knew. He responded with a slight nod. Thinking the conversation was over, he opened the car door.

But his father placed a hand on Matt's arm to indicate otherwise. "I understand you've spent some time with Ms. Jackson this week."

Apprehensive about what his father might know, Matt said, "Yes, sir. I was getting advice from her and her brother, David, for a Science & Technology project." The earlier nausea had been nothing. Matt now felt truly sick as he finished his sentence. After not lying for most of his life, it was now a daily habit.

"I see. What's it about?"

Feeling stupid, Matt said, "Oh, it's…it involves the soil. Their parents taught them a lot about agriculture. I want to keep the project private for now. So I figured I would ask for their help."

"Interesting. Well, as we discussed the other night, a good leader has to make use of the expertise of others. You'll have to tell me about it sometime."

"Yes, sir."

Lying back on his bed, Matt spent a few minutes working through his conversation with his father. He felt he had done a pretty good job with the story about Sophie. He spent the rest of the night wondering what his father meant about watching Richard Sr. Was he suspicious of Richard? If only Matt could ask his father about Richard's murderous activities, he would have his answer and likely many more.

After a while, he began to drift off to another night of restless sleep.

A SATURDAY OUTING

[SATURDAY, SEPTEMBER 5, 2037, 8:00 A.M.]

Matt awoke to a stinging in his eyes, as if he had not slept in days. In fact, he had not slept well in about a week. Thinking about what he had to do, however, gave him plenty of focus. Today he needed to go pay his respects to the scientists who had been murdered just a few days earlier. Then, he would head to the Jacksons' secret lab and attempt to get to the Lincoln Cottage unnoticed.

The ceremony for the three scientists would be held at Arlington National Cemetery, the burial site for everyone since the Storm. Because there was rarely a death in their little community, going to Arlington presented an opportunity to leave the limited confines in which most of them spent their lives.

The first post-Storm RM burials had included a long procession up to the Lincoln Memorial and then over to Arlington across the Memorial Bridge. But now almost everyone simply used the underground Metro from the Smithsonian station to the Arlington station. The train, which ran only on the rare occasion of a funeral, needed only a handful of people to operate. Matt's father said this travel method maximized the time for burial and allowed people to get back to their jobs of running the community.

Matt accompanied his father in his car. In contrast to the previous night, this drive could not have been quieter. Seeing the larger-than-life white, marble figure of President Lincoln looking out over their community reminded Matt of what he and his friends were planning. The sun's rays gleamed off the memorial, as well as the stone-arched bridge.

His father drove across the bridge and through the large, black, iron gates of the cemetery. Thousands of headstones covered the sloping grounds, reminding Matt of the gravity of his mother's message. If he made the wrong decision, everyone might find themselves in the same predicament as those buried at Arlington. He turned away. If he made the wrong decision, who would be left to bury them?

They parked and began their climb to the burial site at the crest of a hill overlooking their city—the perfect location for those who rested there to keep watch over the community. Their ascent was eased by the cushiony grass underneath them. The two of them remained silent, the low whoosh of the robotic mowers and the chirping of crickets providing the only noise until they neared the top. There, the hushed voices of the assembled community mixed with the warm, humid air.

Matt wasn't sure if his increased heart rate resulted from the hike or the sight before him. His eyes darted toward each of the red-shirted IDs who lined the outside of the assembly. Who in this group had helped Richard with the murders?

He joined Lori near the front. As he'd done before each of her singing performances since they'd started dating, Matt held her hand tightly. Today it was cold and clammy. He forced himself to look at her swollen, red eyes, then leaned over and whispered, "I know you'll be great, as always. It'll mean a lot to Stephanie and her family." She managed a smile.

They waited out the final minutes before the ceremony in silence, the soft breeze cooling his skin and providing just enough relief from the heat of the late-morning sun.

Matt's father spoke first. He extolled the great strides of the geneticists, describing how their work had been essential to repopulating the world and bringing humanity back from the brink of extinction. Matt peeked around and saw everyone's faces steeled and focused on the great orator, several with tears inching down them. Next, the family members spoke, followed by Matt's Science & Technology teacher, Dr. Farmer, and a few others who wished to say their goodbyes.

As Matt listened to the eulogies, another marker drew his attention. Even though he had spent only a little time here, he felt strangely at home near his mother's burial site. He tried to remain focused on the speeches, but his mind kept gravitating toward her and her mission.

He rubbed the back of his neck, thinking about the clues. Had she died leaving them? Why—and how—did she leave them? Had she been murdered like the scientists they were remembering now? He had always taken it at face value that she had died in a lab accident. But looking at Stephanie, Matt expected that she, too, thought her parent had merely died in an accident. He wished the ceremony would end so he could rush to the Lincoln Cottage and get some answers.

Finally, it was over. Unlike military burials at Arlington before the Storm, there was no 21-gun salute for the fallen. All of the burials since the Storm were of civilians and, in any event, weapons were banned in their community. Instead, Lori closed the memorial by leading everyone in the singing of "The Battle Hymn of the Republic." Her melodic voice drew Matt to the edge of his seat, his heart beating as if he were about to march off to war.

When she finished, Matt flashed her a great job smile. He then followed his father over to his mother's headstone. Matt stared at it, his hands in prayer, and thought: *I'm not sure what you want me to do. I hope I don't let you down.* After a minute, Matt looked over at his father, whose downcast eyes were watery.

"Dad?" His father looked up. "Uh…I'm going to take the Metro back with Rich and Bobby."

His father stared at him for a moment, then said, "Okay, son. I'll see you later."

He walked over to Lori. "Why don't you spend some time with Stephanie? I've got some things to do."

"What things?"

"You know, with Rich and Bobby." She nodded. "I'll catch up with you this evening for dinner." He kissed her and gave her a quick hug before saying goodbye.

Matt turned and hurried toward the Arlington Metro station, one of the few above-ground stops. The whole way toward the train—down the sloping hills, out the gate, and along the long sidewalk to the stairs down to the Metro station—he felt as if someone were watching him. Every couple of minutes, he looked back, but all he saw was the various members of the community talking with one another as they, too, made their way to the train. He reached the bottom step, turned left toward his friends, and glanced up once more. About halfway up the dim staircase, two eyes focused on him, sending a shockwave through Matt. Richard Sr. was staring directly at him. He turned and caught up with his friends, but said nothing in the mass of people surrounding them.

They boarded the train and sped into the dark underground. During their short journey, Matt tried to shake the fear that they'd been found out.

He looked around the subway car. He guessed that the train had not changed at all from the day of the Storm. Feeling the cushiony orange bench and looking at the advertisements about vacations, colleges, and clothes, he tried to pretend the Storm had never occurred. He imagined that they were just on a Saturday outing. But each dark, vacant station they passed jolted him back to his present predicament.

Upon arrival at the Smithsonian station, they exited the trains and walked up the non-operating escalators, where they shielded their eyes from the bright light. Bobby spotted David and Sophie ahead of them, gliding toward the Botanic Garden. They caught up at the entrance, where Matt took one more look around. No Richard Sr., or anyone else for that matter. "Your parents aren't here?"

"No, they're headed to Lincoln Park, like always."

Matt pushed his way to the front of the group and down into the lab. As soon as Bobby pulled the trap door shut, Matt turned to Rich. "I think your dad knows."

"About what? What we're doing?"

"Yeah. Before we got to the train, I turned around and he was staring at me."

"And?" Sophie asked.

"And what?"

"What else are you basing your conclusion on?"

"How about last night, when Rich all but accused his father of murder? You saw how guilty he looked."

Sophie said, "Yeah, I did. But the way Rich played it was brilliant."

Rich placed his thumbs in his belt loops, thrust out his chest, and grinned at Matt.

Sophie looked at Rich. "From his reaction, I seriously doubt he thinks you know what happened."

"I agree," Rich said. He pointed toward Sophie. "I like her."

Bobby asked, "Is there anything else you can think of?"

Matt considered for a few seconds. "Nothing. But who knows what he knows?"

Rich said, "No offense, buddy, but I think you're being a bit paranoid."

"About a killer knowing what we've been doing, including seeing evidence of his crime? Maybe I am. But consider what we've learned in the last few days and how much more there might be. Why aren't you at least worried?"

Bobby said, "We're all worried. But we haven't done anything yet. As long as we're all following your rules, no one other than the five of us should know what we've seen."

Rich placed his hand on Matt's shoulder. "Bobby's right. We've all kept our mouths shut. Right? No one's copied any of the Neural clues. Right?"

They all nodded and said, "Right."

Matt relaxed onto a stool. "Okay."

"Matt, what did you think about your father's reaction last night?" Sophie asked. "You know, to what Rich said."

He looked up at her. "At first, I thought he was defending his friend, a friend who he might not know is a killer. Then, on the way home, he asked how you were, Rich."

"He did?" Rich asked.

"It seemed normal until he told me that he has to keep an eye on Richard Sr. to make sure he does what's right." That stunned everyone into silence. After a moment, Sophie opened her mouth to speak, but Matt continued. "Before anyone comes to any conclusions, that could mean many things."

Sophie began to raise a hand as if to offer several possibilities. Matt made meaningful eye contact with her and she lowered her hand back to her side.

Matt said, "Even though I desperately want to find out what he knows, we can't risk anything yet. I won't tell him what we've seen or what we're doing. So...what are we doing?"

Rich pulled out four Discs and said, "This...and a few other things. Most of them are standard ID issue, but I've made a few modifications." As he explained the security measures, everyone else stood still, occasionally exchanging impressed glances. The Mislocator program on the Discs most fascinated Matt. When downloaded, a simple code Rich wrote did just what the name indicated. It confused the location programs in their Neurals so that the ID would think they were in one place, when in fact they were in another. It would allow them to create the illusion that the five of them were not together and were not where they shouldn't be.

Matt downloaded the Mislocator and indicated he was at the Botanic Garden. "Do you have anything else?"

"For now, just this." He pulled out four belts like the one he had used with Matt two days earlier to hide their conversation. Rich did warn them, however, that the belt would not work on people who were within a few feet of them.

Matt changed out his belt. "Now, how do we get to the Lincoln Cottage?"

David had this answer. The sewer ran closer to the east wall of the lab than they had initially thought. So close, in fact, they could access it in a matter of minutes with a compressor, a device invented by Sophie's parents to compress a mass of soil into a smaller area. The device looked like a ray gun out of an old science-fiction movie.

The others sat and waited quietly while Bobby helped Sophie with the process. Matt watched David eye the ground. He attempted conversation to help David feel more comfortable. "So, your Magnometers are pretty interesting. Do you have any other inventions?"

"Yes."

"Are we going to use any of them today?"

"No. I didn't come up with any other inventions for our trip to the Lincoln Cottage."

"Your job is to maintain the library, right?"

"Yes."

Rich asked, "I know we need to preserve history, but is there much work for you when we all use our Neurals to research?"

"Not really, but I get a lot of time to read."

Matt asked, "Do you like it?"

"Yes, I get a chance to learn from a different perspective. I see works I might miss if I were just searching on a computer. It's a bit random, which was frustrating at first. But that's how I found the first book I read on theoretical physics. I was dusting one of the shelves and spotted a series of books written by Stephen Hawking. I began reading and couldn't put them down. After that, I found a lot of other books on the subject. I had to learn some complex math to understand most of the books, but that was interesting, too."

Rich asked, "But you've been working in the stacks only since you graduated?"

"Yes."

"And you've learned complex mathematics and theoretical physics by yourself in only a year?"

"Yes."

Rich and Matt exchanged wide-eyed looks.

David asked, "How long have you been dating Lori Ford?"

"For about a year, I guess."

Rich smiled. "Yeah, that's right. It's been about a year since we lost you."

"Funny. Why do you ask, David?"

"Dr. Ford spoke with the president last night."

"Yeah," Matt said, having seen them together before dinner started.

"Dr. Ford spoke to him about you and Lori."

"Wait," Matt said, "You could hear what they said from where you were sitting? I didn't hear anything and I was about the same distance from them as you were."

"Yes," David said very matter-of-factly.

Matt restrained a scoff.

"It's true," confirmed Sophie, coming up suddenly behind Matt. Startled, Matt almost slipped off his stool. Sophie smiled. "Sorry. I was coming back to let you know Bobby's finishing up. Anyway, David could hear it. He used to hear too much and had a hard time filtering out background noise."

"I used to ball up and cry," David said, "because I could hear every noise around me—multiple conversations around a large room, combined with every creak of the floor, the buzzing of flies, and any other noise you've tuned out since you were little. But my parents and sister took the hyper focus that I got with my autism and taught me to focus on one conversation at a time. Now I hear better than any of them."

"It took him years to be able to eat a meal with us," Sophie said. "He can hear you chew your mashed potatoes from across the table. That's why he focuses so hard on his own meal while he eats. So he can block out the noise from the rest of us."

Matt still doubted it was possible for David to have heard his father's conversation. But even if it were true, he didn't want to hear about it in front of everyone.

"Anyway, in case you're wondering," David said, "Dr. Ford seemed upset. He told the president that he and Mrs. Ford have been preparing Lori for you."

Matt's jaw dropped. "What does that mean?"

"It seems the Fords have been training her for years," Sophie said.

Matt turned to Sophie. "You heard the conversation, too?"

"No, I can't hear like my brother. But he told me everything."

"Everything?" Matt asked. "How much was there?"

"Not much else," David said. "She's been trained to follow you since she was a child."

"What? That's crazy."

Rich said, "I'd think so, too. But after this week, I don't know. Think about how she's always there to help you. How she never questions you. Not even about this ridiculous secret project."

David said, "Dr. Ford informed the president you've been hanging out a lot with Sophie this past week. He asked the president to find out what was going on."

Out loud to himself, Matt said, "That's why he asked me about hanging out with Sophie."

"He did?" Sophie asked. "When?"

"Last night on the way home, after our discussion about Rich's dad. I told him I asked you and your brother for help on a Science & Technology project involving soil. I told him I wanted to keep the project private for now."

Sophie asked, "And he bought it?"

"I thought so. He ended the conversation there."

"Well...that's not a bad explanation," she said. "And my joining DC3 will help, but we'll have to come up with something better...assuming you decide to accept the mission."

"I'm done," Bobby said, rejoining the group.

To avoid processing his bewilderment about Lori's training, Matt walked over to inspect the tunnel. To his amazement, it wasn't a simple, small hole that they would have to drag themselves through. It grew from a small hole at the entrance to about five feet tall. Matt's skin tingled as he slid his hand along a smooth surface. He flipped on a flashlight, revealing a 50-foot passageway. Sophie and Bobby had made thick, dark walls of glass with a laser attachment to the compressor. The walls would help protect against a cave-in.

When Matt emerged from the tunnel, Sophie asked, "What's the plan?"

He pointed to the passageway and then to their shoes. "We have our route and our transportation. Let's go."

Sophie handed out the ugly, yellow protective pants and jackets the Jacksons used when conducting their experiments. Everyone pulled them on over their clothes.

Matt led the way through the glass passage. He reached the other side, maneuvered around a filtration system that kept the foul sewer smell from invading the lab, and stepped out into a dark, dank, barrel-vaulted brick tunnel. Despite not having been used in at least decades, the smell was still so powerful that it nearly knocked him out. He struggled to suppress his convulsive reaction by covering his nose, to no avail. *If foul smells could die, this is where they would be buried*, Matt thought.

Four more lights emerged behind him.

"I pulled a box and the table up against the hole," Sophie said.

"That's good," Rich whispered. "Let's not talk until we're beyond the community. The belts don't mute sound, they only change it. The ID might hear us." They all nodded in agreement.

Then they each turned on their Magnometers and glided single file through the sewer.

The minutes it took to glide well past the edge of their city seemed much longer. Matt gazed ahead, his mind flashing from Richard Sr.'s eyes on him to the bizarre idea of Lori being trained.

They reached a curve in the sewer where Rich grabbed hold of Matt's shoulder, pulling him back to their little group. Rich pointed up and whispered. "This is our exit. We're just past Union Station."

Seeing a manhole cover, Matt whispered that he would go first and check things out. His nausea grew with each step of the climb. Upon reaching the surface, he held on with one hand and pushed up with the other with all his might. The manhole cover scraped the surface above and sunlight and fresh air poured in. Matt took a big gulp of the clean air, climbed out, and squinted until his eyes adjusted to the blinding rays.

An eerie scene slowly came into focus. The years of weather and unchecked vegetative growth had turned the once-vibrant area north of the Capitol into an urban jungle. Flora had engulfed the almost un-recognizable streets, like a giant snake devouring its prey. Many vacant cars sat haphazardly with their doors open. Matt could almost sense the Storm-induced terror, the occupants fleeing in a hopeless attempt to survive. He shook off the mixture of sadness and fear and motioned for the others to ascend. After a minute, they popped their heads out of the sewer, one by one. Everyone removed their protective gear and gave it to Sophie to stuff in a pack.

It was a slightly uphill three-mile trek to the Lincoln Cottage. Al-though they had to maneuver around roots and small trees, they were able to find enough flat land to glide there in half an hour. Matt figured that they might have arrived sooner, but the others kept slowing down to inspect strange and interesting sites—from an oak tree growing out of the front hood of a car to a baby carriage tied to the ground by vines of ivy.

Matt pressed forward, more concerned with getting answers that might alleviate their concerns than inspecting a deteriorating neighbor-hood. Each comment from his friends sent another flush of impatient heat through his body. Nearly at the end of his rope, he cooled as they finally arrived at the black iron gate of the Armed Forces Retirement Home—a sprawling site that had housed many retired veterans prior to the Storm, and the location of the Lincoln Cottage.

Rich said, "Can you believe the protection they had for retired soldiers?"

The entrance at the main gate was open, as if to receive them. Matt half expected security to question them at the gatehouse, but, as with the rest of the world outside of their community, no one was there.

The Lincoln Cottage lay directly ahead of them, surrounded by larger three- and four-story dormitories and, miles downhill in the distance, the dome of the U.S. Capitol. Dark trim outlined the windows and the tall roofline of the two-story, dirty, white stucco house. In front of the house stood a life-size, brass statue of President Lincoln next to his horse. It had handled time well.

They walked up the cracked sidewalk and made their way to the front door. Matt had the strange urge to knock, but turned the knob and pushed the rotting, brown door open.

A HOUSE DIVIDED

[SATURDAY, SEPTEMBER 5, 2037, 1:00 P.M.]

Matt was greeted by a musty odor that forced his hand to his nose. The others followed suit as they entered. He adjusted to the smell as he explored.

He walked around a parlor and some rooms intended for tours. Matt shook his head in disbelief at the good condition of the downstairs, then crept up the creaky, wooden staircase. At the end of a hall, he came to a study with a small desk that sat next to a window. Sophie followed him into the sunlit room.

Matt turned to her. "Is this the room?"

Sophie stared at it, unblinking. "Yes."

Matt called out, "Great job, Bobby. You were right." The others filed in.

Matt could hear only the beating of his heart as he waited for some revelation. He scanned the room several times, finding nothing. Then, there it was. The thumping in his chest stopped. On the shelf next to the window stood a book entitled Poetic Observations by Ida Simpson. He walked over and slipped the fragile book from among the other volumes on the shelf. "I can't believe it," he said. "This is the same book my mother left me before she died. The book in which she left the picture of Sophie."

He handed the book to Sophie, who turned it over and read the back. "The author was a resident here at the Armed Forces Retirement Home," Sophie said.

"Do you remember the page you found the picture on?" David asked.

"Page 40. I was always careful to keep it on that page."

Sophie's slender fingers gingerly turned the fragile paper until she reached the right page. As if expecting it, she pinched and slowly raised the loose, antique paper. "It's the House Divided speech by President Lincoln."

After a few moments, Bobby, his chin perched in hand, said, "I think I understand. We have to stand together or we'll fail. All of us need to touch the charm."

The others shrugged. Matt waited for the other four to pinch the charm, then touched it. A minute later, it popped open and revealed five Discs impressed with the letters M, S, B, D, and R.

Four of them retrieved their Discs, while Rich hesitated.

They decided to take them one at a time. Sophie went first. Her Disc told her, "The clock is ticking. Sometimes to solve a problem, you must take a step back. If successful, the day will no longer be Infamous. If not, all will be lost."

Confused by the newest cryptic clue, Matt said, "David, why don't you go next?"

David downloaded his Disc and stared ahead, his brow furrowed.

Finally, Matt asked, "What is it?"

David's face relaxed and he refocused on Matt. "The Disc says, 'With the help of Physics and other Sciences, this chariot can help him complete the journey—but remember its clock is ticking.'"

Matt asked, "Is that it?"

"No. There are schematics. Pages and pages of schematics."

Sophie asked, "For what?"

David smiled. "It doesn't say, but I think I know."

Several others prompted him. "Well?"

"For a time machine."

They all stood there, eyebrows furrowed like David's had just been. A week earlier, that idea would have been ridiculous. But not anymore. "Why would we need a time machine?" Matt mumbled.

"To send you back," David answered very matter-of-factly. Matt suddenly wanted to sit down. But with all eyes on him, he stood tall as David continued. "Along with the schematics, I got an image of you standing with your arms out to each side, your palms face up, and a small machine in your left palm." No one else moved, as if David and Matt were the only living things in the room. "The machine looks like a metallic ball. There are two holes at the top and there appears to be a biometric scanner on the bottom."

The room became quiet, the only noticeable sound a bird rustling in the tree outside. Matt tried to absorb what he had just heard. Traveling back in time was impossible. He leaned against the wall to guard against his growing dizziness.

Sophie got them back on track. "Rich, why don't you go next?"

"Okay. It better not be like my last one." Rich slid the Disc onto his tongue and let it dissolve. He exhaled in relief and said, "It's the same as David's—images and schematics."

Sophie waved a hand in Matt's face, drawing him back into their circle. He heard her voice echo in his ears. "Are you ready?"

"For what?"

"It's your turn."

"Oh...right." He downloaded the Disc and recited the contents. "It includes that darkened circle from one of my other Discs. It also says, 'Without a doubt, Physics and other Sciences will be needed, but to succeed in your journey, you must complete the circle. You have what you need around you and inside you. Remember, the clock is ticking.' What is it with this circle? I would think it means the Circle of Five, but the picture of a darkened circle seems to be indicating something else." No one responded. He didn't pursue the question any further, fixated on the idea of having to time travel.

Bobby said, "That leaves me." He consumed his Disc. "It says, 'You cannot complete the circle without the Arts. To find the answer, you need only look back and up.'" He paused, then added, "I have no idea what that means." Neither did anyone else.

Sophie asked, "Is that it?"

"No, there's one more message…about comBATON."

Rich said, "What, do we have to win the championship?"

"Maybe. It says, 'ComBATON is more than a game. To reach the beginning with the BALL, you have to achieve the end with the BATON. To Discover the date, follow Spain.'"

"The beginning and end of what?" Matt asked. "And what does Spain have to do with this?"

"I think they mean to travel back in time, you have to get to the championship at comBATON," David said.

"How'd you get that?" Sophie asked.

"I was thinking of calling the time machine the Ball."

Everyone stared at David. "Why?" Sophie asked.

"Because that's what the time machine looks like in the schematics. And because saying Ball is less risky than saying time machine."

Matt felt as if the clues had read their thoughts and, by the team's pensive silence, he suspected they felt the same.

"So…" Sophie said.

"The clue is saying that in order to travel back to the beginning—the earliest time in Matt's journey—he has to reach the end with the Baton. The championship in comBATON."

Bobby said, "Wow. That makes sense."

"I don't think David is right," Rich said. "I'm sure he is." He held out a hand to Matt. "Do you have that picture of Sophie with the writing on the back?"

Matt pulled the creased photo from his pocket.

Rich scanned it and nodded. "I think the sequence includes a time and date," Rich said.

"What time and date?" Sophie asked.

"12:01 A.M. on December 7th, 2037."

Matt asked, "How'd you figure that?"

Rich said, "Sophie's clue talks about the 'Infamous' day. The only thing I can think of is December 7th, Pearl Harbor Day. President Roosevelt called it 'a day that will live in infamy' when he addressed the nation."

"Seems like a bit of a stretch." Matt looked around to see agreement in the others' furrowed eyebrows.

"Think about the sequence after 1918. 1-2-0-1-A-0-7-1-2-9-6. Think about the 96. This year is the 96th anniversary of the bombing of Pearl Harbor. As for the 0-7-1-2, I know the 07 and the 12 are backwards, but—"

Bobby cut in. "My clue said we have to follow Spain to 'discover the date,' and the Spanish culture put the day before the month. And December 7th, 2037, is the day after this year's championship."

"Right," Rich said. "Besides, if it means July 12th, we're too late. So, we need to move forward and assume the Infamous Day is December 7th of this year."

Sophie said, "Impressive. But what's the meaning behind the 1918?"

Rich said, "I don't know." Everyone else shrugged their shoulders.

David said, "I don't know about the 1918, but the time makes sense. In my clue with the time chariot, the clock is set to 12:01."

Matt's eyes widened. "Really?"

"Yes," David answered. "It feels like you're supposed to go back at 12:01 A.M. on December 7th." Everyone agreed that conclusion made as much sense as any of their time travel theories so far.

The group discussed what they'd just learned. It all seemed ridiculous on one level, but very serious on another.

"According to what I've read," David continued, "one possible way to travel back in time is to use a wormhole. Theoretically, it would need to be opened on each end. If we were to open a hole on only one end, you might have nowhere to go. Who knows where you'd end up or whether you'd die traveling through another dimension?"

Matt felt colder than he had on the morning of the Speech. He steeled his face to appear confident and to mask his fear of dying in a wormhole.

"Okay, then," Sophie said. "To do this right, we'll have to build the time machine and test it before that date."

"Yeah," Rich said. "And win the championship. Then Matt can go back and do whatever he has to do."

Sophie crossed her arms.

"What?" Rich asked. "The clues require it."

Sophie rolled her eyes. "They don't say anything about winning. Let's stay focused."

Matt exhaled and chuckled. As much as he would have preferred to discuss sports instead of an impending life-threatening journey, she was right. "Okay, I get that the clues seem to say it has to be us and it has to be done at that time. But if we do this and fail, we could do a lot more harm than good. And what would the ID do to us if we're caught?" He thought again of Richard watching him. "Look at what the head of security did just a few days ago. Has it occurred to you that my mother and Bobby's parents might have died trying to do something like this?"

Bobby said. "Yes, that did occur to me." He placed a hand on Matt's shoulder. "And that's why we have to try. They can't have died for nothing."

Matt looked at Sophie.

She said, "I think I speak for everyone else when I say we're prepared to take the risk." The others nodded. "How about you, Matt?"

Matt thought about the risks, but considered the possible reward— saving billions, including maybe his mother. "Yes," he said in a low, but firm, tone.

David added, "I think we can do it. Considering the picture of Sophie and the images of Director Fox must have been taken back in time, it's clear it can work."

"I agree with David," Rich said. "How else could your mother have left us the clues? Maybe there's no guarantee it can be done again, but it's safe to say time travel has been performed successfully at least once."

"There's something else to consider, though," David said. "Let's say you do whatever it is you're supposed to do—like stop the Storm. You might alter the timeline to the point where one or more of us is never born. In which case, how would we succeed in sending you back in the first place?"

Once again, the room fell silent. Then, Rich said, "I don't know, but I would take the risk just to give my father a second chance to do the right thing…and to save billions."

Bobby added, "Matt, we might save our parents. And think about this—I'm the last of an entire culture. Thousands of other cultures were lost in the Storm. If we save them, we've completed the RM's mission."

Matt said, "Okay, it's pretty clear you're all on board." They all nodded again.

"So, what about you?" Sophie asked.

"It's a lot to think about," Matt said.

Sophie asked, "What is? The risks of time traveling? The risk of getting caught?"

"Yes and yes, but like I said, I can handle it," he answered, although his sinking stomach told him otherwise. "It's more than that, though. We've learned a lot this week, but I still need to think this all through." His dream-mother had warned him of a decision, and here it was. He began to perspire. "I know we need to get back soon. I'm going outside for a few minutes." He turned to leave, but turned back and directed, "Rich and David, start working through the schematics…just in case."

Sophie crossed her arms. Matt had become used to this trademark stance of hers—and the remarks that would usually follow. But, instead of the look of someone about to chastise him, her face seemed relaxed, almost sympathetic. "Can I speak with you a minute? Alone?"

"Sure." He nodded in the direction of the stairs, let her pass, and followed her down.

At the ground floor landing, she faced him. "You know why Bobby and Rich are doing this. And my brother will follow me anywhere. But, before you decide, I need you to know why I'm in."

Matt already knew. She had made it abundantly clear over the last week that she did not agree with the current path of the community. Of course she would do anything she could to change it. "Because—"

She placed a Disc in his mouth. "This is why. I found this video and letter in my basement when I was a kid."

The video began to play on his Neural. A young, smiling couple stood in front of Sophie's house, the father holding their baby. But they were not Sophie's family. The time stamp on the video was 10:01 A.M., October 24, 2020. The day of the Storm. The parents crouched several feet apart, facing each other. "Are you getting this, John?" the mother asked. "It's propped on the fence," replied the father.

The mother took one glance at the camera, then smiled back at her daughter. "C'mon, Ava," she said, "You can do it." John said, "Are you ready? Here you go." He let go and held his hands close to little Ava as she took her first steps. She stumbled over to her mother, who picked her up and twirled her around, saying, "We're so proud of you." Ava smiled and giggled as her parents beamed and clapped. A smile wide on his face, John walked up to the camera and shut it off.

The video dissolved, replaced by the image of a water-stained letter. It was addressed to "Anyone who finds this" and signed by "Sally."

I don't know if anyone will ever read this, but I have to write it. John and I have been fortunate to experience so much in our lives. This morning was one of the best. Our girl took her first steps. We were so proud of her—her first steps of independence in a wonderful world. But as the cloud of death approaches, I realize now that these steps are the only opportunity Ava will have in this life. My poor girl will never have the chance to grow up. My sole remaining hope is that someone finds this record of our girl, our amazing little one, and knows she existed. This little light of mine is being extinguished before her time.

Matt struggled to hold back tears as the video ended and he regained his focus.

Sophie stared out a window. "It's not enough. Is it?"

"What?"

She looked at Matt. "Knowing she existed. Remembering isn't enough."

"So, this is your reason?" She nodded. "I guess it's selfless of you to want to risk what we have to save them." He meant it, but a thought popped into his head unbidden. *Although it's my life you're risking.*

"Actually, it's selfish. But not for the reason you're thinking. I know you're thinking I'm willing to sacrifice you to save them." Matt tried to feign astonishment at her accurate insight. "It's all right. Maybe that is what I'm doing. I'm sorry. But if you'd seen that video and letter and woke up most nights to nightmares of that little girl dying or of that mother pleading with you, you'd feel the same as I do." She grabbed Matt by the shoulders. "And now we know we can do something about it. I don't think I'll be able to sleep again if we don't do this. I'm not trying to guilt you. Well, maybe I am. But I thought you should know before you decide." She relaxed her hands and let them drop to her sides.

"I don't know what to say. Thanks for being honest, I guess."

She nodded. "One more thing. I saw you earlier, staring at your mother's grave. Now you know what she wants you to do."

"How'd you know that's what I was wondering?"

Sophie smiled and headed back up the stairs. Matt watched her for a moment, then turned, stepped outside, and leaned against the statue of President Lincoln. Thinking back on his life, he realized he had never had to decide anything of any importance. He had always done what he was told and without question. Even though he feared being seen as a fraud, so far everything had always worked out well for him—the Speech, the assistantships, and especially Lori. But they were all thrust upon him. Now, he had to make a life-changing decision all on his own. On the one hand, he could stick with the status quo and support the society led by his father, a society he had always believed would be humanity's salvation. On the other hand, he and the rest of the Circle of Five could risk everything for his mother's mission—the full purpose of which he didn't know, but might include saving her, his grandfather, little Ava, and billions more.

Out of the corner of his eye, he noticed a small bluebird staring at him from a tree next to the Cottage. He looked around, looked back, and the bird was gone. Matt shook his head and told himself that the ID had not trained birds to spy on people. He had to control his paranoia.

He made his decision and climbed the stairs, holding his stomach to keep it from sinking.

When he entered the study, everyone stopped what they were doing and faced him. He said, his eyes moving from one person to another, "I know that if we all do this, a lot of people could get hurt, even die. I know what you all said about being willing to take the risk. But I'm still concerned." He anchored his eyes on Sophie. "But the thing is, there's something worse than death: living without purpose. I'm in."

Sophie beamed and everyone else cheered. Rich and Bobby slapped him on the back. Matt stood tall, grinned, and nodded at Sophie.

After a few minutes of excitement, Matt quieted everyone down. "Okay. We've got a lot of work to do. But before we begin, I need two promises. First, no one else can know about this. Paranoid or not, I don't want anyone to get hurt. Agreed?"

They all agreed.

"No one outside the Circle."

Sophie said, "No one."

Rich asked, "Including Lori?"

Matt had forgotten that major issue. The others stared at him. "Yes, including Lori," he agreed as the nausea returned. He tried to ignore it. "Okay. The second promise. We must agree to help one another. If an expert on our team tells any of us to do something, we do it. We can ask questions, but in the end we have to follow the expert. That goes for all of us. Agreed?"

Again, each of the others said, "Yes."

"Okay, we have to get back now, but think about the clues and what we need to accomplish our mission. On Monday, we should let Sophie try out for the team before practice to make our story believable. We'll cancel practice on Tuesday so we can meet here again, but we're not going to be able to cancel that many practices. So come prepared." The rest of the Circle began to discuss their strategy on the way out. Even

David was speaking with confidence. Like at the Speech, Matt felt as if he were absorbing their energy. His long strides led them out of the house.

The sun began to set, allowing the cool September evening to descend upon them. Once they reached the tunnel, all discussion of their new mission ceased. They reached the lab and returned to the surface and their lives, acting as if it had been a typical Saturday afternoon.

SOPHIE'S SURPRISE

[MONDAY, SEPTEMBER 7, 2037, 4:10 P.M.]

After school on Monday, Matt grabbed his gear and rushed to the practice field. At the sight of Sophie, a flutter grew in his stomach. Would she be good enough to pass for a member of the practice squad?

It was hot, and Matt was wiping the sweat from his forehead before they had even finished stretching. He smiled to see Sophie paying no attention to the perspiration that dripped from her face as she worked through the basic drills.

Next, they ran passing routes. First Rich passed while Bobby played receiver and Sophie defended. Bobby ran at Sophie, faked a cut out toward the sideline, then cut in across the field. Rich passed the Baton toward Bobby, but Sophie jumped in front, picked it off, and sprinted the length of the field, scoring on a flying side kick.

"Where'd she come from?" Matt asked Rich in wonder. When Sophie and Bobby returned to the huddle, Matt said, "Not bad. Let's see how you do on offense."

Matt surveyed the gathering crowd, which included Lori and several members of DC3. Rich played defense against Sophie. He lined up across from her and tried to stare her down. "You're pretty fast compared to Bobby. Let's see how you do against me."

Matt yelled, "Go!" Sophie ran the route to perfection, but Rich kept up with her. Matt threw the pass high and deep to a spot where only she might be able to reach it, if she had the speed. She edged ahead of Rich. Rich dove for the Baton, but got a fistful of air and a face full of grass. Sophie leaped at the last second, snatched the Baton from the sky, and trotted in for another score.

The chatter in the crowd grew. Matt summoned everyone back to the line of scrimmage. "Where'd you learn to play like that?"

"I've had a lot of time to practice at Lincoln Park while my parents did their work."

"So, let me get this straight," Matt said. "You like comBATON?"

"I like it as a tool for teaching speed, agility, and self-defense."

"So you're good at the martial arts part, too? You know, the kicking, blocking, punching, and grappling?"

"You can judge for yourselves."

"That's enough for me," Bobby said.

"I think we've got a new teammate," Rich panted, his hands on his hips.

Matt called the team over to the sideline. Loud enough for everyone nearby to hear, he said, "As you know, after tryouts last week we were still one person short. I'm happy to announce we have a full roster again," he said, gesturing to Sophie. The news was greeted with enthusiasm.

Jimmy had arrived just in time for the announcement. During practice, he lined up as receiver, while Sophie defended. "Let's see what you've got," he said. Sophie accepted the challenge.

Matt had already seen her defensive skills and was not about to make it easy. He signaled to Jimmy to do a basic curl. Jimmy ran at her for ten feet, planted his foot, and spun around to catch the Baton flying into his grasp. Just as his fingers began to clamp down, Sophie dove in and knocked it down.

Drills over, it was time to scrimmage. Even Matt, Bobby, and Rich had not seen whether she could handle herself in this situation. They got a first-hand look by playing against her, Jimmy, and Sue. On defense,

Sophie eluded blocks, closed on the Baton holder, and landed kicks to the chest to end plays. On offense, she worked with her teammates to find and create openings they could exploit. Toward the end of the scrimmage, Matt's final reservation about Sophie—could she take a shot?—was answered. She caught the Baton and turned smack into Bobby delivering a roundhouse kick to her abdomen. Bobby yelled, "Are you okay? I'm sorry."

"For what? Good kick."

Matt smiled at how her toughness matched her talent.

For the first time this year, Matt felt as if the team had come together. And for a brief time, he forgot about the Circle of Five and its secret mission.

That is, until he saw Lori sitting on the sidelines. The guilt drowned out any weirdness he felt about her possibly being trained for him. Lori was sitting alone and staring into the distance, very unlike her usual perky self. He sensed that she was continuing to struggle with the events of the past week. Adding Sophie to the team hadn't helped.

After practice, he approached her. The sadness that emanated from her reddened eyes tore at his heart. Here was the girl who had always been there for him and, now that she needed him, Matt didn't have a clue what to say. He just sat next to her and held her hand.

The now-typical sensation of time dragging—at least outside of the Circle and comBATON—continued on Tuesday. Finally, the Circle of Five met in the secret lab, traveled to the Lincoln Cottage, and assembled in the study.

"What's first?" Bobby asked.

Matt pulled a page from his pocket and explained his plan. "You'll split into two groups of two. One will help us avoid detection, and the other will build the Ball to send me back."

Sophie said, "After that, hopefully others will be there to help you."

A vision of a slender, blonde woman and tall, dark-haired man, both in lab coats, flashed through Matt's head. He suppressed a smile at the thought of seeing and working with his mother and grandfather, forcing himself to stay in the present. "Right. So, the groups."

"I also think," Sophie said, "a few of us have to learn as much as possible before you go back. Not only about the clues. But about others in the community and where their allegiances lie, about how Matt's mother and Bobby's parents died, about the Storm, and who knows what else."

"Good point," Matt said. "Okay. David and Rich received the schematics." He eyed both of them. "You are clearly meant to build the Ball. Bobby and Sophie, that leaves you to focus on the clues and investigation."

Matt continued, "Obviously, because there are only five of us, we will have to multi-task. Rich, you understand your father and his methods better than any of us. You should take the lead on creating a system to avoid detection. But rely on David." Matt pointed at the Magnometers on his shoes. "We've already seen what he can do."

David stared at the ground as usual, but his cheeks flushed red above his sheepish smile.

"David, I'm sure you were intended to take the lead on the Ball."

David managed to suppress the smile from his still-rosy face and nodded in assent.

Knowing Rich had hesitated around David, and even insulted him at first, Matt watched for Rich's reaction. "Agreed?"

Rich smiled and they both said, "Yes."

"Great. And I'll work with both teams. We've got less than three months to do this. Let's get started."

"Wait," Rich said. "There will be many days when two or three of us should be working, but the others should be seen around the community. That may be our best way to avoid detection. If all of us are always gone at the same time, people may get suspicious."

"Good point, Rich," Matt said. "Okay, let's break into teams for about an hour."

Sophie and Bobby moved into the next room and David and Rich remained in the study.

Matt's pulse accelerated as he moved back and forth between the groups. David made eye contact with Rich as they discussed various pieces of the schematics and how they fit together. Matching Sophie's exuberance, Bobby spoke more forcefully than Matt had ever seen, his hands emphasizing his points.

By the end of the hour, David and Rich had accomplished a good deal on the Ball. They agreed the schematics left for each of them were complementary. They also agreed that the best way to see how their schematics combined, while not allowing them to be easily discovered, would be to write them down and hide them when not in use. In the short hour, they had written out a significant amount of the schematics. Matt thumbed through the designs and stopped on a rough drawing of what he assumed was himself. In the sketch, he stood in a manner similar to the person in the Project RM emblem, palms face up. The Ball, which appeared to be the size of a grapefruit, lay in his left hand. Squiggly lines fed out of one of two holes on top. A small, inside-out tornado hovered near the other hole.

A shiver ran down his spine. To his knowledge, even with all of the brilliant minds throughout history, no one had ever figured out how to travel back in time. Now these teenagers were somehow going to do it. "Interesting. Sophie and Bobby, come on back in." They filed back into the room. "David, why don't you explain what you and Rich figured out?"

David looked down and mumbled, "Based on the specifications…I believe…I mean, we believe…that opening a wormhole requires an amount of energy infinitely greater than man can produce. Therefore, we believe we need a natural source. That's what we think these squiggly lines represent—the Ball collecting dark energy."

Rich said, "Matt, think about it. The same energy from the Big Bang—the energy that continues to expand the Universe—in the palm of your hand."

Matt folded his arms to keep himself from shaking, but grinned to suggest confidence.

Rich said, "Sorry to interrupt you, David. Tell him about the vortex."

Matt's eyes widened a little.

"We believe the Ball concentrates the energy and uses your biometric scan to create a wormhole that connects with a wormhole created by your younger self."

Matt said, "That's a lot of 'we believe' and 'we think.' How sure are you that you're right and that you can do it?"

"I'm almost certain we can do it. The logical explanation for the clues we received is that someone brought them or sent them back in time. But there are a few concerns."

Bobby asked, "What concerns?"

"First, dark energy and wormholes are theoretical. There's no proof that either exist, let alone that one can be used to open the other and that the other would send you back in time to a desired date. Second, I don't understand the energy source needed to power up the Ball in the first place. The configuration of the battery and the collector is strange. I don't see how it starts, let alone how it works. Third, even though the clues will be sent back with you, I'm concerned you could be crushed by unexpected gravitational forces in the wormhole or that the wormhole might not have an atmosphere. Your body might get through and deliver the information we have—the picture of Sophie and the images of Rich's dad—but in the process, you might die."

Matt doubted his mother would send him to his death, but the news still chilled him. He focused on David and spoke a little louder than normal. "I know you'll figure it all out. You've made a lot of progress in only a little time already, so keep at it. Maybe one of the answers is in the clues we haven't solved. For now, let's focus on building the Ball. Have you determined the place and date I'm traveling to?"

They both answered, "No."

"Well, hopefully we can figure that out. It'd be nice to know where and when I'm going to end up. How about avoiding detection?"

Rich answered, "We haven't discussed it yet."

Sophie said, "We did."

Bobby said, "We know that's your department, Rich, but we had a few ideas."

Sophie said, "We agreed that we have to be careful about Neural research. So, we may want to do some old-fashioned detective work. Bobby and I agree we need to consider more than technology in avoiding detection. We need to consider how we'll be viewed in the community. Especially since both Dr. Ford and Matt's father have expressed interest in our...hanging out together."

Matt said, "That makes sense."

Rich added, "I agree."

"Good," she continued. "Because we believe that Rich should appear to be reluctantly working with David on a project for Science & Technology. He could be your researcher. The community will expect you to use him that way."

"Okay," Rich agreed. "But David, just know I don't see you that way." David's eyes performed their typical descent, but a broad smile crossed his half-hidden face.

"Then there's Bobby and me." Matt expected something similar. She paused. "We're going to start dating."

"What?" Matt blurted. "Why?"

"Well, we can't all be working on projects with each other and we can't all act as if we dislike each other. It's just for appearances—not that I wouldn't date you, Bobby, if I were dating."

Bobby's hands fidgeted. "Besides, Matt, it will make things a lot easier for you with Lori. Not to mention Dr. Ford and your dad."

Though it made sense, the plan somehow did not feel right to Matt.

Rich agreed with Sophie. "That'll work. So, Matt, is that it for today?"

Matt barely heard him. "What? Oh…yeah, I think that's it for today. Great job, everyone."

Rich motioned for Matt to follow him into the next room. "Let's find a place to hide these drawings."

"Okay," Matt said, unsure why Rich needed him.

Rich gestured for Matt to bend down to feel for loose floorboards. Both on their knees, Rich whispered, "What's the problem?"

"What problem?"

"They're perfect for each other."

"What do you mean?"

"C'mon, they like the same things. And you told me that it was his speech that got her to come out to our practice. Heck, it got her out of the cap and glasses."

The warmth crept up his neck. "What's your point?"

"Do you like her or something?"

He thought of Sophie and her crossed arms. "What? No."

"Good. Think of how much easier it'll be for you with Lori and your dad." He slipped the schematics under the floorboards. "C'mon, let's go."

They reentered the study, his face cooling. Bobby asked, "So how are we going to do this and still have it look like everything's normal?"

"Good question," Matt said. "Rich and David have the hardest job of building a working Ball. But Rich can't miss too many practices without arousing suspicion. So, on most days, they might have to work on pieces in your parent's lab after school."

"And Bobby and I can go all over and investigate all kinds of things on our 'dates.'"

"True…just be careful about how you conduct your investigation. Questioning RMs and people like Mrs. Peterson will be a dangerous game."

David said, "Before you question anyone, I can do some research in the stacks. The Library of Congress is the largest library in the world. You never know what I might find. For example, maybe I can figure out what caused the Storm or what the dark circle in Matt's clues is—the clues that say we need to look behind the veil of ignorance and complete the circle."

Matt said, "Yeah, that sounds like a safer start." Everyone nodded. "David, do you have time to do all this in addition to your other tasks?"

"Yes, I have time. I'm not in school or on the comBATON team. I can spend all day researching, other than when I'm working with Rich."

"Okay, great," Matt said. "Also, let's keep our eyes and ears open. Try to gauge who we can approach without arousing suspicion. David, let us all know when you have something."

"Or if you think you're not getting anywhere," Sophie added. "We don't have a lot of time to figure everything out and most of your time needs to be spent on the Ball."

"Good point," Matt said. "I guess that's it for today." He turned and led the way out of the room and cottage and back to the lab. Matt couldn't pinpoint why, but the bounce seemed to have left his step.

DOWN TO BUSINESS

[WEDNESDAY, SEPTEMBER 9, 2037 7:12 A.M.]

At Matt's request, Lori met him before the morning stretch. She arrived with a perky smile on her face.

"I'm glad to see you happy again," he said.

"Thank you. I'm just glad to see you."

Matt took her aside. "You know that project I was working on?" She nodded. "It's been canceled."

"Really? I'm sorry to hear that."

"Yeah, it was a total bust."

"Except for getting Sophie and Bobby together," she said.

"You heard?"

"Sure. They make a cute couple. I hope they feel as lucky to have each other as I feel to have you." She leaned in and kissed him.

He reciprocated and held her hand as they joined the crowd at the morning stretch. The awkward feeling he'd had since David had told him about her possible training subsided. It still astonished him, however, that their lives had been so planned. Of course, he should have expected this from his father. His dad never left anything to chance. With all of these thoughts bouncing around in his head, the most basic one was what warmed him on this cool morning—he had the old Lori back.

For the first several days after the Circle of Five split into teams, Rich and David met and discussed the Ball. David also spent his spare time poring through the stacks to find some information that would help in the investigation. He provided little in his initial report to Matt. The only item of relevance was a paper written by Eric in 2010, the year he had become an RM. The paper hypothesized about the possibility of time travel—although David pointed out that Eric had contradicted his own conclusions eleven years later, in the paper he had written after the Storm. David told them this information probably wasn't useful in determining what had caused the Storm, or the meaning of the dark circle in Matt's clues. But hearing about his father's paper on the possibility of time travel gave Matt hope that his father had somehow helped his mother with the clues and had secretly intended for Matt to figure out a way to go back in time and fix everything.

Within days after splitting into teams, Sophie began pestering Matt. "When are Bobby and I going to be able to start investigating?"

"David isn't finished looking through the stacks."

"We don't have time to wait for him to read the entire contents of the library. If we don't begin soon, you may travel back without crucial information."

"I know."

"We have less than three months. This is your opportunity to gain an advantage on everyone in the past. You'll know things that haven't happened yet."

"I know! Let's give David until the end of this week. We'll hear what he has on Saturday. Then you can begin."

Sophie crossed her arms and exhaled. "Okay."

By Saturday, the community was buzzing about just one thing: the comBATON schedule. Anticipation ran high as the competitors and many others waited for the posting of the schedule on the community board at the north edge of DC3's practice field. Each person's warm breath added to the cloudy haze that hung in the cool morning air. Commissioner Turnbull's traditional posting was a bit old fashioned, but it added to the excitement about the upcoming games.

Matt and his teammates barely spoke as they waited. Matt thought back to last year, their first in the league, and wondered who their opponents would be this season. He expected Rich and Bobby were doing the same. The adrenalin rush felt like waiting to open Christmas gifts as a young boy, only amplified.

Rex and two of his teammates eyed DC3. With his typical sneer, Rex asked Matt, "Praying you don't end up in my division?"

Matt was tired of Rex's attitude. On one level, he understood what Mrs. Peterson had explained about his background, but on a more primal one, he had had enough of Rex's attacks.

Before Rex could snarl anything else, Commissioner Turnbull arrived with a long, rolled-up banner. He maintained an imposing, athletic presence even in his forties, standing tall with his shoulders back and chest out. Despite his gentle nature, or maybe because of it, he had garnered a good deal of respect in the community.

"Ladies and gentlemen, before I post this year's schedule, I just want to say that last season was one of the best we've ever had—even better than when your dads and I first won the championship," he said, addressing Matt and Rich. Matt glanced at Rex's sneer, which now dominated his face. "We have some teams who've been there and," he continued, looking at Matt, "we have some talented, young teams that now have experience. Good luck, everyone." He turned and fastened their six-foot long future—at least as it pertained to comBATON—to the board.

The teams of the Red division and their schedules stood on the left side of the banner. Matt scanned the division—the Raiders, the Patriots, the Avalanche, and the Blaze, the team that had knocked Matt and his friends out of the playoffs the year before.

The middle of the banner reflected the Playoff brackets. As in all prior seasons, the winner of each division would face the second place team in the other division in the semifinals, and in the championship, the two semifinals winners would face off.

The teams of the Blue division and their schedules stood on the right side of the banner—DC3, the Tsunami, the Nationals, and the Cyclones. Matt absorbed DC3's eight-game schedule the way David liked to inhale his dinner. Even if there were no such things as Neurals, he would still have no trouble remembering what was on this board. He etched the schedule into his brain. The setup was the same as the previous season. They would play each of the teams in their division twice and two teams in the other division once, and, as with the previous season, the Raiders and the Blaze were the only two teams not on their schedule. From behind him, Rex whispered in Matt's left ear, "Lucked out again, I see. Or maybe it's daddy making you look better than you are."

Matt could no longer contain himself. He wheeled around and exploded. "If you've got something to say, say it to all of us. Otherwise, keep your mouth shut!" Out of the corner of his eye, Matt noticed a disapproving look on Sophie's face.

Rex said, "I bet you'd like to try to shut it, wouldn't you?"

Matt said, "If you're unlucky enough to face us in the playoffs, we'll give you our answer on the field." He turned and headed toward the Botanic Garden.

Marching away with Bobby, Rich, and Sophie in tow, he heard Rex's parting shot. "Only in your dreams, Cane."

When they reached the lab, Sophie said, "Good job, Matt. I thought you were going to go all macho and hit him."

"I wanted to. But this project has to come first. Don't worry. When it's time, we'll confront him as a team."

Bobby said, "Good, because I don't think it'd turn out well. No offense, Matt, but I don't think you could take him. You're pretty good, but everyone says he's the best individual fighter since your dad."

"Yeah, Cane," Rich said in a mockery of Rex's voice. "So you'd better watch yourself." Everyone laughed.

The Circle of Five reached the Lincoln Cottage and Matt bounded up the stairs, eager to hear about David's and Rich's progress. "Okay, this has to be completed in a little over two and a half months. Where are we with the Ball?"

Rich answered as David left the room to retrieve their work. "We're moving along pretty well. We've written out all of the schematics," he said, as David reentered with a small pile of papers and some electronics. "As we'd expected, they seem to be complete." Rich held up one of the pages. "This is the list of the materials we're going to need to assemble it."

"And those are some of the materials?" Matt asked, indicating David's pile.

David said, "Yes. These are the couplers, 40 AWG wire, and—"

"It's the beginnings of the internal meat for the Ball," Rich said. "We believe we should be able to build it with plenty of time to spare, but…"

"But what?" Matt asked.

"But we still have no idea how to operate it. Even if we build it in time, without knowing how to work it? At best, it's nothing more than an ornament. At worst, it's a death trap."

The color drained from Matt's face, but he pressed on. "Keep working on it. We all believe in you. Do you need help?"

David hesitated. "We may need help at some point. For now, Rich and I will handle it."

"Great. How about the investigation? Tell everyone about the paper my father wrote on time travel."

"Several of the principles he espoused in the article are incorporated in the design of the Ball."

Matt smiled. "That sounds promising. Maybe he is with us."

"But David told us he also found the paper Eric later wrote that concluded traveling back in time isn't possible," Sophie replied. She held up a palm toward Matt. "I'm not saying he definitely didn't work with your mother, but he did contradict his earlier premise for some reason. And considering he's the one in power right now, we need to be wary until we have more facts." Matt hated her logic, but she was right. "So can Bobby and I get to work now?"

Bobby put an arm around Sophie's shoulders. "Yeah, I'm ready to do my part."

It didn't look like David would find anything else to help their investigation and he needed to focus on the Ball. "Okay, what's your plan?"

Bobby said, "Sophie and I spoke a few times this week about how we want to look for clues. We'll have to be careful how we ask questions about what happened before and after the Storm."

"So we thought," Sophie said, "it made sense to speak with Mrs. Peterson first, then my parents. We know them the best and it won't seem out of the ordinary to ask questions about Bobby's parents."

Matt said. "Makes sense. Anything else?"

Rich said, "We all need to keep our eyes open and listen carefully. Any of us might see or hear something that indicates who's on which side. One thing, though: if you encounter something suspicious, don't act until we can all meet and discuss it. It could be a trap."

Matt shook off the memory of Richard's eyes on him. "Good advice. I knew there was a reason you were included." Rich smiled. "Okay, let's talk schedule. I know with school and practice we may not be able to keep to one, but we should have a framework to get enough time before

December 7th." He pulled a folded paper from his pocket. "First, we should try to have a working prototype of the Ball by Storm Remembrance Day on October 24th."

Sophie said, "The one Saturday we don't have a game. I like it."

Matt turned to David. He didn't want to pressure his friend, but they did have a target date to meet. "I know it's not a lot of time," Matt said, "but just do your best. We're in this together. Don't feel like the entire weight of this is on you. As soon as you see how one of us might be able to help, ask."

"Okay," David said, although his hesitant tone belied the word.

Matt continued, "Okay, Bobby and Sophie, it's going to be harder to schedule the investigation, as I expect one thing may lead to another and there will always be more information to find out." A thought of someone harming Sophie and Bobby popped into Matt's head. "Just be careful and take your time. I'm available to help. Include me where you can. Now, let's break into our teams for a little while to discuss specific plans for the upcoming week. We may not get here again until October 24th, at least not all together. If you have something to say to all of us, make sure you do it before we leave."

The others nodded in agreement and broke into their groups. Sophie and Bobby went to the front room to talk, while Matt and the others remained in the study.

Matt attempted to follow Rich's and David's technical discussion, but laughter from the other room broke his concentration. His curiosity got the better of him. "What's so funny?" Matt asked, entering the room.

Sophie answered, still smiling, "Oh, nothing. How's everything going in there?"

"Fine. They've got it under control. Do you need any help?"

Sophie said, "Not yet."

Matt knew he had the largest part to play in the end. At the moment, however, he felt unneeded and unwanted.

After about an hour, Matt called everyone back together and asked if there was anything more to add.

Bobby spoke up, looking at Sophie. "Good job on picking the teams, Matt."

Matt did not know what it was, but something about Bobby was getting on his nerves.

The Circle departed the Lincoln Cottage for the last time until October 24th.

LET THE GAMES BEGIN

[SATURDAY, SEPTEMBER 26, 2037, 1:00 P.M.]

Over the next few weeks, Matt became increasingly irritable. He had returned to his normal routine—his daily classes, practices, and dates with Lori—since the last meeting at the Cottage. But he craved more involvement in the Circle of Five, and they didn't seem to need his help.

He pestered the others for information. All he could get out of Rich was, "You'll see." David's unemotional report of "We're doing well" pushed Matt's blood pressure increasingly higher.

Sophie's "Don't worry about it. Bobby's a great partner" left him at a loss for words. Frustrated, he didn't even ask Bobby for a status update.

Just in time to provide Matt with an outlet, the first game of the new comBATON season arrived. He couldn't wait to win and lessen the sting of last playoff's humiliating loss to the Blaze. Today, they would face the Nationals—a strong team of RMs who had played together for years, but whom DC3 had beaten in two close games the previous year.

Each game would start at the top of the hour, beginning at 2:00 P.M. DC3's game, the last of the day, would not start until 5:00 P.M. Nonetheless, the entire team, including the practice squad, attended the opening ceremonies and remained through the end of the day. Matt felt it necessary for everyone to attend. It promoted team unity and provided additional people to scout their future opponents. Most importantly, everyone had worked hard. They deserved to be recognized as members of DC3 as the horn blew to start the new season.

By the time the opening ceremonies began at 1:00 P.M., everyone in attendance was dripping with sweat. The single-toned comBATON uniforms of the competitors clung tight to their protective gear and skin. Matt could barely breathe as he stood with the other athletes on the west sideline of the field closest to the RM Monument, facing the Capitol dome that towered in front of them. Most of the rest of the community sat in a small set of bleachers on the other side or stood on the other edges of the field.

Eric, Richard, and Commissioner Turnbull—who had taken on the role of head league official among his many other duties—faced the teams from the center of the field. The light breeze and Lori's rendition of the Star Spangled Banner brought a brief smile to Matt's face. Commissioner Turnbull followed with a speech about fair play and the integrity of the game. Matt peeked over at the Raiders and the Blaze, the likely intended audience of the oratory. The commissioner finished by pointing to Eric and Richard Sr. as examples of how to win the right way. Matt thought, *If you only knew what we know now.*

Finally, the first game began, a rematch of the prior year's championship battle between the Raiders and the Blaze. Matt didn't blink until time expired. He scouted every move as he tried to determine which of the two teams presented DC3's biggest challenge. The Raiders used their power on offense, with players trying to use the takedown to allow Rex the opportunity to play one-on-one with the Blaze's best player, the

Enforcer. Rex scored three times using his superior speed and timing, landing five-point tornado roundhouse kicks.

The Blaze countered with teamwork on offense, including well-practiced passing routes and variations of the give-and-go to score. With less than a minute left in the game and the Raiders leading 15-13, the Blaze worked their way across midfield. Travis Wilson began to pass until his arm ran into Nick Rounds. The Baton shot off course right into Rex's hands. With no one nearby, Rex took a triumphant jog to a fourth tornado roundhouse kick goal. And that was it—game over. Raiders 20, Blaze 13. The Raiders took a victory lap. As he passed Matt, Rex said, "Boys, it looks like history's going to repeat itself."

With teeth clenched, Matt thought, *Not if we have anything to say about it.*

A long two hours later, it was time for DC3's season to start. Matt chose to begin the game with himself, Bobby, and Rich on the field. The opening charge, with the teams attacking from opposite ends of the field, began with DC3 on the south end and Matt in possession of the Baton. The whistle blew and both teams converged. Matt reached midfield before taking a roundhouse to the chest. On the ensuing plays, Bobby protected Matt, giving him time to complete several passes to Rich. They had no problem reaching the goal zone. In the tighter area, the Nationals—led by RMs CJ Rodney and Joey Townsend—downed them a couple of times. Matt broke free on the third and final play, receiving a no-look pass from Bobby and scoring an easy three-point front snap kick.

On DC3's first defensive series, the Nationals couldn't pass midfield. The months of practice had paid off.

Joey, CJ, and their third teammate, Megan Vogel, changed their coverage on DC3's next possession. CJ covered Rich and the others played an up-back zone. Matt felt this was an easy defense to handle until he forced a pass to Rich. Joey stepped in front, intercepted it, and reached the goal zone before Bobby stopped him. DC3 held their ground for the first two plays. On the third, however, CJ scored on a give-and-go from Megan.

The score remained tied at three for the remainder of the first half, each team stymieing the other's offensive plans. At halftime, Matt looked to regroup. Out of breath, he said, "We need to figure out a way…to get more space. They're smothering us."

Bobby said, "If you'd throw it to me once in a while, that would help. It's like you're only looking for Rich."

Rich said, "Yeah, let's spread it around a little. And what about Sophie?"

"It's the first game. No offense, Sophie, but there's a difference between practice and games. I want to transition you in slowly."

"There's a difference between slowly and not at all," Bobby said. "She can help."

Rich said, "Let's see what she can do." The others agreed.

"Okay. Let's start the second half with our starting lineup. Then we'll switch Bobby and Sophie a couple of minutes in."

A few minutes into the second half, with DC3 in control of the Baton, Bobby called time-out. He scowled at Matt—who still had not substituted in Sophie—and jogged off the field. Sophie ran in to join the game. She created a great deal of anticipation on the DC3 sideline and, given how unknown she was, a great deal of chatter in the crowd.

Matt threw a couple of short passes to her, but continued to focus most of his effort on Rich. With a couple of minutes to go, Matt tried to force an across-the-field pass to him. CJ ran in front and intercepted it. He ran to the goal unimpeded, scoring on a four-point flying side kick. With seconds left, Matt rushed to guide the team downfield for the tie or win. But they never came close to the goal zone.

The final horn sounded and most of the crowd dispersed. Matt's father met with the Nationals to congratulate them. Before departing, he issued Matt one pointed stare, causing Matt's heart to sink even further than it had at the horn.

Matt thought, *It's a good thing he can't shoot laser beams out of those eyes.* He hung his head as he regrouped with the team. "Sorry, everyone. It was my fault."

Rich slapped him on the back. "It's okay. We won't lose again."

Bobby wasn't as encouraging. "We won't if you include the whole team. What happened out there? Why didn't you spread it around?"

"I'm not sure."

"Well...figure it out." In a hushed voice, he added, "You know how important this is."

Matt glanced up at Bobby and nodded. Adding insult to injury—literally—Rex walked past, saying, "Well, maybe history won't repeat itself." He nodded at Sophie. "Nice addition, Cane."

Matt could barely control himself. "You have no idea what she's capable of. You have no idea what we're all capable of. We'll see you in the finals...if you're good enough to get there."

"More words, Cane." He turned, glided away, and shouted back, "Find me when you can back them up."

Matt turned back to the team and said, "I don't know what came over me today, but I can promise you this, from here on out, I'll do more than give one hundred percent. I'll make sure you can give one hundred percent, too. With all of us working together, we won't lose again. That's not a belief, it's a promise."

Bobby smiled at Matt. "That's the Matt I know."

The brief team meeting over, most of the members of DC3 went their separate ways. Matt had just finished packing up his gear when Bobby came over and said, "Let's talk. Come on over to the lab."

Matt's heart sped up. He hoped it had to do with their investigation. He reached the floor of the lab and noticed Bobby was alone. "Where's Sophie?"

"This is just between us. I told her I wanted to talk to you alone and she said we could use the lab if we needed it." He pointed to a box in the corner. "If we run into her parents, we'll say Sophie let us use the lab for my experiment over there."

"What's in it?"

"Nothing, but she said her parents wouldn't check."

"Okay…what did you want to talk about?"

"You know, what I said earlier didn't apply only to comBATON."

"It didn't?"

"Look, you're the leader of DC3 and you're the leader of our Circle. Lately, you seem to just be going through the motions. What's going on? Are you having second thoughts about our new mission?"

"Not at all. In fact, I've been frustrated about how useless I am."

"That's just it. You're the leader. If you want to do more, do more. This is no different than everything else I've ever seen you do. It's great you almost always include everyone and use their strengths. That's what makes you a great leader. But you need to use your own strengths, too."

Matt wasn't sure if he already knew all of this, but hearing Bobby say it woke him up. Time to get out of his own head and into the game—with his whole team. "You're right. What have you and Sophie learned?"

"Not much."

"I think it's time for another meeting. Would you mind asking Sophie, David, and Rich to meet here tomorrow after church?"

"Sure. By the way, just so you know there's nothing going on between us."

"Between who?"

"Me and Sophie."

"Why are you telling me?"

"You know, Matt, you're one of the smartest guys I know, but when it comes to girls…"

Matt rubbed the back of his neck. "What?"

"I'll say this. You're great at reading other people's expressions. The next time you think about her, look in the mirror."

Matt looked away. "Yeah? What am I supposed to see?"

"You'll know it when you see it."

Matt glided home, ignoring the uncomfortable end to the conversation with Bobby. He tried to focus on the agenda for the Circle the following day, but had to put his planning on hold when his father summoned him to the Oval Office.

His father sat behind the large, oak desk, wearing a Neural stare. Matt looked around at the portraits of Lincoln and Washington and began to sit on one of the two opposing couches in the middle of the room. Before he could settle onto the cushions, his father motioned to one of the wooden chairs facing the desk. Matt sat, staring out the large windows into the starry sky as he waited for his father's inquisition on the loss. Finally, his father directed his attention toward Matt. "Tough day on the field, huh. Why didn't you use the game plan we worked on all summer?"

"Sorry, sir. I guess I lost my focus. It won't happen again."

"I should hope not. Listen, you've got to know how to use those around you to your advantage. With your youth and agility, you should've been able to wear them out. Do you remember what I told you on the first night of practice earlier this year?" Matt nodded and his father continued. "A leader who doesn't understand the art of war cannot be respected by his soldiers, nor can he rely on them."

Matt knew from the clues how important the games were, not to mention he hated losing. But war? "Sir, I know, and we'll play better. But do you really think that applies as much in this world as it did in the past? I mean, there hasn't been a war since before the Storm."

"Don't be naïve, Matthew. There are no wars because no one questions my ability. The IDs are the soldiers who ensure peace—and they respect me because of the military prowess I displayed playing comBATON. You can follow in my footsteps by winning at this sport you think is only a game." Matt nodded, hoping his father was repeating the clue intentionally. "And about this Sophie Jackson—is she any good, or are you including her for Bobby?"

Pleased that the news of their so-called relationship had made its way to his father, Matt said, "Actually, sir, she's a great player. I just didn't include her much in the game today."

"If you say so. But don't let her affect the chemistry you have with Bobby and Rich. If I didn't know better, judging by the way you didn't use Bobby or her much, I'd think you were jealous. I shouldn't have to remind you that you need to be very careful about your actions. Women notice these things."

Matt restrained a slight scowl. He was committed to Lori, and she knew that.

"So, how's everything else going?"

"Fine, sir." Matt had no intention of discussing anything else for fear he would slip. He still didn't know if he could trust his father.

His father began to impart some wisdom, while Matt dwelled on the jealousy comment. Why would he think today had anything to do with jealousy? His eyes wandered behind his father's desk to a small table with pictures. Some had been left by prior Presidents, and there were also a few his father had added. One in particular caught his eye—a picture of his parents and his grandfather, Joseph, in a lab. Matt had not seen or thought of it in some time. He stared at their warm faces until he suddenly saw something in the picture that drew the breath from his body.

Eric asked, "Are you feeling all right, son?"

"What? Oh, yes, sir. I think I'm just a bit tired."

"That's enough for now, then. Why don't you get something to eat and get to bed?"

"Yes, sir." Matt stood and made his way out of the office, a tingling sensation running through his clammy fingers.

THE LIFTING OF THE VEIL

[SUNDAY, SEPTEMBER 27, 2037, 10:20 A.M.]

Try as he might, sleep eluded Matt. He tossed and turned, his mind jumping back and forth over what he'd seen in his father's office. What did it mean? He wished David and Rich had already finished the Ball so he could transport himself forward to the meeting the next day.

He glided over to the Botanic Garden shortly after church, yawning. As soon as Matt pulled the trap door open, he saw that everyone was there. "Sorry to keep you waiting. I got caught up in a conversation with my father and a few RMs."

Sophie answered, "No problem. You need to keep up appearances. And if you listen carefully during those conversations, maybe you'll hear something useful."

His adrenalin beginning to flow again, Matt nodded. "I actually do have something new."

David interrupted, staring right at Matt. "Before you go, I've got something I figured out yesterday. It's big."

Matt smiled. "Okay. Go ahead."

"I figured out what the darkened circle is. Here." He quickly opened a book on the art in the Library of Congress and handed it to Bobby, who was standing next to him. Everyone else gathered in close. "There are two murals, one surrounded by the other. The one at the center is called Human Understanding."

"I think David's right," Bobby said. He pointed to a picture. "The woman in the center is lifting the veil of ignorance."

"Hey," Matt said. "The first clue said that to complete the mission, I had to look beyond the veil of ignorance."

Bobby continued, "She's surrounded by another mural called the Evolution of Civilization. It has twelve figures. Each represents a civilization that contributed greatly to humanity. Look at what's below six of those twelve figures."

Matt saw the name of a civilization under each of the figures around the circle. Below the name was the important contribution provided by that civilization. "Look. France—emancipation. Spain—discovery. Egypt—written records. Italy—fine arts. Islam—physics, and the United States—science. Each of these contributions was in our clues. Rich, did you know about this?"

Rich shrugged his shoulders. "No."

"Sophie?"

"Me either."

"Bobby, how'd you know?"

Bobby said, "I didn't remember it until David just showed us this picture. Ah, I get my clue now—you know, 'look back and up?' 'Look back' must have meant to look back in time. During our first year of school, Mom brought me to the Jefferson Building Main Reading Room. She left me there to study while she went to do some work. I remember feeling a little scared being left alone in that big room, but then I looked up and saw the old murals. They were interesting. I asked her about them and she explained they were supposed to symbolize what the RMs stood for: the advancement of civilization. But she said the murals were being replaced by a new image to honor the RM's for their efforts in maintaining and advancing civilization. The meaning was similar to the veil of ignorance painting, but like the RM monument, this would help keep the focus on the RM mission."

Matt said, "Right, I know that one. David, how'd you figure this out?"

"I read a lot at work. There isn't much work to do in the library with everyone using their Neurals. I was looking for older books on local art, hoping to find something about the circle. Yesterday, just by chance, I noticed this book sitting out on the information desk of the Main Reading Room. I'd never seen it before. I sat down, began reading, and found these murals."

Sophie asked precisely what Matt was thinking. "How'd the book get there? Did you see anyone in the room when you found it?"

"I didn't see anyone. I figured everyone else was at the games."

Rich said, "Almost everyone. I never saw Dr. Farmer." Matt tried to think of anyone else who hadn't been at the game, but couldn't come up with anybody. Rich continued, "I guess it's possible he left the book. He and Matt's mother both worked on Joseph's teams. Maybe he knows about Matt's mother leaving us the clues."

Matt interrupted, "And maybe he knows about whoever else is involved, too, including possibly my father."

Everyone's eyes sprang to Matt. "What do you mean?" Rich asked.

"That's what I wanted to tell you. I learned something, too. I was discussing the game with my father in his office last night. Then, while he was giving me one of his lectures, I started looking at the pictures on the table behind him. I've seen this one picture many times, but with everything that's happened recently, I noticed something that hadn't caught my eye before."

With one voice, everyone asked, "What?"

"It was a picture of my father, my mother, and Joseph. It looks like it was taken in a lab. I always thought it was just a nice family photo. But last night, I saw something in Joseph's hand I'd never focused on before. The Ball. Or at least a machine that looks exactly like the one you guys are building."

Everyone else stood in stunned silence. They had decided Matt's mother must have known about the Ball and that she was responsible for leaving the clues, at least in part. And given Joseph's legacy, it wasn't surprising he might have played a large part in the Ball's development, as well. But now they could see that Matt's father, the same person who had openly written that traveling back in time was not possible, must also know about the Ball.

Matt continued, "I know this creates more questions than answers and it still doesn't show where my father stands."

Rich said, "It also means Joseph himself may have been involved in leaving the clues."

"Maybe," Matt said. "But how does that help?"

Rich said, "It guarantees they were working on the time machine before the Storm. Remember David's theory? A wormhole has to be opened on both ends. Now we know it's possible they opened a wormhole before the Storm."

Matt smiled at the thought of traveling back to help his parents and grandfather stop the Storm. He shook himself from the reverie. "It also gives us a direction for our investigation. Think about Dr. Farmer. He worked with my grandfather. He may have left the book for you. I've got some questions for him that might help explain the clues and answer who's with us…and who isn't."

Rich said, "I want to know why my father did what he did and who's on each side more than anyone, but I think we need to listen to the advice on the Discs. We trust no one else for now."

"I agree," Sophie said. "But if and when there's an opportunity to talk to Dr. Farmer, we should listen very carefully to what he says. Maybe he'll give us a clue that he's with your mother, Matt."

Matt said, "Good idea, as usual." He thought he saw her blush as she turned away.

He continued. "Going back to the twelve figures: according to my clue we're supposed to 'complete the circle.' The other contributions in the mural that haven't been in our clues yet are England–literature,

Rome–administration, Judea–religion, Greece–philosophy, Middle Ages–modern languages, and Germany–art of printing."

Rich asked, "And just how are we supposed to find clues for these? The information for the other words was given to us."

Matt said, "I'm not sure, but these words must mean something. The Evolution of Civilization mural must be what my mother intended us to find."

"Maybe she wanted us to have our own veils of ignorance lifted," Sophie added.

Bobby asked, "So what do you suggest? We simply continue investigating with the hope of learning more about our society?"

Matt answered, "Yes, and how it got this way."

Sophie held up a hand. "Something tells me the meaning of the new information will come to us in time. We just have to have faith."

Rich said, "I agree that we shouldn't spin our wheels when we've got a lot to do, but I also don't think we should leave it to chance."

She crossed her arms. "Chance and faith aren't the same thing. It's about doing what we need to do and not worrying that we won't learn what we need to learn. Matt's mother and whoever else left the information couldn't have intended for us to run all over guessing. Every step of the way, the information has been understandable when combined with other information they left. I expect this won't be different. So either we've received that information and need time to think it through, or we haven't gotten it yet."

Rich said, "Or they left it and it was either lost or destroyed, or…"

"They died before they could leave it," Bobby finished.

Unnerved at that possibility, Matt took pains to show no fear. "There's no sense worrying about it. So, let's focus on what we know we have to do. I'll talk to Dr. Farmer…and the vice president. I'm an assistant for him, too. Since he works for my father, maybe I'll learn something from him. David and Rich, keep working on the Ball. Sophie and Bobby, see if you can find anything else that relates to the twelve figures and those clues. Does anyone else have anything?"

David raised his hand. "One of the Discs I downloaded apparently had a lot more on it. I think Sophie's and Rich's discussion about faith and chance triggered the release of the information."

"What?" Matt asked. "How is that possible?"

David said, "I don't know how your mother did it, but there are several ways. She could have hid the file and set it to unlock and open with a specific verbal or visual trigger—like a password—or maybe she set it to open at a specific time. Anyway, this file contains music."

Sophie asked, "Music?"

"Yes, but not like we're used to. It's pretty fast and upbeat. It came with a message: 'For added energy in the game and to help everyone let loose.'"

"It's for comBATON?" Bobby asked. "Why did it get released now? We weren't talking about comBATON."

Rich said, "Who knows? David, can you make a copy of the music? Maybe I can figure out how we can use it."

Matt said, "Okay, well, unless anyone else has new and mysterious information coming out of their Discs, or anything else, I guess that's it."

Matt led the way out. He caught up with Lori at her house and they spent the afternoon doing homework and preparing lessons. After a quiet dinner with her, he took a detour on the way home. Even though it was Sunday, he walked the hallways of the Museum of Natural History, hoping to run into Dr. Farmer. Matt had no idea what he would say if he saw him, but figured he'd think of something. After a lonely half hour of wandering, he headed home.

Suddenly, he found himself running down a long, dark hallway. A domino of dim, fluorescent lights flickered on as he ran. The sound of his feet echoed off of the gray linoleum and pale, cement walls.

Lungs burning and out of energy, his legs carried him as fast as any prey running for its life. He passed door after door. It seemed like an eternity. His only thought: *Reach the door at the end before they catch me.*

He could hear the quickening pace of the pounding footsteps closing in. Fully spent, he carried on by sheer will. He reached the large, metal door, placed one hand on his heaving chest, and slammed his other hand against the biometric scanner. The door clicked and unlocked. He began to pull it open and slip inside, when a gorilla-like hand clamped down on his shoulder and...

He awoke in bed, shivering in a cold sweat.

LET'S GET IT STARTED

[SATURDAY, OCTOBER 3, 2037, 1:30 P.M.]

The following school week was uneventful. Matt focused on Dr. Farmer and the vice president when in their presence. But they never said anything more useful than, "Make sure you review the practical uses of these elements with the class" and "Be sure to go over the many forms of democracy."

These subjects did not appear to apply in any way to their mission.

Bobby and Sophie did not fare any better. They first asked Mrs. Peterson about Bobby's parents and their fate, figuring such questions would be expected from an orphaned son. Unfortunately, the answers revealed no more this time than the many previous times he had asked over the years. "Your parents were great people. The way they lost their lives was tragic. Maybe one day, when we're both ready, I'll tell you more." It had to be difficult for Bobby, who knew next to nothing about his parents, to have their past withheld from him.

According to Sophie, her parents were too focused on their research these days to have any time to talk. She seemed disappointed. Matt knew how she felt and avoided giving her any suggestions. He simply encouraged her to keep trying.

On Saturday, Matt's excitement rose with the sun. With the morning came the first blustery day of fall. Unlike the sweatbox weather they'd had for Game 1, Game 2 would be played in the more typically cool, albeit windy, conditions.

The comBATON team had come together in practice during the week. Matt had begun the Monday practice with the simple statement: "If we play hard and have fun, the wins will take care of themselves." He had taken his own words to heart. He would enjoy playing the game as a team and nothing would get in their way.

DC3 was playing the first game of the day. Their opponents, the Cyclones, were a team of middle-aged RMs who were good, but who hadn't won many times in recent seasons. Jimmy said, "We both lost last week. Whoever loses this game will be in last place."

Rich said, "Forget last week. We're going to win our division. And it all starts today."

Bobby said, "That's right. Let's get it done."

Rich said, "And I've got something to get the fun started." Those in the Circle looked at him as if he were about to reveal a new secret invention. Instead, he pulled from his pocket a little device. "They used to call this an iPod. It plays music."

Matt said, "I've read about those. Why do we need it? We can play all the music we want on our Neurals."

"I've never listened to music like this on my Neural. We have access to so much music, but I've never stumbled across anything like this— and I bet you haven't either." Matt thought about the sheer amount of information to which they had access. He expected that finding a group of songs he wasn't looking for would be like stumbling across a specific blade of grass in the thousands of acres at Arlington.

Rich interrupted Matt's contemplation. "It's synced to the speakers David and I rigged up over there." He pointed to poles he and David had inserted in the ground at the corners of the field. At one pole, Matt noticed David working with the speaker connected to it. "Besides," Rich added, "it's the mission of the RMs to maintain culture. And this was a large part of modern culture at the time of the Storm." Rich took Matt aside and said, "And David finding this iPod in a desk at the library makes it look like he's helping us fulfill the RM mission. It'll make more sense that he's hanging out with us."

"I get it. And what are you going to play?"

"You'll see."

The crowd and the eight teams filed in and assembled as they had in the first week. This time, however, Rich had worked something out with the commissioner in advance. Rather than Lori singing the national anthem, Rich touched the screen of the iPod and immediately Matt heard an incredibly spirited rendition. Everyone stood at attention, watching the American flag wave in the fall breeze and listening to the singer hit every note just right. A strange sensation, the likes of which Matt had never felt before, coursed through his body. After the song ended, everyone clapped and cheered and the commissioner and Matt's father came over and shook Rich's hand. Matt's father gave his son a nod of approval and walked over to his spot on the sideline at center field. The commissioner took the iPod from Rich and retook his place at the center of the field.

Rich turned to Matt and said, "Wasn't that amazing? The singer's name is Whitney Houston." Matt nodded his head in approval. Rich said, "Then you'll love what comes next." Rich looked over at the Cyclones' captain, Will Stromyre, who nodded back at him.

Speaking through a microphone, the commissioner's voice echoed to the crowd. "As our president has said many times, it's our responsibility to protect and preserve humanity's achievements. To do so, we've maintained many traditions. One had been forgotten until this week, when David Jackson discovered this relic that had been stored in a drawer since the Storm." He raised the iPod. "The playing of music to introduce players at sporting events. The Cyclones and DC3 have agreed to play one song as both teams are introduced. So…let's get it started."

The music began to pulse through the speakers. As the words "Let's get it started in here" rang out and the bass began to pound, the strange sensation that had begun with the national anthem crested in a wave of energy that now surged through Matt. Over the music, the commissioner yelled, "And now for the starting lineup for the Cyclones." Throughout the player introductions, the electric beat thrummed through his veins.

By the time he was introduced, Matt was primed, his legs ready to explode and his mind in some sort of hyper-focus. Nothing in the world existed but the field in front of him, his teammates, and his opponents.

Matt heard the distant echo of the commissioner's voice say, "And last, but certainly not least, last year's rookie of the year, Captain Matthew Cane!" He sprinted to one end of the field to take his position between his teammates.

Rich grinned and said, "I think Matty likes it."

The whistle blew to start the game. It seemed the music had affected everyone as both teams converged with attitude. Around midfield, Bobby and Rich collided with two opponents. Matt followed close behind, Baton in hand. He shot through the small gap they had created. It seemed like he and Will would collide at full speed. All of a sudden, Matt faked left. Will started a roundhouse kick in that direction and Matt spun into the clear right, sprinting toward the goal. He leapt far from the goal, spun into a tornado roundhouse, and kicked the goal over the crowd on the sideline. For a brief moment, it was so quiet Matt could hear the rhythmic beat of his heart. Then, the crowd went wild, as Commissioner Turnbull announced "Five points for DC3 on an amazing tornado roundhouse by Matthew Cane."

When he joined his teammates, Bobby said, "That was unbelievable. I've never seen you do that before."

"I feel like I can do anything right now."

Before they knew it, DC3 led 14-0. Matt called for Sophie to replace Rich right before the half. When Sophie got to the huddle, Matt said, "We've got a long field in front of us and the wind's died down. Let's try a deep goal route." Sophie smiled and nodded in agreement. "Bobby, give me time." Sophie sprinted straight up the right side of the field. Matt faked a pass to the outside as she timed a fake move in the same direction. When her opponent took the bait, she cut in toward the goal. In the clear, Sophie caught a deep strike from Matt, and, in full stride, executed a spinning jump hook kick, connecting with the goal for five points. The crowd was silent, likely in shock. Then, all at once, they cheered with approval. Rex remained silent on the sideline, his mouth wide open.

In the end, they won 32-7, by far the best performance in DC3's short existence. Matt caught his father's eye as he left the field and received the approving nod he sought. He felt redeemed after the humiliation a week earlier.

DC3 remained near the field to scout the other teams in the remaining three games. They all went as Matt expected. The Blaze breezed to their first victory after their loss to the Raiders in week one. The Nationals and Raiders also easily won, remaining undefeated.

Dr. Farmer approached the team as they left the field. "Great job. The music really helped you let loose. Joseph would have been proud."

Matt stopped dead in his tracks, said a quick, "Thank you, sir," and looked at Rich, Sophie, and Bobby. Their wide-eyed stares mirrored his.

They rushed to the lab to discuss whether Dr. Farmer's comments were some sort of signal to them. While they weren't sure, they agreed there was a good chance Dr. Farmer was the one who had left the book in the Main Reading Room and who had helped leave the clues.

Rich said, "It was fun using the music today. We should find a way to share it. Here, I made some copies of the songs." Matt, Bobby, and Sophie each took a couple of Discs.

"Okay, well maybe this is one more thing for us to do," Matt said. "If anyone comes up with an idea about the music, please share it with the rest of us."

He turned to leave, adding, "Great game today, everyone."

Matt glided around, switching from song to song. He loved how the rhythms overtook him and made him feel as if he had just woken from a long sleep. They seemed to penetrate his soul. His thoughts were deeper and more emotional than he could remember. It was quite an eclectic mix and Matt loved it all.

The spell of the music was broken when he spotted Lori sitting in the grass near the game field, her head sinking into her shoulders and her eyes brimming with tears. Matt knew that even the slightest wrong movement, let alone the wrong words—which he seemed prone to saying whenever Lori was upset—would trigger a waterfall.

Frustrated at having to exclude her from so much for over a month, Matt realized he finally had something to share with her. He bounded up to her and offered her a copy. She consumed the Disc, stared at him for a moment, then leapt into his arms and squeezed him tight.

THE PLAN

[MONDAY, OCTOBER 5, 2037, 9:15 A.M.]

Matt jumped out of bed and into his day, anxious to question Dr. Farmer. During homeroom, several classmates congratulated Matt, Rich, and Bobby on the game. Lori and Stephanie added their approval of the music, which caused Rich to become unusually silent. Matt knew what this meant—Rich was thinking of a plan for the music.

Matt's interest in Rich's new scheme did not come close to his desire to talk with Dr. Farmer, however. He rushed to Science & Technology, instructed the class to discuss their projects with one another, and approached the man. "Sir, that was some good advice you gave us after the game."

"What? Oh, about letting loose. Well, that was Joseph. You never knew what you would get with him—a party on occasion, or an all-nighter trying to figure out a solution to a complex problem." Dr. Farmer observed Matt. "By the look on your face, I'd say you have a question."

"Yes, sir. I do."

"Shoot."

"Sir, I was wondering how the RMs coped after the Storm. Did they continue to approach problems the way Joseph used to?"

"Interesting question." Dr. Farmer stared at Matt, who felt as if the clever scientist could read his mind. "You know how we handled it, Matthew. We did what we had to do. The Storm cloud lifted almost as quickly as it came. Once we determined it was safe to emerge again, we secured nuclear plants and any other potential safety hazards around the world. Then, we implemented Plan 40, a plan created by your father to maintain our society in one city. The obvious choice was Washington D.C., Project RM's headquarters."

This was not the direction Matt had planned to take the conversation, but the answer piqued his interest. "Why did my father name it Plan 40?"

"Well, I always assumed there were at least 39 other plans. You see, before the Storm, we all had multiple tasks to prepare for the possibility of an extinction-level event. One of your father's tasks was to develop multiple plans, one for each kind of possible catastrophe."

"And he intended Plan 40 for the Storm?"

"I'm sure it wasn't intended specifically for the Storm. He likely intended it for an event that wiped out most of the population, leaving a small number of people behind."

Needing time to process the information and to determine whether Dr. Farmer was truly helping them, Matt stopped his inquiry there. "Thank you, sir."

"No problem, Matthew. You know, your father approaches problems differently than Joseph. And while I like to remember working with Joseph, after the Storm your father led our community out of chaos to safety and prosperity. In my area alone, his leadership style has provided many opportunities to explore scientific advances that might otherwise not have been possible."

Being Eric's son, Matt knew all too well that the "let loose" style was not in his father's repertoire. But his leadership style had succeeded regardless.

Class ended, and he nodded in Dr. Farmer's direction before departing.

The pressure to unload his conversation built inside Matt until he could finally meet with Sophie and Bobby. In the short window between school and practice, he did just that at the lab. They were just as perplexed as Matt as to why no one had ever discussed his father's role before the Storm or Plan 40. They had always been told the same line, "He brought order out of chaos."

The rest of the week was uneventful until Government on Friday. While the other students were researching totalitarian dictatorships, Matt saw an opening to talk with Vice President Silverman. He approached the vice president and, in a low voice, asked, "Sir, do you have time for a question?"

The vice president looked up. "For you, always. What is it?"

"As I continue to work on my leadership skills, I've been thinking a lot about how the president led our community right after the Storm. Considering your position, I assume you must have been a great supporter."

"That's a good question, Matthew. Hoping to follow in your father's footsteps is wise. As for my involvement with him, I certainly was, and continue to be, a great supporter. He had a plan and many of us zealously followed him in implementing it. What makes your father a great leader is he's a visionary, and he doesn't hesitate to actively implement his vision. But you know who was his biggest supporter after the Storm?"

"My mother?"

"Well, yes, she certainly supported her husband. But I was thinking of someone else. Someone with whom you interact on a daily basis."

Matt thought about that for a few moments. There were few RMs with whom he interacted daily.

"I can see you're not sure. Liz Peterson." Matt hadn't even considered Mrs. Peterson. Her style seemed much different than his father's, and she wasn't an RM. The vice president continued, "She was one of the biggest proponents of continuing the tradition of the presidency and of electing your father. For a long time after the Storm, she played a large role in shaping our society. She even came up with many of our rituals, including the T-salute."

When he finished talking, his face transformed from smiling orator into a brief, blank Neural stare. When he came to, it was clear the conversation was over. "If you ever need to talk, I'm available."

Matt maintained a straight face. "Thank you, sir." He returned to his seat deep in thought. What had the vice president just received on his Neural? And what was this about Mrs. Peterson? Since the first day of school, much had been called into doubt. But she had remained the one constant. She would not side with Richard. If he had to doubt his father, however, he had to doubt Mrs. Peterson, too. Until they had objective proof otherwise, his team would have to follow the instruction on the Disc to trust no one outside the Circle.

At a meeting later that afternoon, before the final comBATON practice of the week, Matt disclosed to Sophie and Bobby the discussion he had had with the vice president. They seemed equally surprised and agreed it would be too risky to trust Mrs. Peterson.

Sophie explained her parents were still too busy to talk, but that she and Bobby would continue their attempts to meet with them. In the meantime, they had switched gears and begun asking other RMs about the Storm and their involvement in setting up the current government. Each time, they told the RM it was for History. Each time, they learned nothing useful. Dr. Ford explained how he had established the agricultural system. Principal Franklin discussed how they established the school system. Dr. McCurie spoke about establishing the current hospital, but added that she had done so after she'd become an RM, which meant after the Storm.

And no one seemed to have known about the Storm until it was too late.

The last practice in preparation for Game 3 went well. On the way to the Shed to store the equipment, Rich and Matt discussed the next game against the Tsunami—a group of the youngest RMs, who were well conditioned, fast, and currently tied with DC3 for second place. Rich informed Matt each team captain had now chosen an introductory song for his team. He knew Matt would want to stick with what worked for Game 2.

Before they could pull the handle, the Shed door swung open and Kevin stepped through. "Hi, guys."

Matt wanted to tell him where he could stick his "Hi, guys."

"Keep walking," Rich said. Kevin complied. He was still within earshot when Rich mumbled, "Traitor."

They stored the team equipment, after which Matt swapped his uniform for street clothes. He thought about their mission. "Hey, Rich."

"Yeah."

"Do you think we're being too hard on Kevin?"

"He gave Rex our playbook."

"Yeah, but anyone can get our plays just by watching us practice. Something tells me that he was pressured into giving it. Besides, we've got more important things to worry about."

"Maybe, but trust me when I say—don't trust him."

They stepped outside into the cool, dark night. Matt understood what he meant, but felt Kevin was a good guy. "I guess. Did you hear what Dr. Farmer and the vice president said?"

"A little."

"What do you think?"

"I think we can talk about it later." Rich nodded in the direction of the Botanic Garden across the National Mall. "We'd better get to dinner."

"I'll catch up with you."

"What? I mention food and you have to take care of business?"

Matt smiled. "Yes, actually." He stepped back into the Shed and headed for a stall, and suddenly felt something in his pocket. He reached in and pulled out a Disc. His heart thumped as he looked around. He was alone. Maybe someone had slipped a new clue into his pants while he was a practice—possibly Dr. Farmer. He glanced around once more and consumed the Disc.

At first, there was nothing. No sound, no visual, just darkness. A gray mist faded in, through which a message approached. *Another clue,* Matt thought. The message cleared the mist and Matt stopped breathing. A deep muffled voice recited, "Stop the ops." As quickly as it appeared, the message dissolved, leaving Matt alone with his goosebumps.

TSUNAMI

[SATURDAY, OCTOBER 10, 2037, 7:00 A.M.]

That night and into the next morning, Matt startled himself out of dream after dream. He dreamt of everything from his friends dying in an explosion to a faceless hulk chasing him through vacant hallways. Before dawn, Matt drifted off to what he expected to be one more nightmare.

The dim room filled with a gray mist, through which a tall, thin figure approached.

"Who is that?" he asked.

"Someone who believes in you," his mother said as she stepped through to him.

Matt's mouth dropped open.

She said, "I bet you have a lot of questions."

"Did you leave the message to stop the ops?"

"No."

"Who did?"

"I can't say."

He crossed his arms like Sophie, images of the cryptic clues flashing through his head. "Why not? Are you worried about affecting the future? Considering everything you've told us, I think it's a little late for that."

"I have time only to deliver my own message."

Matt shook his head. "Which is?"

"Don't stop. They don't know what you're doing yet. You can do this."

"Who's they? Do what? Change the past?"

"Save seven billion lives."

Matt's arms dropped. They'd guessed this was their mission, but the clues had never been so direct. "What about Sophie and Lori and everyone else?"

Her hand reached for his shoulder.

In her glistening eyes, Matt saw the reflection of his locked jaw. "You died doing this, didn't you?"

"Yes." She pulled him into a hug, "I won't tell you not to be concerned for your friends. But I will tell you to be brave. You can do this."

"How...how do you know that?"

"I'm your mother."

He smiled. "Any other motherly advice?"

"Two things. First, always be aware of your surroundings, like you are in comBATON."

"And second?"

"Don't tell your friends about the message you received yesterday or this conversation."

His smile inverted. "Why?"

"We'll talk again before this is over. Right now, you need to take care of the Tsunami. Remember, you have what you need inside you and around you."

Ping, ping, ping. The rain pecked at the window. Matt opened his eyes to the howling wind. He slid off the bed and looked outside. Gusts of wind rushed the dark clouds through the sky and ripped the leaves from their limbs. Gazing at his reflection in the glass, Matt knew his mother was right. Time to stand strong.

DC3 was again playing the last game of the day. After another moving broadcast of the national anthem by Whitney Houston, Matt had the opportunity to listen to the other teams' musical selections. The Raiders lived up to their theme song, "Another One Bites the Dust." They dismantled the Patriots, despite the awful weather conditions. The Nationals also remained undefeated and the Blaze upped their winning streak to two games.

When their turn came, Matt heeded his mother's advice. He channeled the music into a hyper focus and relied on his teammates, who did not disappoint. Sophie, in particular, proved to be more than a match for their competition, both in speed and the ability to sense the opponents around her. In the end, DC3 defeated the weather and the Tsunami 25-9.

After the game, Matt motioned for everyone to follow him to the lunch café on the north side of the Mall. He wanted to get everyone together in a more hospitable surrounding.

Drying off inside, Matt eyed his teammates in the Circle of Five. He desperately wanted to tell them about the messages he'd received. Instead, he congratulated the whole comBATON team, including the practice squad, on another successful week. They had faced each of their division opponents once, but he cautioned they would now be facing mostly IDs in the next two games. The RMs they had played so far were athletic, but all of their opposition for the next two games would be young, fast, and have trained in combat.

When Matt finished, Rich stood and said, "There's one thing left to do." He motioned to David, who had joined them for the post-game meeting with Lori in tow. "Dance." David pressed play and the steady beat of the rain was replaced by the electric beat of hip hop. Rich began dancing to the beat and the team followed suit. David stood on the side for the first song, but Matt soon pulled him out on the floor. David did his version of the robot and everyone laughed and did likewise.

After the dancing, in front of everyone, Lori walked up to Matt and planted the biggest, longest kiss on his unsuspecting lips. He knew he should have enjoyed the moment. But he just wanted to pull away and breathe.

The rain and wind did not continue into Sunday, but left an overcast sky. After church, Lori asked Matt to accompany her to the Jefferson Memorial. They barely spoke along the way. Every couple of minutes, Matt heeded his mother's advice and looked around to see if anyone was following him.

The third time, Lori asked, "What's the matter? Are you looking for something?"

"Huh? Oh, no. Just curious."

She half smiled and took his hand until they reached their destination.

They sat on one of the many cold, long, stone steps of the memorial overlooking the tidal basin—a compact, serene, tree-lined reservoir. Leaves of every color adorned the trees and ground. The fresh aroma left by the end of a long rain hung in the air. Fall had arrived.

"That was fun last night," Lori said.

"Yeah, it was."

Lori dropped her head. "Sophie's really impressive."

"Yeah, she is."

"Is that why you didn't want to kiss me?"

Matt froze. "Wait. What? I thought we were talking about her com-BATON performance."

"You know, Matthew," she said, looking up at him, "I just want you to be happy."

"I am happy." He grabbed her hands.

"For the most part, I think you are. The question you need to ask yourself is, why." Matt's stomach quivered. He stared straight ahead, as if the monument across the tidal basin held the answer to why she had asked this question. Lori continued, "You know, I read that poetry book of yours last summer."

A chill ran through Matt, but he forced himself to look into her bloodshot eyes. "When?"

"You were showing me your room when your father called you away. I'm sorry, but that book looked out of place on the shelf next to your cleats and awards. I couldn't resist."

"Did you see anything inside?"

She withdrew her hand and looked away. "Yes. It looks like you've had that photo for a long time."

"It's all my mother left for me." He immediately felt the burn of having said too much.

She placed her hand back on his. "I figured it was something like that. Don't worry. I won't ask you anything more about it. I don't think she knows it, but…Sophie's pretty. I knew it when I realized she was the woman in the picture."

"When'd you figure it out?"

"A few days after I saw it."

"How?"

"It was just a cap and glasses. You know, you're amazing, Matthew, but sometimes you're such a guy. At first, I thought I could compete with a ghost, but when I realized it was Sophie, I assumed that sooner or later…"

"What?"

"I see how you look at each other."

"What are you talking about?"

"Do you even realize how each of you gazes at the other when you think the other's not looking? And the way she looks down every time she sees you start to look in her direction. I'd think it was sweet, if she weren't doing it for you."

Matt sat like a statue, not sure what to say.

"You need to figure out who you want," Lori said.

"What are you talking about? I'm with you. She's with Bobby."

"Until you figure it out, we won't really be together."

"What are you saying?"

"I'm saying it's over. At least for now. Figure out what you want." She tried to maintain a stoic face, but the stream of tears had begun. She stood and wiped her rosy cheeks. "I'll always be there for you. If you realize you want me, I'll be waiting."

She kissed him on the cheek and left Matt alone with his quandary.

NEW ASSIGNMENT

[MONDAY, OCTOBER 12, 2037, 7:00 A.M.]

Matt stepped outside to the first clear sky in days. Inhaling the clean, cool air did nothing to diminish his confusion.

Just before he arrived at the Daily Stretch, he received an N-note from Bobby.

Matt,

I've got a nasty cold, probably from Saturday. I'm going to rest for the next few days. You should take my place with Sophie while I'm out. We're at an important point and you'll need each other to figure things out.

Matt let Bobby know he would step in and told him to rest, then glided up to Sophie.

She said, "So, we're working together today."

He spotted Lori at the other end of the field. "It seems so," he murmured.

"Well, don't act all excited about it."

"Sorry. I've had a rough couple of days." He withheld the urge to tell her about the threat and his mother's second dream visit. Strangely, neither of those things were what bothered him the most. "Lori broke up with me." He could feel the warmth on his face as he wondered why he'd told her.

"I'm sorry." She lowered her head.

Matt thought he noticed her blush and changed the subject. "I think we'll work well together."

She faced him. "Me, too."

"Great. What's the plan?"

"Try to talk to my parents again."

Matt decided to cancel practice for the day, which would give them more time with Sophie's parents.

Lori's words haunted his thoughts throughout the day. He had been blind not to realize her true feelings. If the situation were reversed and Lori had been spending a lot of time with a new guy, he too would have been upset. It was all his fault. But he couldn't abandon his mission with the Circle of Five. He would have to prove to Lori there was nothing romantic going on between him and Sophie, and he had to do it fast so they could get back together. The best way to do that would be to simply focus on the mission while he was with Sophie.

After school, he met Sophie in front of her parents' office. "So, what's the plan?"

"You're in a better mood."

"Am I?"

"Yeah."

"I guess it's because I get a chance to work with you." Hearing his own words and feeling the heat rise in his cheeks, he stammered, "I mean, instead of by myself."

She smiled. "Bobby was going to ask about his parents. That won't work now. So as not to lose time, you can ask about your mother."

Matt hadn't ever spoken to Sophie's parents, at least beyond the normal pleasantries. Considering he had been in their secret lab numerous times, he was glad to finally get the opportunity to do so. "Are they here?"

"No, they're hardly ever here in the afternoon. They split their time between Lincoln Park during the day and their lab at night. They've been working almost around the clock on some important experiment for a while now."

"What is it?"

"I'm not sure. They won't tell anyone."

"So we're going to Lincoln Park?"

"Yup. After I introduce you, let's move the conversation toward your mother and who she worked with after the Storm."

Matt did his best to contain his excitement. "Sounds good."

Sophie and Matt headed for the Jacksons' farm in Lincoln Park. They glided up East Capitol Street, the sun's rays shining through the thinning canopy of autumn leaves. Beyond the trees were the small, green yards that led to the three-story brick row houses where most of the community lived.

On the top floor of one of those houses, Matt noticed a child watching through a window. His dream-mother's warning to be aware of his surroundings spoke to him. Eyes wide, he looked up and down the street, from window to window.

"What are you doing?" Sophie asked. "You think someone's watching?"

How does she know that? he thought. "Maybe. Don't you think it's a good idea to check?"

"Sure, but maybe you shouldn't be so obvious." Her fingers touched his cheeks and pointed his head forward. "Use your peripheral vision."

Matt hoped the warmth of his embarrassment wasn't noticeable.

Before he knew it, they reached Lincoln Park, an agricultural oasis eleven blocks east of the Capitol. Matt doubted it had been kept as it was prior to the Storm. Other than a statue of President Lincoln at the center, any semblance of a community meeting place had vanished long ago. Instead, there were rows and rows of various crops foreign to the mid-Atlantic climate. The vegetation produced a strange concoction of aromas that ranged from citrus, to bark, to corn, to sweet.

"Where are your parents?" he asked, just as a beautiful woman stepped out of the rows of sugar cane and approached. She had Sophie's long, brown hair and hazel eyes. Not having paid much attention before, Matt was now fascinated by the similarities between the two. He would have thought they were twins, had there not been over a twenty-year age difference.

She approached. "Hi, dear—and hello, Matthew."

"Hi, Mom."

Matt followed with, "Hi, Mom...I mean, hi, ma'am."

Sophie and Mrs. Jackson chuckled, causing Matt's cheeks to burn to the point where he expected they looked like the vine-ripe tomatoes growing nearby. Recovering, Matt said, "Sorry, ma'am...uh...I've been thinking about my mother a lot lately. When Sophie said mom, it slipped out."

Mrs. Jackson said, "Your mother was a great person."

Matt asked, "Did you know her well?"

"As well as most other RMs. She cared for everyone, regardless of their standing in the community. I can't imagine how difficult it's been for you all these years. When she passed, she left a void in each of us." Matt's eyes dropped to the moist soil. "You remind me of her, Matthew. You have many of her qualities." Nothing could have pleased Matt more. He could feel a swell of pride light up his face. Mrs. Jackson continued, "Is there something specific you'd like to know about her?"

"Yes, ma'am. Who were her friends? I mean, who did she hang around with the most?"

"Let's see. Before the Storm, she was a lead scientist. So she worked with your grandfather and several other RM scientists."

"What about my father?"

"They worked together, but at some point they were placed on different projects."

"Did you and Mr. Jackson work with her?"

At that moment, Mr. Jackson arrived, seemingly out of nowhere, and placed his arm around Mrs. Jackson's shoulder. He looked like an older version of David, but with a more athletic build. Unlike David, Mr. Jackson held his handsome head up and smiled right at Matt and Sophie. "My ears were burning. Did someone say my name?"

Sophie said, "Hi, Dad." She and Mrs. Jackson glanced at Matt, both likely wondering if he would call Mr. Jackson Dad, too.

Matt flashed the two of them a little smile. "Hello, sir. How are you doing?"

"Fine, Matthew. So, what brings both of you out here today? Don't you have practice? You've got to keep that streak going."

"We will, sir, but there's no practice today. Bobby's sick and I figured the team could use an extra day of rest, considering how hard we've been working lately and being in that nasty weather all day Saturday."

"I see. That sounds like something your grandfather would have done."

Matt liked hearing this and wanted to inquire further, but before he could, Sophie redirected the conversation. "Dad, Mom was just telling us about Matt's mother. We were asking about her involvement with you and Mom."

Matt followed her lead. "Did either of you work with my mother before the Storm?"

Mrs. Jackson answered. "Not really. We always seemed to be on a different project. Your mother's team included her, your friend Bobby's parents, and a few others."

Matt hadn't thought much about this before, but it made sense. The three of them had died in the same lab accident. "How about after the Storm?"

Mr. Jackson answered, "Actually, while many things changed after the Storm, one of the constants was the partnership between Bobby's parents and your mother. They continued to work together, until...well, until that tragic day."

Mr. Jackson stared at the ground, as Sophie's mother began to fidget a bit. Seeing his reaction, Matt understood where David had gotten his sheepish look. He hesitated. But Sophie didn't. "What do you know about that day, Mom and Dad? I mean, what do you know about the accident?"

Five long seconds of silence later, her mother answered, "Not much, unfortunately. We've been working on the same project since before the Storm. We're either here or..."

"In your lab," Sophie finished. "Matt knows about it. He's been there several times with David, me, Bobby, and their friend Rich."

Matt expected Sophie to receive some form of rebuke for revealing their lab. Instead, Mr. Jackson said, "We know."

Matt's stomach caved in.

Sophie eyes blinked wide. "What do you know?"

Mr. Jackson answered, "Just that you kids like to hang out there. It's not a problem, as long as you don't go snooping around. We're working on a special project and we're not quite ready to reveal it."

Matt was intrigued but not about to pry, considering he and Sophie were also working on a special, confidential project. Still, Matt wondered what the project could be. He and Sophie fell silent.

Mr. Jackson seemed to take this as an opportunity to end the conversation. "Well, we've got to get back to it. It was nice speaking with you."

"It was nice speaking with you, too," Matt said. "It's amazing in our little community that we haven't really spoken before."

Mrs. Jackson said, "It is. We'd love to see you again soon, Matthew. Don't be a stranger."

Matt began to turn to leave, but noticed Sophie wasn't ready to go. She said, "I think I'll stay and help here for a while."

Mrs. Jackson said, "No, dear. I'd prefer for you to go back with Matthew."

Matt offered, "I'll walk back with you."

Mrs. Jackson nodded, "Great idea, Matthew. Walks have always given me the opportunity to take a mental step back and reflect."

Matt hadn't thought about not gliding—he'd meant that he would accompany her back. But he liked her advice and offered her a smile.

Sophie asked, "Mom, can we talk for a minute?"

Matt took the hint and stepped away. He took the time to observe the horticultural wonder before him, a field of plants ranging from hearty, northern crops to tall, tropical blends. He shifted his sights to the vacant streets leading out in many directions from the park, like spokes on a wheel. East Capitol Street may have been well manicured and active, but most of the other streets and the houses lining them were abandoned in the same eerie fashion as the streets leading to the cottage.

A gentle touch of Matt's shoulder interrupted his solitary reverie. Sophie had returned alone. "Your parents are nice."

"Thanks. Let's go."

It was quiet at first, as they strolled back toward the Capitol. To break the silence, Matt said, "So, were you looking for more information about their project or my mother?"

"No. I didn't want them to get suspicious about me bringing you to meet them, since I've been dating Bobby."

"What'd you tell them?"

"That Bobby's sick, and that both of you have been wondering about your mother and his parents."

"What did they say?"

"They understand. They said how much they like Bobby and reminded me to be careful about appearances while dating someone. I told them not to worry. You and I are just friends, and you visiting them was Bobby's suggestion."

Hearing those words revived Matt's depressed feeling from the day before. Matt thought, *Why couldn't Lori be here to hear this?* "Good," he replied. "I'm sorry you have to play these games with your parents."

She smiled. "We're all doing what we have to—no need to apologize. But thank you."

"You're welcome. What do you think about what they said? It didn't seem like much, but I guess they just don't know."

"I agree, except...except they've been working on this project since as long as I can remember, and now they're almost finished. The timing is suspicious."

"How so?"

"It could be coincidental, but it's possible my parents are working on a project intended to help us...or stop us."

"I can't say for sure, but I doubt they'd do something to stop us. At least, not intentionally. See what else you can learn from them. In the meantime, from what little they told us, I think it's time to talk to the vice president again," Matt said.

"Good idea. We're on a roll. I'll join you."

"Oh, I was thinking about doing it in class."

"But we made a good team back there. We play well off each other. I can help."

"Okay. I'll figure out his schedule. We can run into him after school."
She smiled. "Great."

An awkward silence descended upon their conversation, and Matt grasped for something to say. "By the way, you're great at comBATON."

"Not like you, but good enough for what we need anyway."

"Are you kidding? You're one of the best players in the league. When you're out there, you seem like you really enjoy it." He thought for a moment. "But it isn't what you want to do, is it?"

"It's all right."

"What would be more than just 'all right'?"

"If things were different, it would've been nice to dance."

"You mean like we did the other night?"

"Not exactly. I've read about the schools for the arts that existed before the Storm. Several of the RMs are expert dancers, but given the current state of the world, they don't have much time to teach dance. It would've been nice to attend a school where I could focus all of my time on it."

"Seeing the way you play comBATON, I think you would've been a great dancer. You have a great deal of grace and balance." Sophie blushed. As soon as he said it, he realized how corny he must have sounded.

Smiling, Sophie said, "Thank you. Here's my house." Her cream-colored home stood out from the mostly red-brick houses that lined the street. She became more serious and said in a low tone, "See if you can figure out where the vice president will be after school tomorrow and we can pay him a visit."

"Sounds like a plan. See you tomorrow." He turned to leave, pleased with the way the day had gone. He felt energized with the anticipation of the next day.

Out of the corner of his eye, Matt spotted a bird perched on a branch nearby. It reminded him of the bird at the cottage. He shook his head. *Whoever is with Richard,* he thought, *it isn't an army of birds.*

Matt revisited the conversation with Sophie and her parents on his way home. They hadn't learned much. But they had learned that they worked well together.

Matt thought about how he would get the vice president's schedule. He knew that when he wasn't teaching, the vice president checked in on many of the other RMs, at the direction of his father. He had no clue where the vice president would be the next day, but figured he could find some way to ask during class. Unfortunately, that would have to wait until Wednesday.

The next morning, Matt woke ready to seize the day. The first thing he did was N-note Bobby to see how he felt. Bobby said he was still sick, but getting better.

The day dragged on until Matt arrived at Human Achievement. He explained to Sophie that their next fact-finding expedition would have to wait until Wednesday when he would see the vice president in class. Not wanting to lose the day completely, he suggested they pay Bobby a visit before practice.

On the way to Bobby's house, they discussed what their lives might have been like had the Storm not occurred. Matt suggested they both probably would have lived in RM City. Sophie agreed, but added that they might have been able to travel a lot more. With so much pressure on the limited number of people in the community, few traveled beyond its small confines.

Bobby answered the doorbell at Mrs. Peterson's standard red-brick house. Matt noticed his sick friend looked a lot better than he expected. "How's it going?" Matt asked.

"Don't worry. I'll be ready for Saturday."

"I wasn't thinking about that...well, not much anyway." Everyone smiled.

Sophie asked, "So, what's it like to be sick? It's really rare these days."

"It's not bad. I get to relax, which we never get to do."

The conversation continued for a few minutes before Bobby said, "You need to get moving or you'll be late for practice. Matt, can I speak to you for a minute?"

The door closed behind Sophie before Matt asked, "So, what's up?"

"You look happy today. I guess you're feeling okay about the breakup with Lori?"

"I'm doing fine," Matt said, not wanting to discuss it.

"How are you and Sophie getting along?"

"Fine. We haven't made much progress yet, but we've got a plan."

"That's not what I meant. Do you like being with her?"

Unsure of where Bobby was going, Matt said, "Yes."

"Good, because...when Stephanie's dad died, I went to see her. And she's come by here a few times. I've liked her for a while and I'm thinking of asking her out."

"How are you going to do that? You're dating Sophie."

"Yeah, but—"

"But what?"

Bobby paused for a moment and then said, "You have to promise to keep this to yourself."

"Absolutely. What?"

"Clearly, you like Sophie."

"Why does everybody—"

Bobby put a hand up to cut him off. "And she likes you."

Matt had an intense desire to end the conversation. "Listen, Bobby. You've got it all wrong. Lori and I are meant to be together. And it's just a matter of time until we are. Not just because our fathers want it. But because *I* want it. Besides, if Sophie likes me, and I'm not sure she does, it probably has something to do with the speech you wrote. That's why she came to me in the first place."

"Don't be ridiculous. You think that's why she likes you?"

Matt's face reddened. "I didn't say that."

"She knows I wrote it and that hasn't changed the way she acts around you."

"Listen, Sophie and I need to get to practice. And feel better."

"Okay, Matt," Bobby said shaking his head. "Whatever you say."

When Matt stepped outside, Sophie eyed him. "What were you talking about?"

The heat increased in Matt's face. "Oh, just guy stuff."

Matt had his plan ready when he got to Government the next day. Everything proceeded normally as he worked with the different groups of students during class. About to leave, he turned to the vice president. "Sir, I almost forgot. I wanted to ask you a question."

"Yes, Matthew?"

"I've got to hurry to Medicine right now, and my schedule's pretty full today. Do you have time to meet tomorrow after school? Say, 4:10?"

The vice president stared at him, as if he were sizing Matt up. "Let me check my schedule." A two-second Neural stare later, he said, "You're in luck. I'm free."

"Thanks, sir. See you here tomorrow."

"See you tomorrow, Matthew."

Matt glided from class to the practice field. As he'd hoped, Sophie had arrived early and alone. They set up the field and Matt explained the plan. It would make sense for her to be with him for the meeting, with both of them going from Human Achievement to comBATON.

They finished their planning just as the others began to arrive, including Bobby. He and Sophie had apparently planned an amicable breakup on his return to practice.

With the team and Stephanie nearby as witnesses, Bobby and Sophie decided they were better as friends. And with that, the fake romance was over.

Matt noticed Stephanie's feeble attempt to conceal a smile.

THE DANCE

[THURSDAY, OCTOBER 15, 2037, 4:10 P.M.]

Matt popped out of bed the next morning and caught a quick glimpse of his face in the mirror. He looked as energized as he felt, ready to seize the moment. Sophie and he complemented one another well. Matt sensed their investigation was about to produce results.

After their last class, Matt and Sophie hurried to Statuary Hall, where Matt had seen the time-traveling chariot in David's clue. Matt looked around with his peripheral vision, as he had been doing since the trip to Lincoln Park. No one was there other than the vice president. "Good afternoon, Matthew...and Ms. Jackson."

"Good afternoon, sir. Sophie and I were just heading from class to practice, to give us time to go over some new plays."

"No problem, Matthew. This was your meeting request. And that's good time management. You'll make a good RM."

That possibility hadn't crossed Matt's mind in the weeks since he'd embarked on their current mission. It was now too remote to bother him. "Thank you, sir."

"So, you had a question?"

"Yes, sir. You spoke to me recently about my father and Mrs. Peterson. In continuing to study leadership styles, I was wondering what else you might tell me about my father's style."

The vice president's hand reached for his chin. "That's a pretty broad question. What could I tell you that you haven't observed yourself? You already know how he works tirelessly to achieve the RM mission. He's been very effective…although, you had another family member whose leadership style was very different than your father's, and just as effective."

"You mean my grandfather?"

"Yes. Not that your father's not likable, but there was something special about Joseph. You felt like he was a friend. He was also a leader. You had no qualms following him and doing whatever he asked. Your grandfather knew how to work as hard as anyone I've ever seen, but he also knew how to let loose and have a good time."

Matt and Sophie flashed each other a smile. Matt said, "I've heard that."

"I'm sure you have. I'm sure you also know he led many scientific teams."

"Dr. Farmer mentioned it more than once."

"Undoubtedly. Matthew, I know you well and know if I ask you to keep something to yourself, you will. Ms. Jackson, can I expect the same of you?"

"Definitely. Even my parents won't hear about this."

"You can trust Sophie with anything," Matt reassured him.

"Well, that's good enough for me. But…" he hesitated, as if he were still unsure whether he should proceed. He rocked back on his heels and, unconsciously copying Dr. Farmer, fidgeted with his hands.

Sophie took a half step toward the vice president. Clasping her hands together, as if she were praying, she said, "Sir, I've always known you to be an honorable man. If there's something you feel you can't say, we understand." She paused to touch Matt's shoulder. "But keep in mind, one day Matthew may be the president. If there's something he should know…"

Matt maintained his focus on the vice president, who rocked forward as if his body were being persuaded to obey. "This may sound strange, but did Dr. Farmer ever mention he was on Joseph's time-travel team?"

Matt had not expected that question and he didn't need to see Sophie's wide-eyed reaction to know that she hadn't, either. Matt said, "No, he didn't."

"People don't like to talk about their failures much. You see, Joseph realized Project RM was established as a reactive measure after the unthinkable. But he liked to think outside the box. What if we could travel back and undo horrific events?"

Trying to remain unfazed, Matt said, "Wow. What an interesting concept."

"Yes. His team worked around the clock. When they encountered a problem, and there were many given the complexity of the undertaking, he would come at it from all angles. He might throw a party or go to a ball game, and then switch right back into work mode. It was his way of stepping away from the problem to see if he could find another way to the solution." The vice president broke off abruptly.

Matt wanted more and became impatient. After a few moments of silence, he asked, "So what happened?"

"In the end, he never succeeded. And of course, your father later discovered traveling back in time isn't possible."

Sophie said, "I suppose Joseph might have been able to figure that out if he had had the opportunity."

"It's possible, maybe even likely. The president formed his conclusion based on Joseph's final test run, which took place right before the Storm...some say his final test may have even caused the Storm."

Matt's heart raced and his skin tingled. The thought that his grandfather might have been responsible for the Storm was beyond comprehension. Clearly sensing his distress, Sophie placed a reassuring hand on Matt's tense shoulder. He asked, "How could a time machine test cause the Storm?"

Vice President Silverman began to rock back and forth again. His face burned bright red. "I don't know. I've probably said too much."

"Why doesn't anyone ever talk about this?" Sophie asked.

The vice president continued to wobble, and his face now paled. "The president said a long time ago that we need to remember Joseph with reverence—that it would tarnish your generation's view of him to hear this. I see his logic, but I thought you should hear a different perspective on leadership. Your father is a strong leader, Matthew, but so was Joseph. His teams followed him until the end. He led them on a mission to save the world, not just to preserve mankind's achievements."

Before the vice president could continue, Matt said, "Sir, you've mentioned Joseph's teams several times. I know my mother was on one of them. Was she on the time-travel team?"

He stopped rocking, leaned forward, and, in a hushed voice, said, "Yes, she was."

Sophie matched his tone. "Who else was on the team? Were my parents on it?"

"No, it was a small team. In addition to Zoe, there were your team-mate Bobby's parents, Dr. Farmer, and a couple of others." The vice president's face blushed once more. "It's time for my next appointment. Remember, keep this to yourselves. I've never said this to anyone and I'll never say it again."

Matt felt the sincerity in his words. Even though Vice President Silverman liked to talk, Matt knew he had taken a chance he would not normally take. Matt focused on the vice president's eyes. "Sir, you can count on us."

"Definitely," Sophie added. "Thank you so much for your time."

"Yes, thank you, sir."

The vice president said, "You're welcome. I know I can count on you."

Matt and Sophie left the building and glided to practice. They decided to meet with the Circle on Sunday to inform them of what they'd learned. They also agreed the next person they needed to speak with was Dr. Farmer. While anxious to do so, they had to be careful not to arouse suspicion. They formulated a plan for Matt to speak to Dr. Farmer in class and try to figure out a logical reason for the three of them to meet.

Saturday was mild and clear, the perfect environment for their style of play. The music continued to have a positive effect on Matt and the ability of DC3 to win. Matt felt unstoppable as almost everything they tried worked. By the time it was over, they had their third blowout victory in a row, 34-9. They had now finished the first half of the season tied for first place, the Blaze having made quick work of the Nationals. The only negative to a perfect afternoon was Rex's snide comment to Matt after the game: "She may play well, but we'll see how good she is after she takes a hit."

Before Matt could do anything stupid, Rich defused the situation by saying loud enough for everyone still at the field to hear, "C'mon, everyone. Let's get over to the café and get the party started."

When he arrived at the café—which Rich had nicknamed the Club— Matt discovered the word party had acted like a magnet, drawing almost every teenager in the community. But he was disappointed to see Lori wasn't there. How could he prove there was nothing between him and Sophie if she wasn't there to witness it?

Rich and David got the music going and everyone else moved the tables and chairs aside. Before Matt knew it, everyone was dancing to the pulsating music and a crowd of boys had formed around Sophie. Matt, suddenly out of breath, turned to leave the dance floor. He hadn't yet reached the edge when Rich stopped the music, causing a disturbance. "Be patient," Rich said. "I'll turn it back on. But before I do, I want to remind everyone this is a victory party. And it's only right we honor those who were most instrumental in making this party possible." Matt expected Rich was going to make some kind of joke honoring himself. "Our two most valuable players today, Matt and Sophie. Will you lead us in the next dance?"

The melody of "Sea of Love" filled the room, as Matt eased his way to the center. He looked over his shoulder at Rich, who was smiling, and thought, *a love song?* He placed one clammy hand on her slender shoulder and the other on her waist. She did likewise and they began to dance. Her intoxicating scent of vanilla captivated him. At first, everyone just watched from the sidelines, cheering them on. But they soon joined in. The rest of the party was the most fun he had ever had.

After almost everyone had gone, Matt leaned over and hugged her. Entranced by the fragrance, he held the embrace longer than intended. After a few moments, he released her. "Good job today."

She smiled. "Thank you. You, too."

Sophie was the first to leave. Matt gathered his things, but stopped when he noticed his friends grinning at him. "What?"

Rich said, "We're happy for you, buddy. You guys make a great couple."

His body flushed as he smirked back. Frustrated by his reaction, he turned and walked away.

The following week was hectic. With everything he was doing, both overt and covert, Matt barely had time to breathe. He most looked forward to working with Sophie on the mission. They would glide around the Mall, talking about who might know what and how they could ask questions without arousing suspicion.

By Wednesday afternoon, they had formulated their plan to meet with Dr. Farmer. Matt had learned from Bobby's research that the doctor shared Sophie's affinity for dance. Matt suggested to him that they should talk, as there were so few people left who truly loved this art. He arranged for the three of them to meet after he and Sophie got out of class on Thursday. He was unsure of how he would turn the conversation from dance to his mother, but at least there was a natural reason to include Sophie.

By the time Human Achievement ended on Thursday, Matt had become anxious. His father had rarely discussed his mother and Matt had loved hearing what little they had about her so far. And from all they had learned, Dr. Farmer had worked by her side for quite some time. Matt hoped that he could shed some light on her supposedly accidental death.

They glided over to Dr. Farmer's office at the Museum of Natural History. The large, windowless room was more of a disorganized lab than an office. The fluorescent light fell on the long workstations, revealing a variety of colors in the partially filled beakers and test tubes. The low hum of the equipment completed the ambiance. Dr. Farmer sat at his small desk in the corner wearing a Neural stare. Matt knocked on the door to announce their presence.

Waking from his trance, Dr. Farmer refocused on them. "Come in. How are you both doing this afternoon?"

Matt said, "Well, sir."

Sophie said, "Yes, we're doing well. And you, sir?"

"I'm doing well as well." They all chuckled. "Matthew tells me you're a dance aficionado like me."

"Yes, sir, although I'm sure the performances I've seen pales in comparison to what you were able to see before the Storm."

"Yes, we do have some great dancers at Dinner Night, and we can see past performances on our Neurals. But I'd have to say it's not quite the same as seeing a live performance at the Kennedy Center."

Sophie's arms crossed, and she gazed past the doctor as if daydreaming about what it would be like to be on stage in front of a large audience.

"You know, Matthew, I attended a few of those performances with your mother."

"I didn't know that, sir. Was she a fan, too?"

"Like most of us RMs, she liked many things."

"I suppose my father attended, too?"

"Actually, he was always at work. He cared so much about the RM mission that he hardly ever took time for recreation."

Sophie jumped in. "So you had a chance to really get to know Matthew's mother?"

"You could say that. It's not like we hung out a lot, like the two of you have been doing recently." Sophie uncrossed her arms and smiled at Matt. Catching a glimpse of the sparkle in her eyes, Matt suddenly realized he had taken Bobby's spot. Not wanting to blow their cover, he returned her smile.

Dr. Farmer's eyes dropped to the left, remembering Matt's mother. "But we worked together and we were friends," he said, smiling broadly.

Matt asked, "Did she have a lot of friends?"

"Yes. Actually, she was friends with everyone. She was one of those rare souls who saw a person for who they were, not for their appearance or title."

Sophie nodded at Matt. "She sounds like an amazing person."

"She was, right up until that tragic day."

Matt said, "Sir, I've always wondered how it really happened. How did she and Bobby's parents actually die?"

Dr. Farmer, hands fidgeting as usual, hesitated. "You know, I'm not sure I'm the right person to answer that question. I wasn't there that day. I'm not sure anyone knows how it happened. I can tell you it was devastating. Your father was despondent for quite some time."

"He was?"

"Well, she was his wife."

"Yes, sir. That makes sense. But my father always seems to...maintain his emotional balance."

"Yes. It's an admirable trait of his."

Sophie asked, "If he was so depressed, how did he regain that balance?"

"I'm not sure, but I suspect it was young Matthew here. He's always been so proud of you."

Sophie said, "I'm sure Matt's mother was just as proud for the short time she was here."

"She certainly was," Dr. Farmer said. He turned his focus to Matt. "She really believed you were important to our future and that you would play an instrumental role in the achievement of the RM mission."

A slight chill ran through Matt, but he played it off with a small chuckle.

Sophie smiled at Matt. "That's interesting."

Matt said, "I wish she could have been here all these years. Sir, I've thought about this for a long time. What was her life like before she died? Other than me, who did she spend most of her time with? I try to envision what life was like for her, but I was too young to remember."

Dr. Farmer hesitated once more. "She certainly spent a lot of time working with her team." He paused again, then changed his tone like he'd received a shock. "Oh, I didn't realize the time. I've got another appointment. Sorry, but I've got to go."

Sophie said, "We understand, sir."

"It was nice speaking with both of you. Have a good afternoon."

Matt and Sophie said, almost in unison, "You too, sir."

After Dr. Farmer left the room, Matt asked, "Was that too direct?"

"Maybe a little, but it was a good question. He had been pretty forthcoming. I wonder why he stopped all of a sudden." Sophie shrugged. "I guess we should get to practice."

THE LESSON

[FRIDAY, OCTOBER 23, 2037, 6:00 P.M.]

On the second-to-last Dinner Night before Halloween, the setting of the golden sun in the clear, cool sky behind the Washington Monument provided the perfect backdrop for a celebration—the annual costume party. Other than Eric, Richard, and Vice President Silverman, who judged the children's costume contest, everyone dressed up as an important person in history. Most dressed as some scientist, doctor, writer, or politician whose efforts had advanced civilization. Matt and Rich had always dressed as their fathers by wearing their presidential and ID shirts. Matt had always gotten the sweats wearing the shirt, but wanted to make his father proud. To avoid drawing attention to themselves, they were continuing this tradition. Matt wasn't as sure of his path these days, but this time his skin was dry—he no longer feared the outfit.

Matt watched as the three judges evaluated the contestants, his father sitting between Richard and the vice president. The three of them were enjoying one another's company, talking and laughing.

After they awarded Peter Jacobsen the top prize for his portrayal of Benjamin Franklin, the festivities wound down. Matt hugged Sophie goodbye, which he tried to convince himself he did just to continue their ruse. He inhaled her intoxicating scent, then reminded himself he would explain everything to Lori when he could.

187

At his father's request, Matt accompanied him home. Matt sat in the front passenger seat and clicked the door shut. "Did you have a good time tonight?" his father asked.

"Yes, sir. It looked like you did, too."

"I did." His father smiled for a moment before his face returned to its natural, serious state. "I'm disappointed things didn't work out with Lori. That Sophie Jackson's an interesting girl. You seem to be spending a lot of time with her lately. Just be careful you don't upset too many people by switching allegiances so quickly. Without the support of the community, it will be impossible to lead."

"I understand, sir."

"You've got a lot going for you right now. Your team's been impressive. And I understand you're doing well as the assistant in both Science & Technology and Government."

"Thank you, sir."

"Just make sure you don't lose your focus."

Matt had heard this before, but something in his father's tone gave him pause. "What do you mean, sir?"

"I mean that post-game ritual you and your friends started."

"That's just a little fun. I won't lose my focus, sir."

"A little fun can grow into a lot of indifference to the tasks at hand," his father said. "We saw that happen in many ways before the Storm. My point is simple. As the future leader, you have to think about more than just how your actions affect yourself. You have to think about how your actions affect everyone."

"I understand, sir."

"Good. I'm glad."

Matt relaxed back into his seat.

The rest of the ride was quiet, until they pulled into the White House driveway. His father flipped on the light in the car. "I understand you've been asking about your mother."

Matt looked up at his father.

"I can understand that with Storm Remembrance Day tomorrow, you must be thinking a lot about the people we've lost, but if you want to know about your mother, you should come to me. Family matters shouldn't be discussed with anyone else." His father stared at his son without blinking. "Do you understand?"

Matt looked away. "Yes, sir."

"Good, because if you want to be a good leader, you cannot allow others to know your weaknesses."

Matt fidgeted. He didn't really agree with his father. He expected it showed, as his father saw the need to continue his lesson.

"Let me put it this way, son. If people know what you're thinking, if they know what drives you, they may be able to exploit it. It's much better to listen and let others speak."

Matt was not fully sure what his father was saying and was much more concerned about who had betrayed him and Sophie. Had his father been the one to leave the message to stop the ops? His voice wavered a little. "Yes, sir. I think I understand."

"Good." He looked away. "There are those in this community who believe only victory brings glory. These same people may use any perceived weakness to achieve that glory."

"What do you mean, sir? No one opposes you."

"There's always opposition. If you don't foresee it, you can't stop them from ruining everything you've strived to create." His father watched him for a moment, studying his reaction. "Do you think those scientists who died last month died by accident? It happened because I couldn't see the opposition until it was too late. Now their poor families have to suffer."

Matt knew that the murder hadn't been an accident, but was startled by his father's unsolicited admission. He acted the part. "What? It wasn't an accident? Who did it?"

"For now, let me worry about that. If we're going to survive and grow as a community, we have to be eternally vigilant. Just think about what I said."

Matt lay in bed, trying to sleep, but the conversation replayed in his head. His father knew the deaths were not an accident, and he seemed to know who had killed the scientists. Despite being confused about many things, Matt feared for the Circle. His mother may have convinced him to continue with the investigation, but now maybe two groups were onto them.

And one of the groups had already killed before, more than once.

THE TEST

[SATURDAY, OCTOBER 24, 2037, 10:10 A.M.]

The dark and rainy conditions outside heightened Matt's anxiety. Storm Remembrance Day had arrived—and, more importantly, the day of the test. With a little over a month left to get the time travel machine to work and the increasing concern of getting caught, Matt knew today's results were crucial to their success.

The community assembled at the Chinatown entrance to RM City. Thick, cold raindrops pounded on their clear umbrellas and raincoats. The annual ceremony began by honoring the billions lost in the Storm. Many dignitaries gave speeches about the infamous day mankind was nearly lost forever. Matt's nerves felt more and more frayed as the speakers brought home the true weight of the Circle's mission.

Immediately after the ceremony, the team assembled in the secret lab. Matt had barely reached the bottom of the ladder before Rich asked, "So, what happened with your father last night?"

Matt felt the heat creep up his neck. "Quite a bit. Let's get to the cottage first."

Rich said, "Okay." The others nodded in agreement.

They journeyed to the cottage in a quiet, single-file line. Each time the wind whistled through the trees, Matt's head jerked around to see if anyone had followed them.

He led the way into the house and up to the second floor study. "So, about my father. First, he knows that Sophie and I have been asking about my mother."

Sophie asked, "Did he say how?"

"He never does. It could be Dr. Farmer, or the vice president, or..."

Rich asked, "Or what?"

"Or it could be the security measures we've implemented aren't working."

Rich said, "You mean the measures I've implemented."

David said, "I doubt that's it."

Matt thought about all the information that had leaked so far, and lied, "I doubt that, too. Your measures are genius, Rich." A vision of the warning to stop the ops flashed through his head. "But we shouldn't rule anything out."

"You're right. I just don't want to be the weak link."

Bobby asked, "So, do you think it was Dr. Farmer or the vice president?"

Matt said, "It seems Dr. Farmer's been helping us. And we all saw the vice president talking with our fathers last night."

Sophie said, "Circumstantial evidence. Not enough to point the finger yet."

"You're right," Matt said. "Then my father said something that made me feel like he was worried for us."

Sophie asked, "How so?"

"He told me he knows that Stephanie's father and his team didn't die in an accident."

Everyone's mouths dropped open, but no one said anything. Finally, Sophie asked, "What?"

"He said they were killed because he couldn't see the opposition until it was too late."

"Who's the opposition?" she asked.

"He wouldn't tell me. He said to let him worry about that. But I had the feeling he meant Richard."

Rich ran his fingers through his hair, as if it would help him unravel the mystery surrounding his father's nefarious act. "I guess it's possible your father's not with my father, but is being controlled by him," Rich speculated. "That would explain why he knew about the murder, but hasn't been able to do anything about it. That might also explain why my father promoted him to lead the community in the first election after the Storm." Rich put a hand over his mouth, as if to hold everything in.

Bobby spoke up. "Do you remember Mom's Rule 5?"

Matt answered, "Two plus two doesn't always equal four. What are you saying? Everything I just told you doesn't mean what Rich and I think it means?"

Bobby said, "Don't get me wrong, Matt. It could. But Mom has always taught us not to come to conclusions without having all of the facts. Of all of Peterson's Rules, she told us this is one of the most important."

The ensuing silence could have been one of contemplation or confusion. For Matt, it was a lot of both.

Eventually, Sophie spoke up. "Whatever it all means, our primary focus needs to be building and using the Ball on December 7th. While we do that, we can figure out how to get as much information as possible to help Matt when he goes back."

Matt nodded. Despite his fear that the life would be squeezed out of his body, he feared even more that their ongoing investigation would get Sophie and the others killed. He prayed the time machine would somehow be ready early. "All right. Let's see the Ball."

David went to the next room and quickly returned with the same machine Matt had seen in the photo in his father's office. He handed it to his sister, who apparently did not realize its extremely smooth, metallic bottom was slippery. She dropped it and a couple of attachments from the top broke off.

"What are you doing?" Matt snapped. "Be careful."

Sophie stepped back. "Geez, sorry."

David said, "Don't worry. I can fix it."

Matt could see the damage his words had inflicted in Sophie's glassy eyes. "Sorry, Sophie. I'm just a bit nervous about the test."

David picked up the Ball and its parts and got to work while the others watched. Within minutes, he put all of the pieces back together. He handed it to Rich this time.

Rich said excitedly, "All right, let's try it."

Matt asked, "Am I going to be squeezed through a meat grinder?"

Rich said, "David has a theory on the meat grinder."

"Yes?"

"Well, I don't think you'll be squeezed," David said. "I don't believe the gravitational forces will be too extreme. I also believe the atmosphere on both ends of the wormhole will be sucked in, creating an atmospheric bubble that will last long enough to allow you to survive the trip."

Matt would have liked a stronger affirmation than "believe," but he trusted David. Matt also reminded himself his mother would not have given him this mission if she thought he would die in the wormhole. "Okay, so how does it work?"

David said, "The biometric scanner reads your genetic signature, triggering the internal battery to activate, which causes the internal couplers—"

"Wait," Matt said. "That's interesting and I want to learn about that later, but right now I just want to know how to turn it on."

"Oh. First, until you're ready to activate it, always hold the Ball from the top. The rest of us can grab it from the bottom because the biometric scanner is set only for your palm print. If you grab it from the bottom, it could activate it early. The schematics included a picture of you with both arms extended straight out to each side, palms face up. When you're in that position, you'll grab the top of the Ball with your right hand, place the bottom of the Ball in your extended left palm, and then return your right arm to its original position. The connection of your left palm with the biometric scanner on the bottom should activate the Ball. So, whatever you do, don't touch the bottom of the Ball until we're in position."

Matt took a deep breath. "It's now or never, right? Let's give it a try and see what happens."

"Hold on," David said, stopping him. "First, you need to enter a special chamber. Otherwise, the Ball's effects could spread for miles. According to the schematics, the chamber we need was already built in the past. It's made of a special type of metal that should contain the effects of the Ball."

Matt asked, "Okay. Where's the chamber?"

Rich said, "You know the little elevator here?"

"Yes."

Rich said, "That's your chamber."

"That's why we were sent to the Lincoln Cottage," Bobby said. "Brilliant."

David added, "We hypothesize that the dark energy attracted by the Ball will be able to penetrate the walls of the chamber, but the wormhole won't be able to."

Matt asked, "And what's your basis for that hypothesis?" He hated to sound snippy, but he was time traveling in an elevator and he wanted facts.

Rich led him to the elevator. "Don't worry about that. Just trust us."

Everyone followed, Rich and David discussing final preparations and Bobby and Sophie in silence. David and Rich finally grew quiet as Matt stepped forward into the little chamber.

Rich said, "Okay. Remember to grab the Ball from the top. If it works, when the bottom comes in contact with your palm, it should produce results almost immediately."

Rich stepped back to close the door. "We'll be able to monitor and speak with you via the video feed and speaker installation in the upper left-hand corner of the chamber." Matt looked up and saw the camera. "Are you ready?" Rich asked.

"I think so. What happens if it works?"

Rich explained, "All we want you to do is place the Ball in your palm and see the effects. As soon as you feel or see anything significant, take the Ball out of your hand. If the wormhole were to open and pull you in, we're not sure where you'd end up, if anywhere."

"Oh, great. How will I know when to stop?" Matt asked, sounding a little more anxious than he intended.

Rich said, "You'll know. If you don't, we'll tell you. So, how does it feel to be the first chrononaut?"

Matt was afraid if they stalled any longer, he'd lose his nerve. "Let's just do what we came here to do."

Rich grimaced. "Touchy."

Matt's heart felt heavy, as if it were trying to pull him down to the floor. He grabbed the Ball from Rich from the top with his right hand. If not for the cool, smooth surface, Matt would not have known he was holding anything—it weighed next to nothing.

Rich closed the door and spoke through the PA system. "Okay, whenever you're ready."

Matt took a deep breath and braced himself. Holding the Ball out as instructed, he placed it in his moist, left palm. The smooth surface slid a bit, then...nothing. He waited a couple of minutes for some delayed reaction.

The Ball might have looked like the one in the picture, but it didn't work. "I think something's wrong. I'm taking it out of my palm. Open up."

The door opened to reveal four faces that reflected Matt's disappointment. They had spent months calculating, building, and hypothesizing. They had risked detection by a murderer. And they had nothing. No one had an explanation and, for the rest of the meeting, they came up with no plausible solutions.

Their journey back to the lab looked similar to the trip there, but felt to Matt more like a funeral procession. For him, it was more than the failure of the Ball to come to life. The entire mission seemed to be falling apart. Despite questioning elders and research in the stacks, they knew almost nothing that would be useful to change the past. With lowered heads, the team members silently followed each other through the sewer.

Matt led the way through the lab and up the ladder. He was ready to go home and sleep on it. Just as he was about to pop the trap door open, he heard a hushed "Stop" from below. It was David. Matt looked down, ready to ask him what was going on. But, seeing David's finger over his mouth and his paler-than-normal complexion, Matt froze.

David mouthed, "Someone's up there."

Matt signaled for the team to descend back into the lab, where David whispered, "I can hear voices up there. Listen."

Everyone became statues. Matt closed his eyes in attempt to better focus his ears. It worked—he could hear Rex's teammates Nick and Travis above them in the garden. He signaled for everyone to remain quiet.

Sophie spoke in a hushed voice. "They can't hear us down here if we speak softly."

"They must have come here because of the Mislocator program. We're all indicating we're at the Botanic Garden," Rich said.

Bobby asked, "What do we do? Sneak up there and act like we've been there the whole time?"

"Too risky," Rich said. "I think we wait them out."

Sophie said, "From now on, we'll have to be caught at the locations where they expect to find us."

"And when we can't be," Bobby said, "we'll have to have alibis for where we are. I suggest we use the Mislocator sparingly from now on."

Rich looked at David. "I don't know what we'd do without you."

Surprising everyone, David lifted his head to reveal a wide grin and a sparkle in his eyes. His reaction was contagious, and everyone smiled.

After a moment, David raised his hand as if to quiet the already silent group. He waited a few seconds, then said, "It's safe. I heard them leave."

The rest of the team patted him on the back. Matt should have been worried that more people might be on to them, but the sight of his teammates had warmed him. "We were brought together for a reason. Listening to each of you just now, especially you, David, and seeing how we've come together, I know we'll succeed." Matt placed his hand on David's shoulder. "I know you'll figure out the Ball. And we'll be here to help."

David said, "Thank you."

One by one, the Circle ascended the ladder. Matt was last, right behind Sophie. She put her hand on a rung, then stopped and turned to face Matt. "We forgot the b—"

Her intoxicating aroma caught him off guard. He leaned in and brushed his lips against hers. They were soft and trembled slightly. An unexpected warmth radiated through his body. After seconds that felt like minutes, Matt opened his eyes to see Sophie's were wide open, staring back at him. He retreated a step and waited for her reaction.

She stepped away and walked past him, her voice a little shaky. "I was saying, we forgot to make sure the box covered the hole in the wall." She completed her chore and approached Matt, her arms crossed ominously as usual.

"I'm sorry."

She stopped in front of him and let her arms fall to her side.

"You know what? No, I'm not."

"Good." She placed her hands on his chest and pushed him back against the ladder. Before Matt knew what was happening, her hands slid up to his face and her lips reconnected with his.

Every one of his nerve endings tingled. He embraced her tightly, as if to say, *I'm never letting go.*

UNDERSTANDING

[SATURDAY, NOVEMBER 7, 2037, 1:00 P.M.]

After months of nightmares, the following two weeks were a dream. Matt and Sophie spent every available moment together. He felt renewed hope that they, or more specifically, David, would figure out the problem with the Ball. Matt was even upbeat about the investigation—despite the repeated warnings—and about figuring out the meaning of the remaining achievements listed in the mural David had found.

Before he knew it, another game day had arrived. This game had significance for two reasons. It was the last game before Veterans Day, meaning there would be a special ceremony before the national anthem. In addition, after their easy win the previous week, a victory against the Tsunami would secure DC3's spot in the playoffs.

The ceremony took place at the RM Monument in front of the Capitol reflecting pool. Matt's father and Richard laid a large wreath at its base and everyone bowed their heads for all those lost in service to the country. Richard led an ID procession in front of the memorial. As they passed, everyone T-saluted. Matt's anger at this false leader directed more power into his clenched fists than he had intended.

DC3 played first in an uneventful match. The team continued its magical season with an easy 37-6 win. They had made the playoffs.

After the game, they watched the last three games of the day. The Nationals broke out of a two-game losing streak, remaining one game behind DC3, and the Raiders clinched their division, beating the Blaze in another nail-biter.

Finally, it was party time. Many of the IDs—including Rex and his teammates—joined this time. Everyone in the Circle of Five, other than Rich, remained quiet at first—all of them probably thinking like Matt: *Are any of the IDs here to spy on us?* But with Sophie by his side, Matt soon allowed the rhythm of the music to take control of his body.

They danced for several songs. Matt and Sophie eventually ended up near Bobby and David. All of a sudden, Rich joined in, signaling for them to hold hands as they swayed to the music. They followed his direction.

The moment they completed the circle, a vision of the Bible flashed into Matt's head—they had unlocked another hidden file from the Discs. Below the picture were the words "Rome" and "Greece." Matt looked around at the others. They all looked like he felt, their eyes open almost as wide their mouths. Matt waited for the song to end, and then escorted Sophie out into the dark night to avoid the eyes and ears of the ID. They sat in his favorite spot on a bench next to the fountain in the middle of the Sculpture Garden. A rainbow of colors illuminated the eight streams of water arching into the center of the fountain.

Matt knew Rich's belt would not work on eavesdroppers who might be closer to them than he realized. Even with the rushing sound of the water drowning out their voices, he was extra careful about what he said. "Do you remember what the Bible verse is for church tomorrow?" Matt asked.

"No, but I was just wondering the same thing."

"Maybe it's Romans."

"Maybe it'll be a story about Judea," Sophie said, and Matt understood from her tone that this was the word she'd seen in her vision.

Matt winked. "I guess we'll find out tomorrow." He knew if they stayed away much longer, they would be missed. "Let's call a team meeting so we can discuss strategy for next week. We can meet after church."

"Great idea," Sophie said, clearly understanding which team Matt meant.

They walked back inside holding hands, which had quickly become Matt's favorite new habit.

After church, the team assembled in the lab. The moment the last person's feet hit the floor, Matt said, "All right, Rich. Spill it. How'd you figure that out?"

"I was standing on a chair, doing my thing as the DJ, when I saw you dancing in a circle. I thought of the clue about completing the circle. It could have meant both the mural, and us. I guessed that we needed to hold hands to complete the circle."

David said, "That's brilliant."

Rich grinned at him. "Thank you. But I have to say I wouldn't have figured it out without you. You named us the Circle of Five."

Matt said, "So, I assume we all got different words along with an image of the bible."

"Why do you think that?" Bobby asked.

"Because I got the words Rome and Greece and Sophie got the word Judea."

Bobby said, "I got Middle Ages."

"I got Germany," Rich said.

David said, "I got England. According to the mural of the twelve achievements, Matt's clues are philosophy and administration—the achievements of Greece and Rome. I'm not sure how that fits. Sophie's is religion, the achievement of Judea."

Rich said, "The Bible is religious. Maybe that explains Sophie's clue. Germany's achievement is printing. After inventing the printing press, Gutenberg printed one of the Bibles on display in the Jefferson Building of the Library of Congress. Our clues might be pointing toward the Gutenberg Bible." Matt's pulse quickened.

"Possibly," David said. "How about Middle Ages, which is modern language?"

Bobby said, "The Gutenberg Bible is written in Latin, the primary religious language in the Middle Ages, at least for Christianity."

David said, "And England is literature. The Bible is the most popular book in history."

Matt put a hand up to interject. "Great, so four of the remaining six achievements in the mural might be tied to the Gutenberg Bible. But how does this stuff fit together and where does it fit with everything else?"

Bobby followed Matt's lead and raised his hand. "I'm the language expert. I think I should go check out the Gutenberg Bible on display. Maybe the clue refers to the passage to which it's opened."

Sophie asked, "And how will you know it's the right passage?"

Matt said, "If I'm remembering correctly, I've heard that after the Storm the RMs opened the Gutenberg Bible to a specific page and it's remained there ever since."

"Do you know the passage it's opened to?" Sophie asked. "Maybe Bobby doesn't need to look conspicuous standing in front of the case, reading the Bible."

Matt said, "No, I don't."

Bobby said, "Don't worry. At some point this week, I'll casually go read it."

Matt smiled at having the first concrete plan in a while. "Great. David and Rich, any progress on the Ball?"

David said, "No. Rich and I have pored through our respective schematics to see what we did wrong. It's frustrating because all we had to do was follow the directions for it to work. Whoever left us the schematics must have given us a complete picture. Otherwise, how could they expect us to figure it out?"

Matt patted him on the back. "Because they likely knew you'd be the one working on it. We all believe in you. Believe in yourself." He faced the whole team. "After Bobby reads the passage, let's meet here and figure out whatever needs figuring out."

Bobby said, "Sounds like a plan."

"Now let's talk about something a little more important," Rich said.

Matt asked, "What?"

"Who do you think we'll play in the first round of the playoffs?" Everyone laughed. They joked and talked for a few more minutes before splitting up. David and Rich remained in the lab. Bobby left, likely to meet up with Stephanie. Matt left with Sophie.

Matt was determined to spend every spare moment he had with Sophie and she clearly felt the same. Every day, they strolled and glided around the community together, doing their part to show the ID where they were. The fact that the weather had turned colder didn't matter. They visited her parents in Lincoln Park a few times, but for the most part they just talked.

Sophie talked about growing up with David. "He's smart, but he's always been behind socially. He's always depended on us if he wanted anything. He'd nag me or my mom until we took care of it. That's all changed since the Circle of Five, and especially since Storm Remembrance Day. Now, if he wants something, he just takes care of it himself."

"I've noticed the confidence. He doesn't hide his face as much anymore."

"I know. My parents can't get over it. The day after the test, David was talking to my mom about you guys. After he left the room, she started to cry. She told me, 'I know there's no cure and I've always loved him for who he was, but those young men have given me the son I always knew was in there. I can't thank them enough.'"

It had never occurred to Matt that his interactions with David had had such a profound effect. Matt smiled and scratched the back of his neck. "Your brother's a brilliant and great guy. We wouldn't be complete without him."

He stopped walking and changed the subject. "I've never told anyone this, but I really miss my mom. I don't even know her, but seeing her in a dream or clue or whatever it was...well...it hurt." He thought about the tears from the brief encounter before the first day of school and lowered his head. Sophie squeezed his hand, causing him to smile. "At least Mrs. Peterson's always been there for me. She's the one I've always been able to talk to. There have been so many times in the last two months I've wished I could tell her everything that's happened." He stared into her eyes. "And now I have you."

She rested her head against his chest. "I know what you mean. I've always been able to tell my parents everything." After a brief, awkward silence, she said, "And now I think I can tell you everything."

Matt's stomach twisted and he nearly lost his balance. "Is there something you want to tell me right now?"

"Lori really cares for you, Matt."

He stared at the ground. "I know. Why are you telling me that now?"

She lifted her head to face him. "Because you need to know she spoke with Bobby and me during Agriculture class right after we started our mission." Matt didn't like where this was going. "She was jealous. And I had been jealous for a long time about her being with you—"

Matt opened his mouth at that, but she placed a finger over it. "I know. I guess that wasn't the best way to tell you, but that's not the point. When we met, she wouldn't stop saying that the most important thing to her was your happiness. I was selfish. I suggested Bobby and I date to see if it would make you jealous."

"It did."

"I know. And I'm sorry. I just wanted you, and knew that was my opportunity."

"Why didn't you tell me earlier?"

"She made me promise not to tell you. And," Sophie dropped her head again, "I guess I was worried you might decide you wanted her, and not me. I'm sorry."

He thought about how Lori had told him he was amazing when she broke up with him. "That confirms she's the amazing one. It also confirms, once again, I didn't make the decision to ask you out. Both of you led me to it." Sophie's eyes remained fixated on the ground. "Now that you've taught me how to choose for myself, I don't know what to say…other than I wouldn't choose anyone but you." Matt drew his body up to hers and inhaled her fragrance. They both stood there, Sophie with her head still down, Matt listening to their hearts beat as one. She slowly raised her head and they gazed at one another. When he could contain himself no longer, he kissed her softly on the lips.

"Why'd you tell me now?" Matt asked, as they resumed their walk.

"Because I don't want us keeping secrets from one another. And just like Lori, I want you to be happy."

"I am."

On the morning of Veterans Day, the ID led a small parade down Pennsylvania Avenue from the Capitol to the White House. Everyone else stood on the sidewalks and cheered them on. Even though there was not a cloud in sight, the sun's rays had little effect on the cold day.

After the parade, everyone gathered on the downward-sloping south lawn of the White House to commemorate all the veterans of the United States military. Most of the IDs remained near the top of the lawn. They were dressed in various uniforms to reflect the different branches of the military at the time of the Storm. Richard dressed as a five-star Army general and Rex dressed as a Navy SEAL. Matt laughed to himself. From what he had learned about the SEALs, he doubted Rex would have ever qualified. Matt watched from afar with Sophie, standing in front of the large water fountain several hundred yards down the lawn. He again felt sickened to see them pretending to be something they were not, but appreciated the rest of the festivities.

He was enjoying his alone time with Sophie until Stephanie approached. "Have you seen Bobby? I've been looking for him since the beginning of the parade."

Matt and Sophie exchanged glances. Matt guessed he had taken the opportunity to do a little reading. They engaged Stephanie in conversation in an attempt to distract her. Luckily, a few minutes later Bobby arrived and hugged Stephanie. "So, what'd I miss?"

Stephanie stared him down, her hands on her hips. "Everything."

"Sorry about that. When nature calls." They all laughed.

"Look at that, up by the house," Bobby said. "That's *some* cake."

Stephanie looked up toward the top of the lawn, where everyone had begun to gather around the five-tier cake frosted in red, white, and blue. Bobby nodded to Matt and Sophie. "I've been thinking. I have a few ideas for the Nationals. I know we don't play them for two weeks, but I expect we'll need to beat them to win the division."

Stephanie said, "It's been an exciting season. Do you all think you can win the championship?"

Bobby motioned in the direction of Matt and Sophie. "With these two, we can't lose."

Matt was about to return the compliment when Stephanie said, "Yeah, you've been great, Sophie."

"Thank you. I'm just trying to keep up with these guys."

"When do you want to meet up?" Matt asked.

"How about after the ceremony? If that's okay with you, Stephanie," Bobby said.

"It's fine. If you want, you can catch up with me after you're done."

"I want. I'll see you right after."

The rest of the ceremony dragged on. All Matt could think about was finding out what Bobby had read.

Everyone finally went their separate ways and Matt and Sophie darted off with Bobby.

They reached the lab and Matt asked, "What's the passage?"

"God said to Noah, 'Come out of the ark, you and your wife and your sons and their wives. Bring out every kind of living creature that is with you—the birds, the animals, and all creatures that move along the ground—so they can multiply on the earth and be fruitful and increase in number on it.'"

"I wonder what the connection is," Sophie said.

"I've had time to think it over. I think the Gutenberg Bible is opened to that passage to commemorate how we were like Noah's family on the Ark after the Storm—which would kind of make RM City the Ark."

Matt asked, "So, how does that help us?"

Bobby said, "I have no idea."

REVELATIONS

[SATURDAY, NOVEMBER 14, 2037, 4:05 P.M.]

The Cyclones presented as much resistance in their second match against DC3 as in their first—none. Due to the victory, Bobby's prediction came true. To win the division, they would have to beat the Nationals in the final week of the season. This would set up the playoffs nicely. First, redemption for last year's embarrassing loss to the Blaze. Next, a championship game shot at Rex and his Raiders.

The after-game party grew again, almost exponentially. Many younger adults had joined the festivities. Matt wondered if eventually everyone would attend. That is, everyone except his father.

Despite the unsolved Ball issue and the confusion as to the meaning of the Bible clue, Matt continued to enjoy each day with Sophie. He felt that as long as he willed it strongly enough, everything would fall into place.

In Human Achievement on Thursday, Sophie informed Matt that her brother wanted to discuss some ideas he had for the game, which was code for meeting in the lab.

Class ended and they rushed over. When they stepped off the ladder, David was waiting.

Matt asked, "Did you figure out the problem with the Ball?"

"Not exactly. But when Sophie told me about Noah and the Ark, it got me thinking," he said, then hesitated.

Sophie asked, "What?"

"Matt, didn't Dr. Farmer say your father named his contingency plan Plan 40?"

"Yes," Matt said, pausing. "You know, now that I think about it, the picture and the copy of President Lincoln's speech were placed at page 40 of the poetry books."

David said, "Considering it rained for 40 days and 40 nights in the story, I wonder if it isn't a coincidence that your father named it Plan 40."

The words sent a chill down Matt's spine. "I guess. Dr. Farmer thought it just meant there were at least 40 plans."

Sophie shook her head in doubt, but she remained silent—likely being careful not to start another argument about Matt's father's motives.

Matt said, "Don't worry, Soph. I'm still holding out hope he's with us, but I know he could be against us."

Sophie nodded. "Let me know if there's anything I can do to help."

"Actually, I think this is one I should do on my own." He didn't know if his father was hiding anything, but he wanted to be able to confront him alone if something strange surfaced.

The color drained from her face. "Okay. Just be careful."

He stared at her, unblinking. "I will."

David said, "Don't forget, Matt, we still don't know how the accomplishments of philosophy and administration fit into things."

"Well…I'll have to find out."

"What are you planning to do?" David asked.

"Beats me. But I'll let everyone know when I come up with something. Thanks for calling the meeting," Matt added, impressed David had become confident enough to do so.

The remainder of the week felt off. Every time they held hands, Sophie's grip felt more like a vice than a sign of affection. Matt knew he had to calm her down before the most important game of the season to date that Saturday. He led her to the lab and hugged her. "I'm not doing anything about Plan 40 right now. We need your best today." He thought about DC3's last two losses—the ugly loss to the Blaze in the playoffs last year and the loss to start the season. "Before we can get redemption against the Blaze, I need a little redemption against the Nationals."

She stepped back and crossed her arms, issuing one of her penetrating looks. "Okay, but promise to talk with me before you do anything?"

He responded with the best assured stare he could muster. "Yes."

"Yes, what?"

"Yes, I promise."

She dropped her arms. "Great, then let's get you your redemption."

He hugged her once more and they headed to the field to join the team.

Because of the importance of the game, the commissioner had set theirs as the last one of the day. The three-hour wait felt like three days. Matt used the time to scout the Raiders and the Blaze, but his primary focus was the Nationals.

Finally it was time. The Nationals were introduced first. The commissioner played "Let's Get It Started" as he introduced DC3. Matt took one more look at Sophie and the energy flew through his body.

He, Rich, and Bobby started, as they had in Game 1. Unlike Game 1, however, Matt spread the Baton around like never before—but five minutes in, DC3 trailed 4-3.

With two minutes left in the half, Matt substituted in Sophie for Rich. After a couple of routine plays, with CJ Rodney bearing down on him, Matt threw a long strike over Joey Townsend's outstretched arms. Sophie caught the Baton in midstride and, in the same motion, executed a spinning jump swing kick for five points and an 8-4 lead. On the last defensive series of the half, they didn't allow the Nationals to reach midfield.

Matt, Rich, and Sophie took the field to start the second half. On the first play, Rich deflected Megan Vogel's pass up into the air. Just as he had done so many times, Matt snatched the Baton in a full sprint toward his opponent's goal. Before the Nationals knew what had happened, Matt struck with a tornado roundhouse to score five points for a 13-4 lead.

He jogged back to the huddle and said, "Let's finish them off," which is exactly what they did. Playing like a well-oiled machine, DC3 passed, kicked, and scored in perfect harmony. The Nationals never scored again and DC3 won 21-4.

ERIC'S ALLEGIANCE

[THURSDAY, NOVEMBER 26, 2037, 2:15 P.M.]

The time had come. Matt couldn't postpone investigating his father any longer. He had to know, now.

Despite having promised Sophie he would talk to her before doing anything, Matt decided the risk was too great. It was better and safer for her to find out after the fact. He would search his father's office during the Thanksgiving Day Parade, then catch up with Sophie. The plan had the bonus of providing the perfect alibi for Sophie. She would be out in public with the rest of the community.

This parade would follow the same route as the Veterans Day Parade, but would go in the opposite direction, starting at the White House and ending at the Capitol. There, everyone would eat dinner in the Rotunda amid richly textured wood tables and fine china, as well as exquisite, albeit pre-recorded, classical music.

Matt discussed his plan with Rich, the Circle member most familiar with security measures. Rich offered to take care of the monitoring system. Matt disagreed at first, but relented when Rich truthfully told him, "You can't pull it off without me."

On the misty, chilly Thanksgiving afternoon, Matt accompanied his father to the annual pardoning of a turkey. The whole time, he kept hoping he would find proof that exonerated his father.

They returned from the ritual in time for the parade. Sophie found Matt in front of the White House just as the festivities began.

Matt looked back toward the Oval Office.

She caressed his shoulder. "Are you okay?"

Her voice drew him back to reality. "I think so. I'm just a little nauseated." This wasn't a lie. The possibility of being caught snooping around his father's office sickened him.

"Let me take you inside," she said and grabbed his hand.

He took her free hand with his and pecked her on the cheek. "That's okay. Go enjoy the parade with your family. I'm going to lie down for a while. I'll catch up with you for dinner."

"Are you sure?"

"Yes."

Sophie ran off to find her family and Matt hurried inside, heading straight to the West Wing.

Reaching the door and praying Rich had done his job, Matt entered the Oval Office.

His heart rate accelerated. He had never been inside without his father. He edged around the furniture, looking at the pictures he had seen hundreds of times. The photo of his father standing with his mother and Joseph drew his attention. He shook his head to take his focus off of the time machine in Joseph's hand. He looked at the desk. It was clean, as usual.

Matt realized he would have to look inside the drawers if he wanted to find anything. Having come prepared for first-class snooping, Matt pulled on a pair of latex gloves and took out a master key Rich had made. He took a deep breath, plunged the key into the lock, turned it, and opened the top left-hand drawer. He thumbed through the papers and, seeing nothing about Plan 40 or anything else that looked interesting, made sure the papers were just as he had found them before closing the drawer. He continued the same process in the other two left-hand drawers and followed the same procedure on the right side.

After finding nothing, he released a long breath. He could abandon his search and join everyone else.

Before he took the first step for the door, an image popped up in his head. It was a portrait of George Washington, in front of which were the words, "Without choice, there is no freedom. Choose to be free!" A shiver went down his spine.

The image disappeared, leaving him staring across the room at the same portrait hanging near the door through which he'd entered. He walked over and pulled at the portrait. To his surprise, it was on hinges, and it swung open to reveal a safe that had a keyhole on the right side. He pulled Rich's key from his pocket and shook his head before plunging it into the slot. Success. Rich was craftier than Matt had ever realized. He pulled open the safe to see one thin folder, marked with the words Plan 40.

Matt looked around the room and listened for any hint that someone else was in the building. Hearing no one, he checked the time and pulled out the folder. The parade would last a little while longer, but he would need to finish what he was doing quickly and catch up with everyone to avoid detection. He yanked it open and began reading.

The first few pages covered how the government should be reestablished if an event like the Storm were to occur. It was just as Dr. Farmer had told him, except the government described in Plan 40 was much looser than the one his father had established. Then he saw a handwritten page headed Humanity's Harmonization. Under it, Matt saw a handwritten diagram showing the government he knew. The president was at the center and all other governmental functions reported to him. This included the legislature, the courts, and the ID. Matt didn't think much of it, considering this centralized model had allowed them to maintain stability for years.

The next page was headed Goals. Below it were several bullet points. The first few items were checked off, including Establish ID, Eliminate Weapons, Establish Recreational Ritual and Show Prowess, Establish

Daily and Weekly Rituals, Reestablish School System, Limit RM Program to One Entrant Per Year, and Establish Uniform Dress Code.

Below the checked items were some unchecked ones. First, Establish Genetically Determined Arranged Marriage, next to which was the justification: "Reduce risk of defect and promote stability." Thinking about it, he realized that was probably the reason why Lori and he had been matched.

He continued down the page, the laws becoming harsher. Second was Penalties for Failure to Comply with Arranged Marriage. Third was Proscription of Sin Products. On the right side of the page, circled and in capital letters, were the words NEED MAJOR EVENT. Unsure of what that meant, Matt turned the page.

It was titled Weaknesses. Many members of the community were listed. The first line was "Richard: Guilt, Richard Jr., and Gloria." Matt almost passed out when he saw a line for his mother. About halfway down the page was the line: "~~Zoe: Matthew and JP.~~" His father had crossed out his mother's name like the completion of any ordinary task. Sweat trickled down his forehead. He stared at the names. "Who's JP?"

Below his mother's name was his own: "Matthew: ~~Need to please father, Lori, Bobby, and Richard Jr.~~ Sophie Jackson." Sophie's name was written in a differently colored ink, no doubt indicating she was a recent addition. Matt leaned against the wall and slid to the ground.

Feeling ill, Matt flipped the page to New Dawn, below which the genetic repopulation team was listed, including the three geneticists who had died earlier in the school year, and Dr. Farmer. The names of the three deceased scientists were struck through. For some reason, next to the names was the statement: Dinner with Matthew.

Below the names was the heading Genetic Repopulation. The first test was Genetic Therapy on Human Subject, next to which the comment "12/7/2019—Successful!" was written. Matt wondered who the test subject might be and what had been successful.

Further down the page was Human Cloning, next to which "8/31/2037—Failure" was written. That was the day the scientists had been killed.

At the bottom was the title Primary Cities to Repopulate. The first city listed was Washington D.C. and the second was New York City.

On the next page was a list called The First Forty, below which were the names of forty people. At the top of the list were Eric and Zoe. The list also included other RMs and a broad array of recognizable names, like Einstein, Washington, Franklin, and Disney.

The last page of the folder was titled People to Remove on Successful Completion of Cloning Technique. He covered his mouth to conceal a gasp. Half the community was named, including Richard Sr., Dr. Farmer, Vice President Silverman, Principal Franklin, David, and… Sophie. Sophie's name was crossed out in the same color ink in which she had been penned in as Matt's weakness. Matt thought, *He doesn't plan to kill them. Does he?* The sweat now dripped down the sides of his face. He closed his eyes and breathed in slowly.

A noise outside the office sprung him to his feet—footsteps coming down the hall. Realizing he needed to get out of there as fast as possible, he reassembled the folder as he had found it, shoved it back in the safe, locked it, and placed the portrait back in its proper position.

He froze at the sound of someone on the other side of the door. He didn't have enough time to hide or get out another way. He went to the door, ready to fight. The door knob turned. Matt stood to the side.

The door creaked open. Matt could feel his heart pounding, sweat freely running down the sides of his face. Fully in attack mode, Matt was shocked to hear an unexpected voice.

"What are you doing?" Sophie whispered, out of breath.

"I thought you were my father or an ID. We need to get out of here. Now!"

"That's what I was coming to tell you!"

He led the way out. His plan was to get out of the house and back to the parade, but as they neared the front door, Sophie said, "No, not that way. Your father saw you weren't with me. I told him you were sick. Then David overheard him tell Rex to come here and check on you. He's only a minute behind me. Go to the bathroom. *Now.*"

Matt moved quickly, shutting the door just as the front door opened. "What are you doing here?" Rex asked.

"Matt's sick, so I left the parade to check on him," Sophie said.

Matt made some retching sounds.

Rex said, "You know, you've been lucky all season. Your team hasn't played anyone good. The Blaze are going to crush you guys on Saturday."

"Why are you telling me this? Do you actually think I care what you think?"

Matt took this as his cue to exit the bathroom. "Is everything all right out here?" he asked, wiping his forehead with a washcloth.

Rex said, "Everything's fine. Your father's concerned about you. Are you okay?"

"Tell him I'll be fine. Sophie's taking good care of me."

Rex turned and left.

With Rex safely out of earshot, Matt turned to Sophie. "Soph, how did you—"

"Don't Soph me," she cut in with her angriest voice. "We'll talk later. Right now, let's go to dinner."

They didn't speak on the trip to the Capitol. She refused to hold his hand and focused straight ahead as if he weren't there. Matt caught one glimpse of her steely face and couldn't look at her the rest of the way.

He tried to process what he'd just seen. He had always known that his father would do what he had to do to maintain order, but this was far beyond anything Matt could have imagined. Did his father plan to kill all the people on that last list? Had the scientists been killed because they had learned of his father's plan? *Did my father order the killing of his own wife?* Matt thought as they arrived at the Rotunda. The dinner had just started and he caught sight of his father at the head table. Feeling dizzy, Matt stopped several tables away.

Matt's father called them over to his table. He said to Sophie, "Thanks for bringing Matthew, but he doesn't look well." He placed his hand on Matt's forehead, causing Matt to shudder. "Son, maybe you should go home and get some sleep."

Matt didn't say anything. He just stared at the man he called Father, the possible murderer of his mother.

Sophie said, "Don't worry, sir. I'll get him home."

"Are you sure? I could ask one of the IDs to take him."

"It's no problem, sir. They should enjoy their meal. I've got him."

She led Matt out of the south side of the building, allowing them to pass by the Botanic Garden on the way home. She said, "You look really bad. Let's go to the lab."

He followed her in and stumbled down the ladder. When they were safely inside, he looked at her and shook his head. "I'm sorry. I wanted to keep you safe."

"That's no excuse. We need each other. I need to know I can trust you."

"I know. It won't happen again."

"Fine. What did you find?"

"First, how'd you know where to go?"

"David overheard your little planning session with Rich." Matt's brows furrowed. She continued, "And don't be mad at David. If he hadn't overheard, you'd have been caught." Matt's face relaxed and he nodded in assent. She added, "I wasn't happy with the plan, but I figured you guys knew what you were doing. Clearly, I was wrong."

"It was a good plan. It was no different than Bobby's trip to the Gutenberg Bible."

"Right, except you're the president's son and your absence is much more conspicuous than his. Oh, and he simply read a book in a public place. You broke into the Oval Office."

Color rushed into Matt's face as he realized that his plan had not been as well planned as he thought. "Okay, so it wasn't exactly the same."

"I thought you and Rich were smart." She took a deep breath. "All right, what'd you see? Judging by your reaction, it couldn't have been good."

He stared blankly in the general direction of the ground. "I think he murdered my mother."

She froze for a moment. Then, she came to him and hugged him tightly. She whispered "I'm sorry" in his ear. For a few minutes, nothing else was said.

Ready to move forward, Matt said, "There's more." Sophie released her comforting embrace as he continued, "I understand the last clues now. His idea of 'administration' is he tells everyone what to do and they obey. And his 'philosophy' is to exploit others' weaknesses. I should have realized when he told me about being careful not to let others figure out my weaknesses. He has a list of everyone's weaknesses to make sure his *subjects* obey."

"He does?"

"For my mother, he listed me and somebody named JP. And for me—"

"You were on the list?"

He nodded. "For me, he replaced everyone and everything with you."

Sophie waited a few seconds, then asked, "What about mine?"

"Yours are your parents, David, and me." He didn't want to tell her about the last page. But he felt he had no choice. "It gets worse."

"Worse?"

"Much worse. First, sit down." Sophie sat on the floor, likely figuring it would be unwise to take the news sitting on a stool. Matt sat next to her. "Once the genetic repopulation technique is perfected, he plans to…"

"What?" she asked, her voice shaky.

"He plans to *remove* certain people."

"What do you mean remove? You mean kill?"

"I think so. And…David's on the list." Matt didn't think telling her she had recently been reprieved would help matters. Sophie began to shake. Matt wrapped his arms around her and held her tight. "It's going to be all right. Remember, I'm going back in time to fix everything." He wiped her tears with his sleeve.

After a couple of minutes, she crossed her arms and hardened her expression. "Tell me everything, and I mean *everything*, you saw."

He took a breath. As he exhaled, everything else began to flow out, from the additional clue about choice and freedom to the full contents of the folder. "Let's meet tomorrow before our last semi-finals practice and I'll tell everyone else," Matt said. "I don't know how Rich has done it. How has he been able to live with his father the last few months?"

Still shaky, she said, "I don't know. He's a lot tougher than I've given him credit for. Don't worry. We'll stop your father. Like you said, we'll send you back and you'll stop this nightmare before it begins."

Somehow, hearing his words reiterated by Sophie wasn't as reassuring as he'd hoped. They were running out of time and they might not succeed. Not wanting to diminish her confidence, he replied, "Yes, I will."

They ascended the ladder and stepped outside of the Botanic Garden into the cold, dark night. He shivered and reached out for one more warm embrace. She willingly responded, then kissed him goodnight.

He moved to leave, but she held his hand. She offered a plastic smile. "Let's try to get a good night's sleep. We'll think more clearly in the morning. And Matthew—sweet dreams."

Matt couldn't help but smile back. "You, too." He turned and took his time on the way home.

Matt glided up the driveway and his father pulled in behind him. He stepped out of the car. "I would have thought you'd be in bed sleeping by now."

"I felt too sick to make it home...sir. Sophie let me into her parents' office for a little while."

"You really care about her, don't you?"

The question had a different meaning than it might have had the day before. He pretended to be indifferent because his father was now listing Sophie as his weakness. He replied, "She's all right," but he could see his father wasn't fooled.

"If you say so, son. But watching you with her the last few weeks reminds me of myself and your mother."

Matt growled involuntarily. He masked it by leaning over as if his stomach hurt.

"You better get to bed. You've got a big game on Saturday. I want you at your best."

Matt mumbled, "Yes, sir." He turned and went straight to bed.

BLAZE OF GLORY

[FRIDAY, NOVEMBER 27, 2037, 6:30 A.M.]

Matt awoke early the next morning to another cold, dreary day. His pulse quickened as he snuck away from the White House grounds. He managed to avoid his father, but the Circle of Five wouldn't meet for hours. Matt glided to his favorite spot in the Sculpture Garden.

He sat on the cold, stone bench and gazed at the streams of water flowing into the center of the fountain. He shivered uncontrollably at the thought of opposing his father. Matt had hoped for months that his father might be on their side, but now he knew better. Despite everything his rational side understood about how vile his father was and about the importance of his mission, Matt still harbored a strange feeling that he was supposed to follow the man who had given him everything in life. That is, until he reminded himself that everything in his life had been a facade, behind which his maniac father had left a trail of destruction. Matt shook with anger. He suddenly felt the urge to destroy something or someone.

He was plotting his next move when the crackle of leaves drew him up into a fighting stance.

"It was pretty bad, huh," Rich said.

Matt's arms relaxed. "You could say that."

"We can talk about the details later, but how bad?"

Matt looked around, then dropped back onto the bench. "Let's just say my father's the ring leader and your father is one of his trained acts."

"Sorry."

"Soph's sorry, too. But I'm the one who should apologize. I had no idea what you've been going through."

"I wouldn't wish it on anyone. You know what helped me?"

"What?"

"The four of you. If I didn't have that, I'm not sure what I would've done. You've got Sophie and the rest of us."

"For now."

"Don't worry. After you travel back, we'll be with you in spirit. C'mon, let's go work out."

Matt tilted his head quizzically.

"Trust me. It helps."

They stood to leave. "How'd you know I was here?"

"C'mon, we've been friends as long as I can remember. In some ways, I know you better than you know yourself."

Matt chuckled. "By the way, good job with that key."

When the five of them gathered in the lab, Matt explained Plan 40. First, he told them that Sophie, Bobby, and Rich were all on the list denoting everyone's weaknesses—but David wasn't. Bobby's weaknesses were Mrs. Peterson, Rich, Matt, and Stephanie. Rich's weaknesses were his parents, Matt, and Bobby.

Next, he discussed the timeline for genetic testing, including the dates of the tests. David found it interesting that the successful genetic therapy listed in the plan had occurred prior to the Storm. "I've read that altering your genes is risky. You might get the results you want, but you might also get unintended consequences, like a change in your chemical levels. Do you think your father was the test subject?"

That thought hadn't crossed Matt's mind. The sinking feeling he had had in the Oval Office returned. "I guess it's possible," he mumbled.

David continued, "There's something else."

"What?"

"When's your birthday?"

"August 28. Why?" Before David could answer, Matt eyes popped open in understanding. "Wait. You don't think whatever he did to himself got passed to me?"

"Possibly. But unless you were born early, you would have been conceived before the therapy began."

"Actually," Matt said, as all eyes turned to him, "I *was* born a few weeks early. That means—"

"Whatever your father did to himself may have been passed to you," David finished.

Bobby's and Rich's slack-jawed look didn't help. But Sophie's crossed arms were a strange comfort. "Matt, I'm sorry to inform you, but you're nothing like your father." She finished her statement with a smile.

Matt hoped Sophie's assessment was accurate and not meant to placate him. Either way, he knew they had to continue. He spoke directly to David as he explained the contents of the last page. He expected David to freak out, but David just nodded.

Sophie said, "I told him about it last night. I thought he had a right to know."

Bobby placed a hand on David's shoulder. "Don't worry, buddy. We're going to change all of this. Matt will go back and fix everything."

Rich said, "Yeah, we'll just finish the Ball, send Matt back, and change the future."

David said, "It's okay. I know it's a tough task. But we'll do it. We haven't been risking our lives for months for nothing."

"But seeing my father's view of you and others, realizing he thinks you're expendable…I hope you know how important you are to us. If my father saw what we see, you wouldn't be on that list. No matter what, we won't let him hurt you."

David smiled.

"Maybe I should go back to his office and get the proof I should've taken in the first place. If I show everyone his insane plan, maybe we can stop him before he hurts anyone else— whether or not we use the Ball."

Sophie said, "I thought about that, but it's too risky. If you get caught, we'll jeopardize the entire mission. Besides, even with the evidence, the ID would support your father. The last thing we need is a war with them."

"Sophie's right," David said. "Thanks for being willing to do that. But I'll take my chances with the time machine."

Rich smiled at Matt. "I agree. We'll call your crazy second break-in idea Plan B. Let's focus on the Ball for now."

Bobby said, "I agree."

"It was just a thought," Matt said. "But you're probably right. Anyway, now we have a much better idea of what we're dealing with. David, we know you'll figure it out." Addressing his athletic team, he said, "I know comBATON doesn't seem like it matters much at the moment, but let's not forget about the clues. We have to make the championship. And we're going against the best of the ID tomorrow and next week. Let's give them something to worry about in case our mission comes down to a fight."

He put his hand in. Everyone else followed suit, shouting, "One-two-DC3."

The next day, the sun broke through, its radiance creating comfortably cool conditions. It was the perfect atmosphere in which to make a statement.

The games were to be played at 2:00 P.M. and 3:00 P.M. Because the Raiders were the only undefeated team, they were given the choice as to their game time. Rex chose the earlier time.

The playoffs included a bit more pomp and circumstance than the regular season. Before the national anthem, some of the former champions were introduced, including Richard and Matt's father. They waved to the crowd, their first championship medals gleaming on their chests. Matt ignored them and finessed the remaining points of the strategy for today.

Finally, the first game started. Matt had mixed feelings. He knew what he would be up against if they were to play the Nationals, but he wanted a shot at Rex. What he wanted quickly became a moot point. The Raiders pummeled the Nationals and finished the game 30-3.

Between games, Matt ran to the restroom. On his way out, he heard Rex's snide voice. "What are you *doing* out there?"

Kevin answered, "Playing comBATON."

"Hardly."

Matt peeked around the lockers just in time to see Rex's fist land in Kevin's gut.

Kevin clearly did not expect it, and a low moan escaped his mouth along with his breath. He grabbed his stomach, stood tall, and said nothing.

"What're you gonna do? Go run and tell mommy and daddy?"

Matt shook his head and returned to the field. These IDs needed to be taught a lesson and now was the time to do it.

The Blaze were introduced first to "We Will Rock You." With the bass pounding, the Blaze's star, known as the Enforcer, stomped his foot and pointed at Bobby in sync with the chorus, "We will, we will rock you."

Next, DC3's introduction song played, but Matt heard nothing and saw only the field in front of him.

DC3 had the Baton first. They started conservatively, methodically working their way down the field. Their progress was slowed by some cheap shots from the Enforcer and his two equally bulky teammates,

Rick and Mark—a kick to the back, a punch to the face—none of which were called. They had timed their fouls perfectly for when the commissioner was focused on another area of the field. Matt barely avoided a side kick Mark directed at his knee.

Despite the questionable plays, Bobby's forceful pushing kick cleared the goal zone and Rich scored five points on a tornado roundhouse.

Before the next series, Matt called time-out and his team huddled.

"I'm sick of this illegal bull," Rich said.

"Me too," Matt said. "I'm going to follow my father's advice." In response, Sophie and Bobby each cocked their heads to the side. "He always says I can earn the respect of the ID by winning this game. Fine, let's earn their respect. And let's show them we can give as well as we can take. For the rest of the game, I want a fist or foot in every opening. Everything legal, but I want them on the ground. That goes for everyone but Sophie."

"Don't leave me out of the fun," she protested.

Matt hesitated. "Okay." They broke the huddle and, on the way back to the field, Matt whispered to Bobby, "Help me protect her." Bobby nodded.

After the Blaze's first offensive series, during which they couldn't get past midfield, Matt substituted Sophie for Rich. On the first play, he handed off to her, ran toward the corner of the field, and then cut toward the goal. He looked up to see a perfectly placed pass coming at him. In one move, he jumped, caught the pass, and spun into a jumping back side kick, scoring five points. The crowd erupted. At first, Matt thought it was for his score. Then, he turned to see the true source of the commotion. Bobby stood over the Enforcer, who was laid out on his back in a daze. Matt approached and Bobby pointed down at his fallen opponent. "Rock this." When Matt asked what had happened, he learned the Enforcer had been running in from behind, directing a flying side kick at Sophie's back. Before he could reach her, however, Bobby had blasted him with a side kick to his chest.

As Rick and Mark helped the Enforcer off the field, Matt said, "Okay, let's keep this going. Rich, you're in for Bobby." He turned to Bobby. "Thanks."

The rest of the half, Matt, Rich, and Sophie traded turns clearing the way with palm strikes, punches, and kicks. They scored three points apiece for a 19-0 lead.

Matt grinned at his team during halftime. "Are we having fun yet?"

"Yes!" they answered.

"Good, because we're not putting on the brakes now. I want every one of those ID jerks to know who they're dealing with."

That speech seemed to motivate Rich, who switched back and forth between takedowns and scores for most of the second half. With just over a minute left in the game and DC3 leading 34-0, Rich said, "You know, I don't think I've thrown a scoring pass this year. Matt?"

Matt caught a glimpse of his father. "Okay, you got it. Sophie, switch with Bobby."

She smiled. "Okay."

Bobby came in and Matt said, "Give Rich a little time."

"Yes, sir."

Before the play started, Matt jogged out to the sideline. At the same time Rich yelled, "Go," Matt struck the Enforcer's replacement, Jason Tucker, with a tornado roundhouse to the chest. His defender fell and Matt took off. Rich stepped back and threw a pass that was way out of reach. All of a sudden, Matt turned it up another gear, caught the Baton, leaped into a jumping back side kick, and scored as the horn sounded, ending the game. Matt and his teammates didn't celebrate wildly and they didn't acknowledge their opponent. They met at midfield, put their hands in, and yelled, "One-Two-DC3!" He hoped his father and the ID got the point.

After the game, everyone got cleaned up at the Shed while Rich sped over to the Club.

Matt began to walk over with his friends, but his father stopped him. "Could I have a minute with you?"

His chest tightened. "Yes, sir." He told his friends he would catch up with them.

"That was an impressive game. Rich played his heart out and Bobby has become a heck of a player."

"Soph's great, too."

"Yes, she is."

"And you played extremely well, but…"

"But, what…sir?"

"But you still haven't reached your potential yet. I may be old to you, but I'd still win if we were to play each other." He chuckled. "I have a few things left to teach you."

He forced a smile. "I'll remember that, sir."

"Good. Now go catch up with your friends."

Matt caught up with his teammates at the Club, where almost everyone in the community had congregated. His eyes scanned the dance floor for Sophie. They found their mark next to Rich. There she was, in a form-fitting, red dress that accentuated her slender curves. He closed the space between them.

Her blushing face tilted downward. "My mother gave me this. Silly, huh?"

"Silly is not the word I'd use." He gently lifted her chin. "When I saw you, my heart stopped. Because my eyes had found the most beautiful woman I've ever seen." She hugged him, then leaned back to reveal the sweetest smile.

Once again, DJ Rich orchestrated the music, while everyone else partied the night away. After an hour, Matt led Sophie outside to his favorite spot. They sat on the edge of the fountain, the illuminated streams of water jetting up behind them. After looking around to ensure they were alone, he told her what his father had said. "He is my comBATON coach, but do you think he meant something else? Do you think he's onto us?"

She grabbed Matt's hand and stared into his eyes. "I don't know what your father meant, but I've never seen anyone do what you did on the last play."

"What do you mean?"

"I mean the entire play you were almost superhuman. You took out Jason like he wasn't there. You ran faster than I've seen anyone run, caught an uncatchable pass, and flew. I've never seen anyone fly so far."

"You mean jumped."

"Yes, but it was such a high jump, it was like you were literally flying. We should call you Superman."

"Please don't."

"Okay. I wouldn't want it to go to your head."

Matt laughed, then stopped abruptly at the sight of the glimmering light dancing on the waves of her hair. "Soph. Stay right there and keep smiling."

"Why?"

"Just do it." He stared at her, then said, "Thank you. That was it."

"That was what?"

"I just took the picture I've had for sixteen years." He smiled at her and wanted to say I love you, but the party began to spill into their private space. He led her back inside.

His feet had barely made it through the door when DJ Rich stopped the music and announced over the microphone, "Superman has returned."

Matt issued Sophie a cross look.

She said, "I told you I wouldn't call you that. I can't stop Rich from saying it."

The rest of the night they relaxed and had a lot of sorely needed fun. David danced with Lori, while Bobby and Stephanie were inseparable, as usual.

At the end of the night, Matt said, "David, why don't you come with us? I'd prefer it if nobody walks around alone right now."

David said, "Okay."

Matt enjoyed the walk home. When they reached the Jacksons' house, David stepped inside to give them some privacy.

Sophie took Matt's hand. "Are you going to glide home alone?"

"What? Should I call my daddy to come pick me up?"

"Funny. Just be safe."

"I will." They hugged and kissed for a few minutes. Matt somehow pried himself away, said goodnight, and glided toward home up East Capitol Street.

Suddenly, Bobby raced toward Matt in a panic.

LAND OF CONFUSION

[SATURDAY, NOVEMBER 28, 2037, 10:00 P.M.]

"Why are you alone? Why didn't you wait for Rich?" Matt asked, afraid.

Out of breath, Bobby said, "They took him."

"What do you mean? Who's they?"

Bobby doubled over, held up his hand, and took a gulp of air. "The ID." Matt motioned for them to go somewhere else to talk, but Bobby said, "Listen to me—there's no time. A couple of minutes after you left, Rex and a team of five other IDs came inside. Matt, they were carrying some kind of rifles."

Every muscle in Matt's body tensed. "What do you mean, rifles?"

"Yeah, I know they're banned, but they had them. Anyway, Rex told Rich he needed to go with them. Rich said 'I don't think so.' Then, they did some trash talking about comBATON."

"Bobby, focus."

"Okay, then Rex said, 'We have our orders.' Rich said, 'Whose orders? My father's?' Rex said, 'It doesn't matter.' After that, the Enforcer and Nick took him by his arms and escorted him out. I made a move to stop them, but Rex and the others pointed their weapons at me. Rich shouted at me not to do anything, that he would be all right. So I just stood there as they marched him out at gunpoint."

"There was nothing more you could have done." Matt patted his friend on the back. "But there's something I can do. I'm going to talk with my father."

"I'm going with you."

"Thank you, but I need to do this alone." Matt turned to leave, then stopped. "I've got a much more important job for you. Go to Sophie's. Make sure she's okay."

He glided home, his thoughts fixated on one question: How much did his father know?

Matt's contemplation was suddenly rocked by a nearby explosion that nearly knocked him to the ground. His ears rang from the blast as he looked around. He saw no one. His only thought was Rich. Dizzy and legs shaking, he sped toward the large fireball. Before he could reach it, the Enforcer intercepted him. Matt's body stiffened at the sight of the rifle pointed at his chest. "Your father wants to see you."

"Where?"

He nodded toward the White House.

Matt stood tall and glided up the driveway, aware that the Enforcer and his weapon followed close behind. "I suppose he's in his office?"

In reply, he received only a nod in that direction.

The door to the Oval Office pulled open and Matt stepped in. At the sight of Eric, Matt's legs weakened and his heart pumped fast. The president stood from his desk and walked over to face his son. Rex and the Enforcer surrounded Matt on either side.

"Where's Rich?" Matt managed.

His father nodded toward Rex. Matt's nose latched onto a peculiar smell, similar to his first experience sparring. He turned to confirm with his eyes what his other sense had detected—blood. Blood spattered all over Rex's face and ground into his knuckles.

Out of the corner of his eye, Matt saw a fist flying at his face. Then everything went black.

The next thing he remembered, the two IDs were lifting him off the floor.

Rex joked, "It seems your father's come out of retirement. He dropped you with one punch."

Matt's head felt like it was ready to explode. Dazed, he heard his father say, "Sit him on the couch and leave us."

Rex asked, "Are you sure, sir?"

Eric growled, "Yes. And get that smirk off your face."

Eric stared at Matt from the opposite couch.

Matt thought it was best to wait to see how everything played out. He waited for his head to clear.

Finally, Eric spoke. "You've been a busy boy lately."

"What do you mean, sir?"

"Don't play stupid with me. By now, you know nothing happens in this city without me knowing about it." Eric leaned forward toward the coffee table in between them. His hand rested on a file on the table. Matt strained his eyes to focus and his chest tightened at the sight of the Plan 40 folder. "I will assume you've seen everything in here."

Matt exhaled. "Pretty much."

"Do you know what it takes to maintain order? Do you know what it takes to ensure the community is well taken care of?"

"Yes."

"No. You don't. It takes actions you would consider cruel. Those actions are a necessary means to realize the desired end."

"What end?"

"What end? How about a kingdom for mankind? A kingdom you could inherit. A kingdom I've spent years building, I might add. And a kingdom you seem intent on destroying. Well, I'm not going to let even my own son do that." Eric picked up the folder and threw it in a small, metal wastebasket. "I see your hand in your pocket. Pull it out and give it to me."

How does he know? He pulled out the picture his mother had given him.

"That's it. Give it to me. It's time you grew up. I'm tired of the way you've held onto that picture since you were a child."

Matt knew it would be best to obey. His head throbbed as he lifted the photo. Eric seized it and, without looking, threw it in the wastebasket. Then, he pulled out a lighter.

In an instant, his most cherished possession and all the evidence against his father disappeared in the flames.

"I know from my personal surveillance camera that your girlfriend didn't see that. Having scanned your Neural, I also see you didn't copy it. So, the two of us are the only two who've seen it."

Matt felt like the world as he knew it had been destroyed in that fire. The last remnant from his mother was now just ashes, along with the last remnant of his father's integrity. He shook his head. "Where's Rich?"

"I'm afraid I have some bad news."

Tears welled in Matt's eyes.

"It seems young Rich was quite the saboteur. We learned tonight he was responsible for the deaths of the scientists."

"That's a lie!"

"How would you know?"

Matt had had enough. *"Where is Rich?"*

"It saddens me to tell you that Rich has had a tragic accident. When the IDs were interrogating him, he stole my car in an attempt to escape. He crashed. There was a horrible explosion and…well, he didn't make it."

Matt slid off the couch and trembled, tears now streaming down his cheeks.

Eric stepped around the coffee table and stood over him. "It's all right. There's still hope for you and Soph. That's what you call her. Right?"

A surge of adrenalin flooded Matt. He got to his knees, acting like he was about to get up and sit on the couch again. Instead, he jumped up with all of his might and landed a massive uppercut to Eric's jaw, knocking him to the ground unconscious.

Realizing Rex and the Enforcer were still right outside the door, Matt groaned as if his father had just hit him. He slipped out the side glass door, escaping through the trees and bushes on the side of the South Lawn.

He turned off the community interface on his Neural and sped away from the White House grounds as fast as he could, finally stopping to catch his breath and get his bearings. In a moment, he knew what he had to do—get away from the community, retrieve the Ball, and activate it so he could go back and fix everything. That is, if he could get it to work. But before all that, he had to know that Sophie was all right.

He decided he should take the long way around to get to Sophie's house. Thanks to David and Rich, he could glide around undetected, as long as no one saw him. His route took him just outside of the inhabited areas: first around the World War II Memorial to the west of the Washington Monument, then past the Jefferson Memorial, and finally down the streets that paralleled the abandoned interstate.

Matt's adrenalin rush wore off as he neared Capitol Hill. He alternated between rubbing his arms to stay warm and his temple to sooth his pounding head. The closer he got to the likely heavily guarded East Capitol Street, the trickier it was to stay hidden. He used abandoned vehicles, low walls, and vegetation for cover, arriving within a block of Sophie's house.

As he got ready to sprint to her back door, someone tapped him from behind.

RETREAT

[SUNDAY, NOVEMBER 29, 2037, 1:00 A.M.]

He turned around, expecting to see a rifle directed at him. Instead, Bobby crouched down and pulled him into a bear hug. Bobby's low voice cracked. "I know...about Rich. The IDs sent a community N-note."

Matt's eyes began to tear up again.

"Come on." Bobby released Matt and motioned for him to follow. They cut through the overgrown vegetation, away from Sophie's house. He led Matt behind a large, oak tree, put his hand in the dirt, and pulled up.

But it wasn't dirt. It was a hidden trap door, similar to the one they used to gain entry to the secret lab. He motioned for Matt to climb down.

Twenty feet down, Matt found himself in a dark tunnel. He hopped off the ladder and Sophie's arms wrapped around him. "Thank goodness. I thought you were—"

"Dead? Not yet." He lowered his head. "But Rich..."

Matt could hear David crying nearby.

Sophie sniffled, "We know."

A minute of silence later, Matt asked, "What is this place?"

David cleared his throat. "Our parents built it a long time ago. Someone thought it would be useful one day."

"Where are they?"

Sophie said, "At work, as usual."

Matt said, "Good. It's better we don't get them involved."

His eyes now adjusted to the absence of light, Matt could see Sophie staring at him with worry. She asked, "What happened to you? Did the ID do that to your face?"

"Do what?" Matt grimaced as he felt his tender left cheek. It was split and swollen. "No, that was my father. At least that's what Rex said happened—he sucker punched me."

Sophie's hand shot to her mouth. "How'd you get out of there?"

"It's a long story. First, we need to get out of here and get to the Ball."

David said, "And we need to get moving before they mobilize."

"I'll go up first," Bobby said.

Matt said, "Has everyone turned off the community interface on their Neurals? They may have figured out Rich's program."

"We're way ahead of you," Bobby said.

"Good. Let's go." He stopped for a second. "But where are we going?"

Sophie said, "Just follow me."

Matt smiled. "Okay."

Bobby was the first one back to the surface. He gave the all clear and David followed, then Sophie, then Matt, who closed the trap door behind him.

The moonlight illuminated the packs on Sophie's and David's backs. Matt nodded at them in approval of their preparation.

Sophie waved to them to follow her and they glided as far and as fast as they could. Matt shivered and struggled to keep up, as if his batteries had worn down.

After about ten minutes, Sophie looked back, slowed, and walked up to one of the many abandoned row houses. Matt had no idea where they were. "Why are we stopping?"

"You look awful. We can rest here. David and I used to play here while our parents worked in Lincoln Park. We're about two miles east of the park. You can wait here with David while Bobby and I get the Ball."

"No way. If they know about the cottage, they'll get you," Matt objected.

"We have to risk it," Bobby said.

"No, we don't," David said. "If they know about it, it's too late. If they don't, resting a little first won't hurt. Either way, it doesn't matter."

She crossed her arms, then sighed. "Okay." She walked up to the door and pushed it open, the others following. She and David dropped their packs and she said, "Assuming they don't know about our gliders, we should be safe here for a while."

Matt said, "Good thinking." He held his arms to control his shivering. "I guess we won't be able to light a fire."

Bobby said, "Probably not a good idea."

Sophie pulled a blanket from her pack, placed it over Matt's back, and hugged him. The shivering slowed. They filed into a family room. It looked like the room that time forgot, with wood-paneled walls, a couple of brown, velour couches, and a large television. The space had deteriorated a good deal, but the reading glasses on the end table and the drinking glasses on the coffee table made Matt feel as if the owner might return at any moment.

Sophie sat on one of the big, cushiony couches and patted it. Matt fell into the spot next to her and she tended to his split cheek. "What happened?"

Matt described the whole story. He told them his father had framed Rich for the murder of the geneticists and had their friend killed. Matt stopped for a moment to let it all sink in. His friend was dead.

"How'd you get away?" Bobby finally asked.

"When I heard Rich was dead, I just slid off the couch. I didn't think I could even stand at that point. But my father stood over me and mentioned you, Soph, and before I knew what I was doing, I caught him with an uppercut."

Sophie placed her hand over his red knuckles. "What did he do?"

Matt smiled a little. "He crumbled. I took advantage of him being unconscious and snuck out the side door." Looking at the raw hand Sophie was now caressing, he added, "I wouldn't be surprised if his jaw was broken."

Bobby grinned.

"Bobby, what were you doing out there when you found me?"

"Looking for you. When I went to check on Sophie and told her they had Rich, she immediately asked where you were. I told her you had gone to see your father. She took me to the tunnel, got the packs together, and was about to go after you when I stopped her. The only way I could keep her from going was to promise to look for you myself. Luckily, I saw you pass by as I came out of the tunnel."

Matt refused to think about what would have happened had Sophie or Bobby gone to his house looking for him. He embraced her and pulled her back to lie down. For a while, he relaxed to the rhythm of their heartbeats. Then, Sophie got back up and pulled a mobile printer out of her pack.

"You really came prepared. What are you doing?"

"There's no way I'm going to risk you growing up not thinking of me every night." She turned on the printer and pulled his hand over to the metal plate lining the side. Matt thought a print command, and out slid the picture he had watched burn just a little while earlier.

They smiled at one another and lay back down on the couch together. He hadn't felt this warm in a long time.

Matt awoke to the comfort of Sophie still there with him. It was dark and everyone else appeared to be sleeping. The buzzing that had been building in his head was gone, as if a noisy air conditioner had shut off, leaving only silence.

He realized he could no longer put Sophie and his friends at risk. Matt would only risk his own life from here on out. He inched off the couch to avoid waking Sophie and took a long look at her, her chest slowly rising and falling, her angelic face emotionless. He picked up the picture and crept over to the packs to look for a pencil and paper, his hands fumbling. He froze at sudden movement next to him.

"What are you doing?" David whispered.

Matt motioned for David to follow him into the next room.

"I need to get to the Ball."

"Right. I'll wake up the others."

"No. I need to do this alone."

"Why?"

"Because Rich died for this. I can't risk any more of you getting hurt. If Sophie were hurt or killed, I'm not sure I could go on. And that's what my father's counting on. Do you understand?"

"I do."

"Good. Please explain it to her. And get as far away as you can. Hopefully, I'll figure out the problem with the Ball. Then I can go back and fix everything." Matt looked into David's wide eyes, stepped forward, and hugged him. "You know, you really are more like a brother to me than a friend." A tear trickled out of David's eye and down his cheek.

Matt began to head for the door, but David placed a hand on his shoulder. "I may be able to figure it out. Next Sunday morning at 6:00 A.M., turn on the community link on your Neural and look for an N-note from me. I know it's a risk, but I believe I can help."

"Thanks."

David handed Matt a jacket and a pack. Matt took them, smiled, and left.

Dawn would arrive in an hour. Matt knew if Rich had broken under interrogation, his father would already have the Ball. Nonetheless, he sped toward the cottage to retrieve it under cover of darkness.

He reached the eastern side of the Armed Forces Retirement Home in a half hour. Rather than take the long way around to the main entrance, he jumped the fence and worked his way up the hilly grounds until he could see the cottage. He hid behind a nearby tree and looked for movement. Seeing none, he walked up to the door and stepped inside. He almost jumped at a creak in the floorboards, but no one attacked.

Matt crept up the stairs and found the board under which Rich had hidden everything. He exhaled at the sight of the Ball and schematics. But as he lifted them, he realized the ID might be waiting for him to reveal the Ball's exact location. He stopped and listened for a sound. His shivering returned, and cold sweat beaded on his forehead and ran down his face. He had to get out of there as fast as possible.

At the front door, Matt sighed and took one more look around. He was sure about one thing at that moment. Rich must have been very brave when he died. He hadn't given up their secrets.

He decided to make camp at the compound. First, he foraged for food in the Scott Building, which was located next to the cottage. He guessed that many retired veterans had lived there prior to the Storm. Exhausted and nauseated, he finally located enough canned food to feed an army. The uncooked, chicken-noodle soup tasted surprisingly good going down. Unfortunately, it didn't taste very good coming back up.

After cleaning himself the best he could, Matt found a bed and collapsed. He dreamt he was the president and Sophie was the first lady. They had four children in their happy family.

Matt woke to reality. His chest felt like it had been hollowed out. Rich was dead and his friends were in mortal danger. And he had no idea how to operate the Ball.

He shook himself out of his mood. There was no time for fear or cowardice.

He walked over to the cottage, stepped into the chamber, and got to work. The figures and formulas on the schematics might as well have been in Mandarin Chinese. His primary thought through the hours of flipping pages: *How did David figure all this out?* In retrospect, it had been a huge mistake not to bring him along.

He tinkered with the Ball and hoped something would click. But he also hoped that if it did, he wouldn't accidentally open a wormhole before the appointed time. Otherwise, Matt would never be able to bring back Rich, his mother, his grandfather, and the other seven billion. Moreover, he would be lost forever, endlessly traveling through space and time.

Every so often, he placed the bottom of the Ball in his palm, hoping there would be some sign that it worked. But it continued to stubbornly just sit there.

By the end of the first day, Matt had slipped into a routine. He spent his days at the cottage, where he progressed from knotted stomach to empty chest during hours of fiddling with the Ball. At night he returned to the Scott Building, where he daydreamed about Sophie as he ate and had nightmares about Rich and his friends as he slept.

On Friday night, he again dreamt about running down a dimly lit passageway, passing several entrances before reaching a large, metal door. He tried to open it as pounding footsteps closed in. The vice-like grip on his shoulder sent a shock through his body. He shot up in bed, drenched in sweat despite the frigid conditions.

It was still dark out. Moonlight shone through the blinds, and Matt could make out a shadow in the corner of the room. "Who's there?" he demanded, shivering.

"Someone who wants you to be happy."

BETRAYAL

[SUNDAY, DECEMBER 6, 2037 4:41 A.M.]

"Lori?"

"Yes."

"Who's with you?" he blurted.

She stood from her chair in the corner and approached. "No one. I promise."

He bolted out of bed, pushed past her, and stared out the window, but couldn't see any sign of movement.

"I told you, no one's with me."

He pushed past her again to the door, watching and listening. But he only heard his sweat droplets crashing to the floor and his racing heart. "How long have you been here?"

"I've been in your room since you fell asleep and at this complex since yesterday afternoon."

"How'd you know where to find me?" he asked, not sure who had given up the Circle's secret location. Had Rich succumbed to Eric after all? Had Sophie and his friends been captured?

"Calm down," she pleaded. "Give me a second to explain."

Realizing there was no escape if she were lying, he marched up to her. "All right, but get to the point."

Tears filled her eyes. "I will, but you're scaring me. Just calm down first."

Matt backed off. "How did you find me?"

"There was some sort of information embedded in the music you gave me."

He froze. "What information?"

"There was a message and a map." She hesitated. "I don't know how, but they were for me."

"What do you mean, for you?"

"The message started with 'For Lori Ford.' The rest of it said, 'The charm was intended for you, too,' whatever that means. It also said, 'Tell him that he knows Sophie was right. Now's the time to admit it.'"

Matt dropped onto the edge of the bed. He remembered one his of clues saying she was right, but he didn't have to admit it yet. And he hadn't. In fact, he hadn't revealed that part of the clue to anyone. He forced himself to look into Lori's anxious eyes. "She was right. She knew there were huge problems with our perfect community. I believe you. Was there anything else?"

"Yes. It said, 'Soon, he'll have to run. Find him at the cottage.' There was a map of this complex, followed by the statement, 'He'll need your help before it's over.' I would have told you, but the instructions said not to tell you until I found you here."

Matt had spent months wishing he didn't have to exclude Lori. As he neared the end, he realized the irony. Now her life was in danger, too. "Was there any other information embedded in the music? Was there anything about a Ball?"

"What Ball? No."

He hesitated, not sure yet whether to divulge the Circle's secrets to her. "Are you sure you weren't followed?"

Her eyes dropped. "Yes, even though the ID has had me under constant surveillance."

"I've been...thinking about you since I got here. I hoped that with the way our relationship ended, you'd be safe from that lunatic I used to call my father." Matt had been frustrated there was no way to check on Lori, but knowing she was no longer on Eric's list had provided some comfort.

She glanced at him. "He's imposed martial law. The IDs are patrolling with rifles. Can you believe it? I didn't even know they had weapons."

"Neither did I, until last week."

"And since last Sunday everyone has been required to check in on their Neurals at least once an hour. Some of the IDs claimed that Rich killed Stephanie's father and that you, Sophie, Bobby, and David were also involved."

Matt stared into her eyes.

"I don't believe them, of course. Neither does my brother. He wants to confront the ID. I think a lot of people do."

"How did you get away?"

"I wasn't allowed out of my house for days. Finally, I convinced my mother I had to go. She helped me slip out undetected."

Matt stood and walked over to the window again.

"Don't worry. I turned off the community interface on my Neural. And with the route I've taken over the past two days, I'm sure I wasn't followed."

"Two days?"

"I wasn't about to lead those goons to you." He opened his mouth to ask another question, but she cut him off. "First, you need to get out of those clothes."

"What?"

"You're drenched. You'll catch pneumonia if you don't change." She opened a pack she had brought, pulled out clean clothes, and tossed them at him. "Don't worry. I won't look. I know you're in love with Sophie."

Silence filled the room. She stepped into the hall, adding, "She's a real take-charge kind of girl."

Matt hadn't thought much about it, but Lori was right. Her take-charge personality had attracted him from the start, even when he hadn't admitted it to himself or anyone else. She was always willing to take the risk and she always said what was on her mind. She stirred every emotion in him. Sophie made him feel alive. As he changed, he said, "I wanted to prove to you there was nothing, but—"

"There was something. It's okay. So, where's everyone else?"

"I snuck away. I didn't want them risking their lives. I'm alone."

"I don't know what you're doing, but you're not alone."

"I'm done," he said, having finished changing his clothes.

She reentered, picked up a spare blanket, and placed it around his still-shivering body. Sitting beside him, she wrapped her arms around the blanket. "You don't look so good."

"I've felt better. With everything that's happened, I can't sleep."

"I noticed. Well, I'm here now. Do you have a first-aid kit?"

He nodded in the direction of his pack. She retrieved it, pulling out the crisp, new picture of Sophie. Lori stared at it, eyebrows raised. He waited a few seconds, then gently took the picture from her. She glanced at him for a moment and got back to work.

She rebandaged the cut on his face and he resumed the conversation. "Were you ever going to tell me about your deal with Sophie and Bobby?"

She looked away, her face reddening. "She promised she wouldn't tell you."

"Don't be mad," he said. "There wouldn't have been too many people willing to do what you did. It was underhanded, but it was also selfless."

Her head dropped, similarly to the way Sophie's head had during their conversation on the subject. "It tore my heart out."

"I'm sorry."

"Me, too."

There was a short silence.

"So, I noticed you've been spending some time with David," Matt finally said.

"He's nice."

"And misunderstood."

"Yes."

"Is there anything there?"

"Who knows what the future holds. So, what have you really been doing this whole time? And don't give me any of that bogus secret mission for your father stuff," she said, smiling.

Matt figured she was intended to be included at this point. He exhaled and the information he had withheld began to flow. When he finished, she shook her head in disbelief. But when he pulled the Ball from the closet, the color drained from her face.

"I expect that's what I looked like when I first realized what we had to do." Before he could explain the clue Rich had received about his father or what had happened on and after Thanksgiving, a Neural reminder told him it was 6:00 A.M. *Time to link to the community network and find out if David has the solution.*

He linked up. Many N-notes bombarded him, but they were all either from his father or Richard Sr. He flashed through the list once more. It's not here. Matt feared that the others must have been caught. Just as he was about to unlink, it came in. David's N-note was short enough to read in preview mode without opening: "Still working on a solution. Don't give up. Sophie misses you, but understands." That was it. Matt quickly unlinked.

"At least they're okay," Matt said.

"David hasn't figured it out yet?"

"No."

"What are you going to do?"

"I've got eighteen hours to figure it out. I'm heading over to the cottage to work on the Ball, like I've done every day since last Sunday."

She looked out the window for a moment. "Not like you've been doing since Sunday. I'm here now—teach me how it's supposed to work. Maybe teaching it will trigger the solution."

"Interesting…let's go."

They sped over to the cottage, stepped into the elevator on the first floor, and worked through the morning. Matt had finally begun to understand some of the schematics, but he was no closer to his goal. They took a break in the early afternoon. He had just sat down against the wall of the chamber when he heard a noise near the front door. Lori's wide-eyed stare reflected his own. "Stay in here," he whispered. "When I yell 'Now,' run to the door and follow me out." He exited the elevator and shut it.

His heart began to race as fast as his mind. If the ID had located him, the cottage might be surrounded. He hid next to the door, ready to subdue the first intruder, get Lori, and escape with the Ball.

A man stepped through the door and right past Matt, who sprang into action. He collapsed the man's legs with a side kick behind the knees and followed with a knifehand strike to the pressure point at the base of the neck. The man fell to the ground, unconscious. Matt rolled him over. It was Rich's father, Richard Sr.

Matt wanted answers, but he played it safe. He found rope in his pack and tied Richard's legs and arms. He looked out the building's windows. Seeing no one else, he yelled for Lori. She came bursting out of the elevator, ready to run.

"We're okay. And we're not going anywhere. At least, not until I get some answers."

She looked down and saw Richard. "What are you going to do to him?"

He thought: *I'd like to kill him.* "Find out what this murderer knows."

"He didn't kill his own son," she gasped, her hand covering her mouth.

"I don't know about that, but Rich had proof that he killed Stephanie's father and the other scientists."

"What? That was an accident."

"He's waking up. Get back in the elevator and listen. Whatever you do, don't come out. They may not know you're with me or that you're now part of this."

Matt flipped on the PA system in the elevator so Lori could listen. He pulled up a chair, kicked Richard in the legs, and sat down.

Richard opened his eyes and struggled against his bindings. "What's going on?"

Matt sat him up against the wall. "I thought you could tell me. Who's with you?"

"No one. I came alone. And I wasn't followed."

"Why should I believe you? You're a murderer."

Richard's sagging shoulders drooped further as he looked down. "I'm here to help."

The heat began to grow within Matt, but he struggled to maintain his composure. "How can you possibly help? You're just one of my father's minions. Did he send you to kill me?"

"No. I want to fight him, with you. Listen, I did something long ago. Something I shouldn't have done. Your father never lets me forget it. He likes to remind me how he's protected me and how that protection might not last forever." Richard began to sob. Matt had never seen a grown man sob this way before. "Nothing could hurt worse than watching them kill my son."

Matt narrowed his eyes to avoid shedding his own tears. "Were you there?"

"No, they were in RM City. I saw it from a live video feed in my office. I'd give my life a million times if I could have a second chance," Richard wept. "He wasn't even eighteen."

Matt wanted to believe him. He wanted to believe something about his life until now had been real. He stared into Richard's eyes. "I know what you did to those scientists."

"Did my son know?"

The flame within Matt rekindled at this implied confession. "Since the first week of school. He saw images of you planting the explosives and retrieving the evidence as they lay there dying."

Richard's head dropped into his hands. "That explains a lot."

"Why'd you do it?" He held his hands stiffly at his side to avoid trying to smack more remorse into the killer.

"Your father said they were saboteurs. They were threatening to destroy their research. They had just learned about Eric's plans to eliminate any babies with abnormalities." A shock ran through Matt's body. "I know. It's horrible. But your father was sure that if they had carried out their threat, they would have put us years behind. We might have been too late to save humanity. For the mission, they had to be eliminated. He told me what to do."

Matt shook his head. "And you just took him at his word and did it?"

"I know it doesn't excuse what I did, he threatened my family. Once again, I did his dirty work. I convinced myself he was right and that I had to do it for humanity and...and for my son." Richard lifted his head and faced Matt. "You kids have been tough to track."

"You can thank Rich for that. And I'm sorry to disappoint you, but I'm the only one here."

"I know. I've known where you are for several days."

"How?"

"I do have a few secrets of my own." Richard looked satisfied with himself. "Even your father doesn't know I created a small drone to relay your movements."

Matt thought for a moment. "You mean that bird?"

"Yes."

"And the warning to stop the ops?"

"Yes. I prepared that message, but not as a threat. I was trying to scare you into stopping before someone got hurt."

Matt thought about the warning and about his mother's message. He slumped against the wall and covered his face with his hands to hold back the tears once more.

"I know what you're thinking. But it's not your fault. It's my fault. It's your father's fault."

He pulled his hands away and stared into Richard's eyes. "If I'd listened, Rich would be alive right now." Matt straightened up, resolute. "But he will not have died in vain."

Richard looked away.

"Have you found the others?"

"Your father kept too close a watch on me after I spotted you last Sunday morning. I haven't used the drone since. But I'm afraid the ID found your friends this morning when David Jackson sent you a message."

Another shockwave surged through Matt's body.

"Don't worry. They're safe…for now. That's why I was sent here. Eric realized that I'd been tracking you and demanded I give up your location. When I denied knowing where you were, he said, 'Let me make this simple. If Matthew isn't at the championship game tonight, there might be another accident. And this time, it could claim the lives of three young adults…and your wife.' So I waited until I was sure no one was monitoring me and snuck away out of a secret passage under my office."

What is it with all of these secret passages? Matt thought. "What does he have planned for us?"

"I don't know. He is a cruel man. I watched Rex use a knife to dig my son's Neural out of his head."

Matt shook with anger. "What did they find on the Neural?"

There was great pride in his response. "Absolutely nothing. My brave son had done something I've never seen anyone do. He wiped his Neural before they could dig it out. It was clean."

Matt tried not to think about his friend just yet. He had a mission to complete. "So you've come here to tell me I need to give in." He looked Richard straight in the eye. "Would you?"

Richard stared into space. "No. I would've fought for my son's life."

"And that's what I'm going to do. For your pitiful life, and mine, and everyone else's." He pulled the Ball from the pack and Richard's eyes shot wide open. "You've seen this before?"

"Not this one, but yes. What do you plan to do with it?"

"Go back in time and give you and the others a second chance. That was Rich's wish, that you get a second chance."

"That's a noble mission, Matthew, but that thing has the ability to do one thing and one thing only…kill. That's a death machine."

Matt tensed. "Why would you say that?"

"Did you know Joseph experimented with a machine like this?"

"Yes."

"Did you know your father was involved?"

"Yes."

"Did you know that both times this machine has been used, people have died?"

"You mean both times that you know of."

"Did you consider *you* could die using this machine?"

He nodded. "Yes. But if I can save the world, it's worth the risk."

"You sound like your grandfather."

"Thank you. Besides, we know it's worked before. We've received information that could only have come from someone who'd traveled from the future to the past."

Richard paused, then shook his head. "Just because information was sent to the past, don't be so sure that the machine is safe."

"Wouldn't that be a logical conclusion?"

"Did you consider information might have been successfully transmitted to the past, but the person holding the information might have died on the trip?"

Matt swallowed hard. Figuring he had nothing to lose, he said, "We haven't figured out how to operate it yet. You wouldn't know anything about it, would you?"

"I'm afraid not. Quantum mechanics isn't one of my specialties."

They remained silent for a few moments. Finally, Matt said, "Okay, you can tell my father I'll be there. I've got a championship to win."

Richard shook his head.

"I have no idea how, but I'm going to get my friends and we'll figure out how to work this Ball. And I'm going to complete the mission."

"You've got no chance."

"Maybe. But I have to try." Matt stared him down once more. "We'd have a better chance if you'd help."

"How?"

"I don't know yet. But you could start by pretending to continue to follow my father."

Richard remained silent for a moment. "Okay, I'll do what I can."

"Great. Rich would be proud."

Richard began to cry once more. "I always taught my son to do the right thing. In the end, he was the one who taught me. You know, someone told me long ago it was never too late to change. I hope he was right."

Matt now felt he could trust Richard Sr., and unbound him. "I read my father's plans. They include eliminating you and your wife."

"I guess I shouldn't be surprised."

"Before you go, I've got one question that's been bothering me since Rich told me about you killing the geneticists."

"Did I kill your mother?" Richard stared into Matt's eyes. "No." He turned and left.

As soon as the door clicked shut, Matt said, "He's gone. You can come out." The elevator doors opened and Lori slid out, sobbing. He held her up. "I know. We're not exactly living in paradise, are we? Can you walk?"

She whispered, "Yes."

"Good, because I've got to get something from the complex before we go. First, let me go pack up." She waited as he entered the chamber. A few minutes later, he exited. "Let's go."

He led her to a nearby building on the Soldier's Home grounds. "What did you leave here?"

"Something extremely important." She followed him up to the second floor to a bedroom, where he picked up a decaying newspaper from the end table and stuffed it in his bag.

"We came back for that?"

His hand organized the contents of the bag. "Mhmm. Information about the past. You'd do anything to help me, wouldn't you?"

"You know I would."

"So there's no chance of talking you out of coming with me."

"None."

"That's what I thought." Matt hugged her. While he held the warm embrace, he reached his left hand up to her neck and plunged in a sedative-filled syringe.

She flinched and grabbed her neck. "Why?"

"Because I care about you too much to allow you to get involved."
As she slipped into unconsciousness, Matt caught her and laid her on the bed. "Don't worry, it'll all be over before you wake up."

He kissed her on the neck where the shot had done its job. Then he headed toward the Mall and his destiny.

ALL OR NOTHING

[SUNDAY, DECEMBER 6, 2037, 4:42 P.M.]

At the Chinatown entrance to RM City, Matt took a sweep of the surroundings. He didn't know what to expect, but relaxed slightly at the realization he was alone. He felt in his pack one last time for the smooth, cool metal of the Ball and the now partially creased picture of Sophie. Exhaling at the touch, he hid the bag in a receptacle near the entrance, then headed for the game.

He neared the field as the sun set behind a thick blanket of clouds and the floodlights installed for the championship clicked on. Other than the Raiders, every member of the ID surrounded the field, each with a rifle.

His chances of escaping alive were slim, but for the mission to succeed and to save Sophie and his friends, he would have to play Eric's game. Matt edged closer and hid behind a bush. Through the leaves, he saw just about everyone in the community in the stands, hours before game time. Behind each set of bleachers was a tent—one on the east side for the Raiders and the other on the west side for DC3.

Under different circumstances, Matt would have thrilled at the electricity in the air. This day was supposed to be one of the most important in his life. It still was, but now for a much more pivotal reason.

He took a deep breath and stood—and found himself face to face with Mrs. Peterson. He stumbled back a step.

"Matthew, we need to talk."

Matt didn't know whom he could trust, but since she wasn't in the stadium among Eric's flock, he had a small hope. He nodded.

"I've never discussed this with you, but I knew your mother well. You know those rules I've taught you?"

"Peterson's Rules."

"Not exactly." She pulled a small, black book from her pocket and offered it to him. "I was instructed not to give this to you until December 6, 2037."

He accepted the book from her. On the first page was the familiar handwriting from Sophie's picture. It read: Mom's Rules for Matthew's Success. Matt was speechless. The rules Mrs. Peterson had taught everyone for years were his mother's rules—his mother's rules for *him*. A small jolt ran through his body and he straightened up. "Who told you to wait until today? My mother?"

She nodded. "And her team."

"Thank you." As if attempting to touch his mother's hand, he ran his fingers over the words she had written so long ago. He felt a slight bump and turned the page to find a Disc fastened to the other side.

He looked up at Mrs. Peterson, who stared down at the Disc, then back at him. He plucked the Disc off the page and placed it on his tongue.

Mrs. Peterson disappeared from view and a video began to play. It was nothing but a dark screen at first, and then the welcomed voice from his dreams spoke. "Matthew, if you're hearing this, I'm sorry for putting you and your friends in such a tight spot. As your mother, you need to know I love you. As your somewhat absent team member, I want you to know that you and your friends can do this. Trust yourself and your teammates and you'll get through it. You know what's at stake. I've got some important information for you and I'm sorry you have to find out this way. Once you've seen and heard everything, delete it all."

An image of a young Eric phased into view. "Your father was a wonderful young man." Much of his physical features were the same, save the muscles, the scar, and the serious demeanor. He seemed happy, at least happier than Matt had ever seen him. "Even as a teenager, his theories on time travel were groundbreaking. Your grandfather—my father—took notice. He offered to bring your father into Project RM. While Eric had come from a well-to-do family, he was an only child whose parents obsessed over their careers. Your grandfather took him in and became his father figure. We were the same age. He was shy and cared more about his brains than his brawn. Just my type of guy. I fell for him instantly."

Another image appeared. This time Eric appeared to be in his early twenties. He looked like an older version of the boy, except the determined look had taken hold. "The early years with your father were the best of my life. We grew up happy and were married. Unfortunately, that's where the tale turns. He was frustrated that he was a true prodigy in only one discipline and he was embarrassed of his 'scrawny build,' as he put it. None of that mattered to me—but it consumed him. He constantly told me I deserved more, even though I always told him he was everything I wanted."

The image changed once more. His father was the same age as the last image, but now looked like a younger version of the father Matt knew, still sans the scar. "I found out too late that your father had been experimenting with gene therapy." Matt remembered the genetic therapy task of Plan 40. "He had found a way to alter his DNA. Almost overnight, he became a physical specimen. Unfortunately, the experimentation changed more than his muscles. It took me a while to notice, but his rational thought—the place in his brain that understood moral complexity—had vanished. The void was filled at first by constant rage, a rigid grasp of right and wrong, and later...well, you've probably got a pretty good idea." Matt's stomach tightened at the thought that his father had passed this change on to him. "This gets me to my point."

A voice from afar jerked him out of his Neural dream. He tried to refocus his eyes on the Disc, but the younger Eric on the Neural now morphed into the actual monster standing in front of him. The only change in his appearance over the last time Matt had seen him laid out on the floor of his office was a large bruise around his left jawline. "I asked," Eric said, in a slightly irritated voice, "if you shouldn't both be at the stadium?"

Before Matt could ignore the beast and refocus on his mother's voice, an odd sensation swept through his head. It wasn't quite dizziness, but he felt empty. He squeezed his eyes shut to try to relocate the contents of the Disc, but found nothing. In fact, he couldn't access his Neural. It wasn't there.

With her lips tight and her brows furrowed, Mrs. Peterson bored into Eric with a glare. She turned to Matt and exchanged the fury for her matter-of-fact teaching expression. "You know, Matthew, for years I've been careful not to show my allegiance. However, after what happened to poor Rich, it's worth the risk. You need to know that I'm with you and your friends."

Eric leveled his gaze at her. "Who else is part of this little conspiracy, Liz?"

Mrs. Peterson's lips tightened once more.

Eric shook his head. "Nothing? Fine, arrest her." Several IDs approached, two of whom grabbed her by the arms.

"For what?" Matt blurted.

"Treason. To stand against the president is to stand against the government, and to stand against the government is to stand against humanity."

As she was handcuffed, she looked at Matt. "Don't worry. Go do what you have to do. I'll be okay." Matt doubted that was true. He narrowed his eyes at Eric.

"Hold her in the stands until after the game. Then I'll interrogate her personally. Now leave. I need to speak with my son."

Before they could turn her toward the stands, Mrs. Peterson winked at Matt.

Alone with his son, Eric seized his book—the book his mother had written for him. Matt had no idea what his father would find beyond the first page, other than the rules Mrs. Peterson had taught since his first year of school. Eric thumbed through the pages. Matt's heart beat harder and faster. Eric finished flipping the pages, pocketed the book, and lifted his eyes to meet Matt's.

Eric said, "We both know you're leading a team in a futile effort to undo everything I've worked years to build." Matt watched his moving lips, but heard little. He could not believe the man speaking to him was his father. The man he had looked up to his whole life. The man who he had thought did his best for everyone's welfare. Eric continued. "If you hadn't started this nonsense, young Richard would be alive today and you would be playing for your place in history. Instead, he isn't and you won't. So, don't blame *me* for what *you* did to your friend."

How could I be responsible for killing Rich? Matt thought.

Eric's eyes pierced through Matt's, as if they had seized his mind. "The person who puts the wheels in motion bears the responsibility. Now, as for the game, you *will* play...and you *will* lose."

Matt said nothing.

"I'm not sure who started you down this unfortunate path, but some-one has poisoned your mind. You've always been loyal to me. That's an admirable trait. Over the last few months, someone has been turning you against me. They've done such a good job that you're willing to risk certain death. I'm going to give you one last chance to display your loyalty to me. And you will do so in front of every last living human, by losing this game."

"Why?" Matt shouted. "So that I'll never be as great as you?"

"Calm down. You need to control your emotions. To answer your question, no. I know how important this game is to you. You'll lose to prove you're willing to do whatever I say. Then, with your friends observing, you and I are going to destroy the time machine. That's right. I know all about it. After that, you'll tell me everything about who's helping you. And if you don't…" Eric pointed in the direction of the IDs surrounding the field. "Well, we shouldn't think about that."

Eric turned to leave. "Oh, and by the way, in case you're wondering why your head feels strange, after we copied everything on your Neural, we wiped and crashed it. You can thank your friend, Richard, for that idea. In fact, all of your friends' Neurals have been shut down. So don't plan on forwarding this conversation to anyone. It never happened."

Matt felt numb. He didn't know what to do next. When it came to strategizing, he couldn't match his father. He watched Eric stride off toward his seat in the first row at midfield.

His body warmed the moment he saw Sophie in DC3's tent. She smothered him, her fragrance refilling the emotional tank his father had just emptied. "You shouldn't have come back."

"I had to."

David was in the tent with the team. "Why? You couldn't figure out how to operate the Ball without me?"

Matt's index finger sprang up to his mouth.

Bobby said, "Don't worry about it." He pointed to his belt. "They may have shut down our Neurals, but Rich still had one trick up his sleeve."

Matt smiled.

David asked, "Where's the Ball?"

"Hidden. Any chance you've figured it out?"

"Not yet."

"You will."

For the first time, he noticed the rest of DC3 was standing next to Sophie and Bobby, listening in. They obviously knew what was going on by now and what was at stake. Matt said, "When the moment's right, we'll make a break for it. Oh, and we're supposed to lose the game."

Bobby asked the obvious question. "Why?"

"Because my father told us to." Matt ran his fingers through his hair. "And the clues said we had to get to the end, which we've done. But…I don't feel much like doing what he says these days."

The team stacked their hands and then broke them upward. "For Rich," they shouted as one. "One-two-DC3!"

Matt stepped into the center of the huddle and looked around from teammate to teammate. "No matter what happens today, it's been an honor to play with each of you this year."

Jimmy said, "Matt, the honor's been all ours."

The game wasn't scheduled to start until 8:30 P.M. Matt sat quietly with Sophie, David, and Bobby, discussing his mother's Disc and his fear that he might be just like his father.

"You're nothing like your father. You *may* have inherited the physical attributes, but you can distinguish right from wrong. He lost that ability eighteen years ago," Sophie said.

Having calmed Matt's nerves on the subject, they moved on to another topic—what his mother had been about to say when Eric once again stole her away from him. It could have been almost anything, from discussing people he had killed, to his other co-conspirators, to her mission for the Circle, to how to operate the Ball. They agreed they needed first to focus on a plan of escape.

While Sophie and Bobby brainstormed, Matt turned to David to discuss the Ball. Each solution seemed less likely than the last. After exhausting the possibilities in his mind, Matt asked David, "Have you ever read the book *The Prince*?"

"Yes. With your expertise in government, I'm surprised you haven't."

"Why? What's it about?"

"It was written by Niccolo Machiavelli in 1513. It's a political strategy book about the best ways for a prince to gain and keep power. Why do you ask?"

"On the Disc my mother gave me, my father was holding the book after he had changed."

"Based on what we know, that doesn't surprise me. The book subscribes to the idea that the ends justify the means."

Matt contemplated this for a moment and considered Rich's and the geneticists' deaths. "Morality be damned?"

"Exactly."

"It's interesting my father never mentions that philosophy."

"Actually, he does. Remember some of his lessons you discussed with me and Rich?" Matt nodded. "Like about impressing the military with your prowess in comBATON?"

"Yes—you think those were from that book?"

"I don't think so. I know so."

"I guess," Matt said, smiling a little, "that even though I never got my mother's intended message, I did get a message from her."

"Maybe it was intended."

Others on DC3 took turns periodically looking outside the tent. Each time, they saw the same menacing IDs with their rifles. Sophie and Bobby agreed there would be no escape before the game.

With four hours to go before Matt had to activate the Ball, the teams took the field, warmed up, and lined up on the sideline. Matt listened to the national anthem and the teams' introduction songs, but the energy that used to course through him was absent, replaced by hollowness. It was as if nothing good had ever existed.

He jogged onto the field and passed Rex, who said, "Maybe I'll get another chance to bloody my knuckles."

An image of Rex beating a defenseless Rich flashed into Matt's head. Unable to control himself, Matt transformed into a wild animal. An unrecognizable guttural cry issued forth through his clenched teeth as he pounced on Rex, landing a right cross to the eye. Matt stood over Rex, who lay on his backside, holding his eye and sporting a wide grin.

Commissioner Turnbull yelled, "Penalty!" Regaining his sanity, Matt couldn't believe what he'd done. Still, what would the penalty be? They hadn't even started the game. Commissioner Turnbull wore a Neural stare as he walked to the center of the field. "Matthew Cane has been suspended for the first half."

That was one way to lose. Matt glanced at his dejected teammates. Sophie's slack expression spoke for the rest of the team. How could he have taken the bait? He looked at his smirking father, who'd likely set it up for him. Then he saw Mrs. Peterson, who sat handcuffed near his father. Unlike so many others in the community sitting nearby, who hung their heads, she stared back at Matt and offered a small nod.

The cold breeze seemed amplified as Matt witnessed the brutality of the first half from the sideline. All he could do was yell at the commissioner for each illegal shot. Jimmy and Bobby took the worst of it. Rex landed a cross to Jimmy's cheek and Nick struck Bobby with illegal kicks to his back. Unlike in the semifinals, this time the IDs didn't even try to hide their cheap shots. In fact, with every strike Rex offered Matt a sneer. Near the end of the half, Rex jogged by Matt. "Don't worry, Cane. I'll save a few for you."

Matt growled, "In the second half, you're mine."

Sophie avoided the minefield of fists and feet and even engineered a scoring drive that ended in a three-point goal by Jimmy. Despite the effort, DC3 limped back to their tent trailing 15-3.

Matt addressed the team. "I'm sorry for losing it."

Bobby said, "I bet it felt good."

"Not as good as you'd think." Matt managed a little smile, then his face turned to steel. "We'll get them in the second half."

Sophie and the others smiled.

Matt said, "Did you notice how dead the crowd is right now?" They all nodded. "Our only hope is to create a huge celebration in the middle of the field. That won't happen if the Raiders win. But if we win, we might have a chance to escape."

Jimmy said, "But the Raiders haven't given up 15 points all season."

"Yet," Bobby responded.

Matt said, "That's what I'm talking about. Huddle up. This is how we're going to win." He laid out a simple game plan that would focus on the strengths of each of them: Bobby's power, Sophie's speed and instincts, and Matt's ability to read the defense and jump. After they went through the plan, Matt called David into the huddle. "You too, David."

Everyone put their hands in and yelled, "One-two-DC3!"

They broke the huddle, Matt's focus as clear as ever. With the team headed for the line up, Matt said, "Soph, go ahead and lead them out. I'll be there in a minute."

When only Matt and David remained in the tent, Matt told him where to find the hidden pack.

"Why are you telling me?"

"Because you may be able to sneak away more easily than the rest of us. If anything happens to us, get to the Ball, make it work for you, and get that picture to my mother."

The color drained from David's face. "I don't think it works like that."

Matt turned to leave. But Kevin stepped through the tent entrance.

Matt said, "I think you're in the wrong tent."

"No, I'm not. I won't take much of your time, but we need to talk… in private."

David began to leave, but Matt placed a hand on his shoulder. "Anything you have to say to me, you can say to both of us."

Ready for the second half and everything else to come, Matt strode back to the sideline. Rex greeted him with his sneer. "Glad to see you back, Cane. I was worried you'd chicken out."

Matt ignored the insult and huddled with his team. He only had one statement. "Now's our time."

Matt started the second half with an amazing cut that brought Nick Rounds to his knees. Bobby and Sophie got in the way of the other defenders and Matt galloped to the goal for a five-point jumping back side kick. His teammates responded with a combination of smothering defense. They intercepted the baton and Sophie scored on an acrobatic jumping back swing kick. Rex and his teammates were out of words and out of breath. The crowd, on the other hand, sounded like they'd just arrived. They screamed and cheered.

With less than three minutes remaining, the Raiders held the Baton and a 15-13 lead. Rex grinned as he and his teammates began to chew up the remaining clock. "Looks like you're out of time, Cane."

Matt called a time-out and, with a glance at Sophie, knew what they had to do. "We need to let them get down the field or we'll run out of time."

Sophie asked, "What are you thinking?"

"Remember the code on the back of the picture?"

"Yes."

"What were the first four numbers that we didn't understand?"

"1918," Bobby said. "That's a dangerous game, Matt. You want to let them score, but to make sure it's only 3 points."

"Right. We'll have time to counter and tie the score. It'll work. I know that's what we're supposed to do."

Bobby said, "You're the captain."

Sophie nodded.

On the next play, Bobby let Nick Rounds by him. Nick rambled all the way to the goal zone, where Matt stopped him with a roundhouse to the chest. Rex's grin widened.

Matt jogged back to Sophie and Bobby, "Okay—Bobby, defend like you did in the first half so they have no choice but to go for the quick three."

They nodded.

On the next play, Bobby clogged the middle. He didn't see Nick's attack from the side. With Bobby on his back and out of the way, Rex had a clear path to the goal and an easy four-pointer that would effectively end the game. But Sophie quickly dove in Rex's path. Rex half-growled, half-laughed as he landed a pushing kick that knocked her to the ground. Her diversion gave Matt more than enough time to recover, get in Rex's way, and force Rex to settle for three points with a quick front kick to the goal.

"It's over, Cane," Rex shouted.

Matt ignored him and jogged back to the huddle. "Sorry. You okay, Soph?"

"No big deal. It worked. What's next?"

"We have time for two plays," Matt said. "Soph, on the opening attack, take your defender long, like we're trying to score in one play."

"Okay."

"Bobby, I'll get you the pass. Get as close to the goal zone as you can."

"Got it."

The play worked as Matt had drawn it up. Nick stopped Bobby midway between the midfield line and the goal zone.

Matt called their last time-out and the team regrouped. "Anyone tired?"

They chorused, "No."

"Okay, this is our last chance. With the little time we have left, they'll probably be in a man defense so we don't slip through their zone again. Can both of you take down your opponents?"

Each replied, "Yes."

"Good. Draw your defenders toward the goal so they think they're covering you and making it impossible for me to pass."

Bobby smiled and said, "And we know what to do from there."

Matt approached the line of scrimmage and the crowd went wild. Everyone was on their feet. Sophie and Bobby ran to opposite ends of the line of scrimmage and Matt yelled, "Go!" His teammates bolted toward the goal.

With less than thirty seconds left, Matt held the Baton at midfield, Rex standing in his way. Matt scrambled back and forth, looking up field.

Rex snarled, "Nowhere to turn, Cane." The clock reached 11 seconds.

Matt faked like he was going to try to run around Rex and score from the side. In midstride, Matt spun into a jumping back side kick to Rex's chest and ran over his fallen opponent.

Rex's teammates looked back toward him, and Sophie and Bobby each landed double roundhouse kicks to their chests. This gave them the right to take their opponent to the ground, which they did. They grappled with the downed Raiders and rolled over at the last second so their opponent was on top. Matt didn't have time to run around the obstacles and, with a feeling of invincibility, he accelerated toward the mass of downed bodies. Matt felt the tingling of energy flood his body as he jumped off one Raider's back onto the other's, then leaped toward the goal. He seemed to fly the last ten feet, spinning into a tornado roundhouse and tying the score at 18 as time expired. The crowd erupted.

The team went wild. "Way to fly, Superman," Bobby said.

Eric growled orders to the IDs surrounding the field and they shot their rifles into the air. The weapons were some sort of laser rifles that shot red sparks. They produced no sound, but had the intended effect. The crowd fell silent.

Once again, it seemed Eric was several steps ahead. Matt decided he would let events play out.

Commissioner Turnbull called DC3 and the Raiders to midfield and explained the overtime rules. Each starter on each team would have one opportunity to try to score a point in a one-on-one sparring match with an opponent. The first team with two points would be the champion.

Rex held up his hand to stop the Commissioner. He spoke through his sneer. "Cane, let's make this a bit more interesting. Let's decide this with one old-fashioned sparring match. No protective gear, no light contact. One rule: the first one knocked unconscious loses."

"This is a team decision," Matt said.

"Go ahead. Huddle with your little friends and ask permission." Rex scanned the perimeter of the field and added, "But hurry back. We don't have all night."

Matt no longer cared about Rex's ridiculous insults. He turned and met with his team about twenty yards away from midfield.

Bobby said, "I don't think you should accept Rex's challenge. He's the best fighter around. You're pretty good, Matt, but I'm not sure you can take him."

Matt said, "Don't worry about that. We all have a job to do." Matt turned to David, who had joined them. "Did you figure out how to make it work?"

"Yes," he said, bouncing from foot to foot. "At least I think so."

Everyone on the team leaned in.

Matt said, "Great. What is it?"

"It's inside you."

Everyone's wide-eyed expressions matched Matt's.

"What do you mean? What's inside me?"

"Adrenalin. A lot of adrenalin."

"So. Everyone has that."

"I don't think anyone has as much as you have, except your father."

Matt asked, "How'd you come to that?"

"Seeing your reaction in the tent made me start thinking. And watching you play the second half confirmed the tests I ran before the second half. Your adrenal gland is twice the normal size and your cardiovascular and pulmonary systems are stronger than any I've ever seen."

Matt said, "I don't understand."

David asked, "Do you remember one of the clues said you would have what you needed inside yourself?"

"Yes, but I thought that meant for me to think about what's important."

Sophie said, "It was. But it must be literal, too."

David continued, "Yes. Your body can produce and tolerate an amount of adrenalin that's off the charts. There's also some chemical in your blood I've never seen. It could have something to do with your energy levels, too. The clues must have said to make the finals so you would fully realize your abilities and be able to start the Ball."

Sophie nodded. "I thought you flew last week. But what you did tonight was amazing. Your speed was unreal. And I think you could have scored from another ten feet away."

Matt knew there had been something special going on in the second half. But though David's news had revved up his heart rate, there was no time to fully process his strange physicality. "How does this extra energy start the Ball?"

David said, "Energy transference."

"What?" Matt asked.

David asked, "Sophie, I bet you think Matt's a great kisser?"

Her cheeks flushed. "What are you talking about, David?"

Matt thought this was an odd line of inquiry, but waited for her answer.

Sophie said, "Okay, not that it's your business, but yes. Even though I've never kissed anyone else, I know he is."

"Do you feel a surge of energy when he kisses you?"

"Yes."

David said, "Energy transference. I believe that you produce so much energy, you can conduct it through your skin to the biometric scanner, which also serves as a conductor."

Matt exhaled at the thought they might finally have a solution. Before he could answer David, everyone looked behind Matt. Each DC3 member stood tall, arms crossed, at the new figure in their midst.

Richard Sr. tapped Matt on the shoulder. "Put this in your pocket."

Matt pocketed the Disc he'd been handed. He felt the heat emanating from the rest of the team. "I don't have time to explain, but we can trust him. And at this point, we don't have a choice." He turned to his friend's father. "What are you doing here?"

"The president convinced me to remind you of his offer."

Matt said, "I suppose as soon as this is over, we're all going to be detained."

Richard eyed everyone, then lowered his head. "Actually, I think they plan to execute you. All of you. Even you, Matthew. They plan to keep one of you alive long enough to lead them to the time machine."

Shoulders and jaws dropped.

But not Matt's.

"We just need to find a way to get out of here and to the Ball. I'll take out Rex. From there, we need a plan to get through my father and the ID."

"The moment one of you makes a move to leave, they'll shut off the lights. The IDs will put on their night-vision goggles and begin firing. The president intends to end all possible insurrection tonight."

They all stared at Matt. "I wish I could tell you I know how to stop laser rifles with my bare hands. I don't. I've never even seen them used until a few minutes ago. But right now, that doesn't matter. After we win, everyone try to stay together and get to the lab. We can use the tunnel to sneak away. If we get separated, get there any way you can." Matt looked around. David trembled. Bobby and the others were wide eyed with fear. But Sophie stood steady.

He eyed each of them. "We'll get through this." His gaze settled on Sophie.

Sophie said, "I know we will. And I love you, too."

Matt's face broke into the largest smile imaginable. Continuing to look into Sophie's sparkling eyes, he said, "Energy transference. Let's see if David's right." He crossed the huddle and interlocked his fingers in hers. Their palms connected. Still smiling, he yanked her tight and softly touched his lips to hers. The power radiated from his head to his toes.

Her body shuddered. She stepped back and leaned over with a gasp. She raised her head with a smile. "David's right."

Everyone in the huddle laughed.

Matt shook his head to regain his focus. "Before I go finish Rex and we get out of here, I've got some new information." He smiled at Richard. "Your son's alive." He looked around at everyone. "Rich is alive.

For his own protection, I don't know where he is, and I won't tell you who's helping him. But he's alive." Matt briefly thought a *thank you* to Rich's savior, Kevin, who had revealed his deed in the tent at halftime.

Richard seemed about to faint, but his smile radiated through the hand that had shot to his mouth. Everyone else stood tall in excitement and relief. Feeling the hope return to his team, Matt finished, "I know they think they can easily defeat us. But they don't know who they're dealing with. We will complete the mission. For Rich."

They threw their fists in the air. "For Rich!"

Matt turned and marched to midfield with his team, Richard, and David following close behind.

Rex said, "It's about time. So, what's it gonna be?"

Matt removed his gear, his eyes never leaving Rex's.

"Excellent. Time to end you, little Cane."

Matt looked back at Sophie and received the boost he sought.

The commissioner dropped his hand and yelled, "Start." Matt switched to a back stance, inviting an attack. Rex stormed in, checked like he was going to kick, then threw a right hook toward the same cheek where Eric had connected just a week earlier.

With a flick of his arm, Matt blocked the punch, then stepped back. "Come on," he snarled.

Rex rushed in and double punched at Matt's gut. In one motion, Matt's arms blocked the punches and continued forward into a double palm strike to Rex's chest. Rex stumbled backwards, holding his ribs.

Matt smiled at his opponent, who charged in with a series of quick strikes. Matt blocked every fist, elbow, knee, and foot, finally landing a side kick to Rex's stomach and backing up.

Rex attempted to land a speed side kick of his own. Matt caught Rex's leg in his left arm and landed a right hook to the side of Rex's knee, dislocating it. Following with a knifehand strike to Rex's throat, Matt sent him reeling to the ground.

He writhed in pain and gasped for air.

Matt kneeled next to him and growled, "Stay out of our way." Matt then stood up and crashed back down with a hammerfist to Rex's uninjured eye, knocking him unconscious.

The crowd erupted. The commissioner announced, "And our new—"

A loud explosion erupted in the direction of the Capitol. Matt couldn't hear anything other than the deafening sound ringing in his ears. His head spun toward the Capitol, where a fireball rose and pieces of the RM Monument flew in every direction. He motioned for the team to move, but David just lay on the ground and screamed, his fingers in his ears. Matt pulled David to his feet and began to run.

They had barely taken a few steps before the lights went out. Red sparks flew toward Matt from Eric's direction. He didn't have enough time to react. But Richard did, jumping in front of Matt at the last second. The sparks disappeared into his abdomen and he fell to the ground, dead.

Everyone else scattered, except Bobby, Sophie, David, and Jimmy, who surrounded Matt.

Matt braced for the inevitable volley of fire. But it never came.

The moon shone through a narrow thinning in the blanket of clouds, providing enough light for Matt to see several members of the ID attempting to fire their weapons. But nothing was coming out.

He didn't wait to find out why. He yelled to his team.

"Go!"

RACE TO FREEDOM

[SUNDAY, DECEMBER 6, 2037, 9:47 P.M.]

A melee broke out all over the field. It was hard to make out who was fighting whom.

Matt and Bobby easily subdued the two IDs blocking their escape. After a futile attempt to try to activate their Magnometers, the team ran for it.

They entered the Botanic Garden and looked back. Seeing no pursuers, they sped into the rainforest area, flew down the ladder, and pulled the secret door closed.

They all remained quiet for a minute and listened in the dark.

Matt said, "I don't think we were followed."

"Why won't the automatic lights turn on?" Sophie asked.

His fingers still in his ears, David shouted, "I think someone's firing an EMP."

Matt asked, "How'd you get that?"

"I can't figure out any other logical reason why everything electrical isn't working. First the laser rifles, then the gliders, and now the lights."

Sophie said, "Hold on." She turned a stool on its side and axe kicked it to pieces. With the others' help, she used the lab equipment to fashion several torches.

By the light of the first torch, Matt saw Jimmy. "You shouldn't have come with us. You're risking your life."

"I don't completely know what's going on, but I'm with you no matter what."

Matt smiled at him.

"What is this place?"

Bobby said, "Don't worry about that right now. We need a plan to get to the Ball. We've got less than two hours."

Matt said, "Right. Let's use the tunnels. Maybe we can get to it without being noticed." Matt paused, then a hand shot to his mouth. "David, do you think the EMP affected the Ball?"

"Don't worry. It's made of the same protective metal as the walls of RM City, which blocks electrical interference. Rich took some metal from an inner wall of a room near a secret entrance."

Matt's hand dropped and he exhaled. "Good. For a minute, I thought this was going to be difficult."

Everyone laughed.

David finally pulled his fingers out of his ears. "It may be a little easier than you think." He walked over to a table on the far side of the room and opened a box. "Remember Sophie and I told our parents we had a private experiment in here?"

Matt nodded at the thought of the empty box.

"I did." He pulled out a baton, walked over, and said, "Matt, hold this in your right hand until you're ready to activate it."

Matt grabbed the baton in his right hand. It looked just as smooth and felt just as light as the ones they used in comBATON. "Is this—"

"Yes, it's a time machine. Rich and I argued about me going off the schematics, but after the test you told me to trust myself."

Matt smiled. "I did."

"Besides, didn't the clue say to achieve the beginning with the Ball, you have to reach the end with the Baton?"

"Yes."

"Like so many of the clues, I figured this clue had a double meaning. Reach the championship game and—"

"Make a time machine out of a Baton," Sophie said.

"Exactly."

"But what about the Ball part of the clue?" Bobby asked.

"I think it means a Ball is being used to open the wormhole on the other end, at the beginning. Not only is this an improved model, but even your father won't know it's a time machine."

Jimmy said, "I still don't know what's going on, but if you're supposed to use a time machine, just do it."

"We can't," Bobby said. "If Matt sets it off here, the effects will spread and everyone but Matt might be pulled into a wormhole to nowhere."

Jimmy's mouth dropped open.

Sophie said, "We have to get this to RM City. Matt can set it off safely from inside. David, do you think the IDs' Neurals are fried?"

Everyone turned to David. "Even though the implants are made from the same metal as the Ball and the Baton, the Neural Network server isn't. It should be fried."

Matt said, "I suppose that helps even things a little. Okay, let's get moving."

Sophie placed a hand on Matt's shoulder. "Wait. Just in case this is the last time we have to talk—"

Matt said, "I know. I feel the same way."

"That's great, but I was going to talk about what we just saw."

Matt flushed. "Oh."

"All those months of investigation can't compare to actually watching the civil war out there, even if it was mostly in the dark. Who did you see fighting your father and the ID?"

"I didn't see anyone. I just saw it as our chance to escape."

Bobby's head sunk. "Me, too."

Sophie said, "Then you didn't see Mrs. Peterson take down the Enforcer with a leg sweep and a knifehand strike to the neck."

Matt smiled. "No. I guess that confirms she's on our side. Did you see anyone else?"

She said, "I saw Dr. McCurie and Commissioner Turnbull fighting ID. I also saw the vice president grappling with Nick. He wasn't doing bad for his age."

David's hands shot to his hips. "I saw Mom and Dad take out a few IDs."

Sophie smiled with pride.

"Good. Anyone else?"

Jimmy said, "I saw Dr. Farmer run away."

Matt shook his head. "Disappointing, but useful." He looked around and waited for any further intelligence reports. "All right. If that's it, let's get going. It's too risky to go back out to the Mall and try to get to the Smithsonian entrance to RM City. It'll be easier to get in through the Capital One Center entrance in Chinatown."

Matt started toward the tunnel, but stumbled into a table. It felt as if his turbines had suddenly turned off.

"Are you okay?" Bobby asked.

He propped himself up with one hand and held his foggy head with the other. "Yeah."

Sophie rushed to him. "What's wrong?"

"I don't know. I'm...exhausted. Maybe...my body just realized everything that's happened since Thanksgiving."

David said, "That may have something to do with it, but it's probably because of all of the adrenalin you used tonight. It's typical to have a rush of energy, followed by a depletion of energy."

Matt asked, "What? But I have to activate the Baton in the next couple of hours."

"Yes. And because your energy peak is greater than anyone else's, your energy low might be greater than anyone else's, too."

Everyone stared anxiously at their leader. He had the same concern—he might have used the needed energy for the Baton on something as trivial as a game. Realizing they needed him to be strong, he said, "One thing at a time. We've got to get to RM City. We can worry about my chemical levels later."

Sophie helped him over to the entrance to the tunnel, where he stopped her.

Sophie asked, "What's the matter?"

"Do you think the tunnel's going to explode when the flames from these torches hit all that sewer gas?" He smiled as he finished the question.

She slapped him on the back. "That's not funny. I thought you were about to pass out or something."

"Sorry, just trying to lighten the mood. Rich isn't here and we needed a corny joke to break the tension. Let's go."

Despite the foul stench in the sewer, despite everything else they'd been through, and despite the gravity of their final task, Matt relaxed into step with the beautiful woman beside him. "It seems like I've been saying goodbye a lot lately."

She smiled. "You're not going to be able to get rid of me."

Matt returned the smile, but as he looked at her, he could not prevent a few tears from trickling out of his bloodshot eyes. "I wish that were true. If it works, I could change the past in ways we don't want. What if I do something that causes you to get hurt or die or to not be born?"

"There are all kinds of possibilities in this world. But I know no matter what happens, I will always exist here." One hand pressed into Matt's chest. With the other, she placed a Disc in his hand.

"What's this?"

"You think Richard's the only one who can give you something to help you in the past?"

"What's on it?"

"You'll see."

He kissed her on the lips.

"Just promise me one thing."

"Anything."

"Do whatever you have to do when you get back there." He nodded in understanding. Her hand still on his chest, she stared him down. "I mean it. No matter what it is."

"But," he began, but stopped short at the sight of the torch fire dancing in her eyes. "I promise." They continued on their way in silence, his arm over her shoulder.

Even without their gliders, the team quickly reached the exit point just north of Union Station. They extinguished the torches and Bobby helped Matt up into the chilly night. Once they were all out, Bobby said, "We're about a mile away. We don't have time to walk. Matt, are you up to running?"

"I think so."

Matt jogged as fast as he could. They ran through the weed-filled streets past block after block of empty buildings and abandoned vehicles. Matt nearly heaved several times, but in minutes they neared their destination. A couple of blocks away from the Chinatown Metro entrance, Matt stopped to catch his breath. "We need…to be more careful now." He looked around. They were alone. "Wait a minute." He reached into a garbage can, pulled out the pack, and felt metal.

Bobby asked, "What's in there?"

"David's not the only one who hides time machines in strange places."

"You hid the Ball here?" Sophie asked.

"I wasn't sure we'd have enough time to get back to the cottage. I guess we think alike."

She smiled.

He pulled the Baton out of his belt and dropped it in the bag, the metal from the time machines clunking together. "You guys need to get out of here."

"We're not going anywhere until you're inside," Bobby said. Everyone else stood with Bobby and nodded.

Matt wanted them out of there, but he didn't have time to argue. "Fine. As soon as I get inside, get as far away as possible. Hopefully, within an hour, everything will have changed."

They neared the escalator down to the Metro, where Matt realized they were not as alone as he had thought. Fifteen IDs approached from the street and trapped them, the entrance down to RM City at their backs. "Eric's waiting inside," one of them said. "We were a little surprised to see you on the monitor. Thanks for making this easy for us."

David whispered to Matt, "It looks like the EMP didn't affect the electronics in RM City."

Another ID said, "Let's go."

Matt asked, "Where?"

"Down there," the ID said, motioning toward the subway.

Matt held the pack tight, hoping they didn't know about the time machines. He whispered to his team, "There's too many of them and we can't risk damaging these. I'm sorry you'll be down there when I set the thing off."

David whispered, "We wouldn't be anywhere else."

Matt said to the ID, "Okay, let's go."

They descended the non-operating escalators into the dark Metro, Matt holding onto Sophie's shoulder to avoid stumbling. When they reached the bottom, one of the ID ordered Bobby to open a door that led to a dark staircase. A couple of flights down, Matt asked, "So, what does the president have planned?"

The chuckle he received in response didn't faze him. He was just pleased they hadn't taken his pack. Either Eric hadn't seen it on the monitor or he had not told them to confiscate it.

When they reached the bottom, one of the IDs slipped past them, opened a door, and ushered them through. Matt had heard about RM City his entire life, but this was his first visit. His father had said the RMs could honor those lost in the Storm best by staying above ground.

Now Matt knew the real reason his father didn't want anyone to go there. From what Richard Sr. told Matt about Rich's interrogation in RM City, Matt knew that his father now used this once vibrant underground city as his personal torture chamber.

The warm, stale air, and greying walls did not minimize Matt's awe. Even in the dimly lit extremities of the room, he could see this space dwarfed the Great Hall. It reached four stories high and stretched a couple of hundred yards. Dozens of smooth concrete columns ran along either side. A several-story high, aged painting of the original Project RM logo—with a slightly less muscular Vitruvian Man than the current logo and without the insignia above the man's head—adorned one of the walls. Another Project RM logo mirrored the original from the opposite wall—this one with a woman in the circle. Matt hadn't seen that one before. He guessed Eric had something to do with that.

At the center of the room, a bright fluorescent light accented what must have been a majestic sight years earlier—a decaying tree with thin and thick trunks strung together to form one large trunk. The broad, bare branches twisted three-quarters of the way to the ceiling.

Shockingly, it seemed like almost everyone in the community was inside. Many were tied up along the wall below the painting of the Renaissance woman. How could he set off one of the machines with almost every last human in harm's way?

The IDs escorted Matt and his friends to the base of the tree, where Eric waited.

The IDs encircled them and Eric spoke calmly. "You were a little lucky earlier. But your luck has run out. I appreciate you saving me the trouble of hunting you down, Matthew. And if I'm not mistaken, you have your little machine with you." He grabbed the pack from Matt and gestured around the hall. "You can see that we don't need weapons to maintain control." He pulled the Baton from the pack and tossed it to Jimmy. "Keeping mementos of your short-lived championship. Cute."

Matt couldn't keep the corners of his lips from curling a little.

"Proud, are you? Maybe you won't be so happy after I do this." He pulled the Ball from the bag, tossed the bag back at Matt, and smashed the Ball against the ground. Pieces splintered everywhere. "What do you have to say now?"

Matt pulled the pack onto his shoulders. "You were right," he said, causing his father to flinch. "ComBATON is more than a game. Go."

One of the IDs turned and knocked out another. It was Kevin.

Each member of Matt's team attempted to subdue the other agents. Matt dropped to his knees, punched an approaching agent in the crotch, and followed with an uppercut to the jaw. Bobby knocked out two more with one swing kick across their faces. Sophie fell to the ground and kicked up into the jaw of an oncoming agent. Matt and Bobby turned to help David and saw him land a series of hand strikes to an oncoming ID, finishing him off with an elbow to the temple. Matt stood in shock for a moment, then stumbled to the ground, lightheaded.

More agents streamed into the room, along with many RMs who supported Eric. Greatly outnumbered, Matt wasn't sure if he would be able to get away in time to activate the Baton.

In his peripheral vision, Matt noticed movement. The RMs and others against the wall were no longer bound. Mrs. Peterson, Sophie's parents, and the others rushed the ID.

Matt began to break for an exit when Eric grabbed him from behind. "Ready for round three?"

Bobby stepped in and engaged Eric. "Get out of here," he yelled at Matt.

Matt, Sophie, and David ran toward the other end of the hall.

Jimmy yelled, "Catch," and threw the Baton in a perfect strike at Sophie.

She caught it on the run and shoved it in the bag.

About to turn the corner, Matt saw the IDs and Eric's supporters overwhelm Bobby and the others.

Kevin yelled, "Everyone's inside," signaling to Matt that, after saving Rich's life, this is where he hid Rich.

They started down a long corridor as stark as the hall, the lights flickering on as they ran. It seemed strangely familiar. They reached the end of the passage, where two IDs grabbed Matt from behind. He stumbled back.

Sophie jumped and landed weak kicks at the chest of each one. Off balance, she was easily subdued. She yelled, "David, get him out of here."

David pushed Matt around the corner. "We don't have time to look back. Go."

Matt looked down the next long, dark hallway. "I know this place."

"How?"

"From my nightmares."

David stumbled. "That doesn't sound good."

"At least I know where to go."

They kept moving, and Matt was suddenly aware that he had to reach the room behind the large metal door. Somehow, he knew setting off the Baton anywhere else in RM City could kill every remaining person in the world. That thought, along with all of the running, just about finished him. He began to drop. David propped Matt up against a wall, pulled off his shoes and threw one down each of two nearby corridors. The lights in both hallways flickered on. He opened the door next to Matt, pulled him in, and closed the door. The lights turned on to reveal an almost empty studio apartment. David sat Matt on the one piece of furniture, an orange, cloth couch next to the door. "Are you okay?"

"Yeah, just give me a minute."

David looked around. "Okay, but no longer. You've got less than ten minutes left."

"Hey, where'd you learn to fight like that?"

"How do you think my sister got so good at comBATON?"

Matt smiled. "Let's go."

They stepped out of the apartment and two more IDs spotted them from the end of the hall in the direction from which David and Matt had come. David ran toward the agents to fight them off, yelling, "Complete the mission!"

Matt ran the other way. He realized he had entered the last stage of his nightmare. His terrifying memories guided him down the corridors.

Footsteps closed in behind him. Matt used what was left of his strength to make one last dash for the door. The last sprint seemed to take forever. The pounding feet of his pursuers grew louder.

Physically spent, his lungs burning, he reached it. He slammed his palm against the biometric scanner, pulled the door open, slid inside, and yanked the door shut. The lock clicked just before a body pounded the other side.

If he hadn't felt so empty, Matt would have been pleased it had ended differently than in his dreams. But he now had no adrenalin left to activate the Baton.

The lights burst on to reveal a large, metal chamber, with computers and other electronics lining the side walls. He pulled the Baton out of his pack just as a voice emanated from a PA system.

HOME STRETCH

[SUNDAY, DECEMBER 6, 2037, 11:57 P.M.]

"Turn on the video screen, Matthew."

Matt pressed the button.

Eric appeared just outside of the chamber, hands on his hips. "Good. It's about time you listened to me. If you open the door right now, this will end. Everything goes back to normal. But if you persist, you and your girlfriend will meet the same fate as your friend Richard and his father."

Matt heard the words, but felt nothing. He inspected the chamber and saw the walls, floor, and ceiling seemed to be made of the same metallic material as the Baton. He hoped this meant everyone else would be protected if he were able to activate it.

He reached behind his back, pulled the Baton out of the bag, and placed it in his left palm. And...nothing. Matt slid to the ground, laid the machine down, and stared at it.

Eric's scowl transformed into a sneer. He turned to an ID. "Bring her here." He turned back to Matt. "Tonight, you finally realized all of your abilities, which is why this current situation is such a disappointment. You're just like JP."

Matt remembered the Plan 40 file. He had wondered about the name. "Who's JP?"

"The uncle you never knew. Your mother's brother."

"Did you kill him…and her?"

"I didn't kill your mother. He killed her, along with himself and your friend Bobby's parents by involving them in a scheme not unlike yours."

Matt could not follow Eric's twisted logic.

"I fear that you and your friends are repeating history. How will you feel knowing you could have saved them? Bobby, David…and especially Sophie."

The heat began to rise in Matt's gut.

"She'll be here shortly. Maybe she can talk some sense into you."

"You have the ability to stop all of this. Why do you insist yours is the only way?"

"You don't know what it was like before the Storm. So I don't expect you to understand. The world was in chaos: terrorism and war everywhere. The structure humanity had depended on for millennia was quickly eroding. Because of its very structure, our government was incapable of functioning. Everything was always deadlocked."

"And you knew how to do it better?"

"Yes. Isn't the last sixteen years proof of that?"

"I used to think so. Now I know the truth. Look at what you're doing. You're risking humanity's existence."

"No. I'm saving humanity. I'm completing the RM mission. What I'm doing will guarantee humanity flourishes."

"By cloning only those you deem fit and removing anyone who isn't?"

Eric didn't respond.

"So, you've got your list. And you and Mom are at the top."

More silence.

"And then you plan to simply get rid of anyone who isn't worthy?"

"You need to understand. Humanity will always be on the brink of extinction unless we learn to work together in harmony. The last sixteen years are proof that we can. By carefully selecting the most fit and the most compatible, I'm speeding up the evolutionary process that would have occurred anyway and ensuring success."

"You sound as if you're happy the Storm happened."

"Considering I started it, yes."

Matt blinked. He couldn't have heard that right. "Wait, you…you started the Storm?"

"That's right, son. Now do you realize who you're dealing with?"

"Yes, sir, I believe I do." Matt's anger surged. He felt his body charging. "And I suppose you're not going to tell me how you did it?"

"No, I will." He exhaled, took a deep breath, and continued. "You kids are not as clever as you think. You certainly couldn't compare to the team that designed the real time machine. It took the most brilliant RMs years to build a prototype they thought would work. Convinced Joseph could stop an extinction-level event, the government supported the project with all of the required funding and secrecy. They didn't know I'd taken the research, which was nearing completion, and built a working prototype—well, almost. It would open a wormhole on only one end."

"You turned it into a death machine." Matt stood up. "I guess that's what Richard meant when he said it only has the power to kill."

"He would have known."

"What does that mean?"

"Enough of this. Bring Sophie here," Eric commanded. Matt's body burned with rage.

An agent appeared behind Eric. He had Sophie. Eric grabbed her arm. "Good. So how are we going to finish this?"

Matt looked into Sophie's eyes. Her smile triggered a surge of energy that flooded Matt's body. The clock on the video screen read 12:01 A.M.

He picked up the Baton, placed it in his left palm, and felt a shock. The taste of metal enveloped his mouth. A rushing noise filled the chamber. Within seconds, the room began to change. A large vortex opened just above him. It quickly grew bigger and stronger. As he was lifted off the ground, he realized he was not alone. A sharp pain stung his chest as a second vortex sucked in Lori. She reached out to him, her eyes wide, as she was pulled into a separate wormhole, a wormhole to nowhere.

Dark, silent, and quick. In his drained state, Matt saw and felt nothing. That is, until a tiny, distant light sped toward him. The closer it came, the more it grew, until it reached him and...he caught a glimpse of himself in it, like speeding by a mirror. As quickly as his reflection had approached, it sped away in the direction from which he'd come. The light shrunk to the size of a pinprick, and Matt refocused ahead.

Within seconds, another light approached—this one dimmer and broader. When he reached it, he floated out of the wormhole down into a dark chamber, the same one he'd just left—metal lined and computer filled. He dropped slowly, buoyed like a cushion by a deflating atmospheric bubble David had predicted might enter the wormhole with him. Softly, he landed on the cold, smooth floor. The time machine hadn't worked and might have killed Lori. *How did she get into the chamber?* Matt thought.

Nausea consumed him. He wondered how long it would take for them to come and get him. What had happened to Lori? Was Sophie safe? Were his friends already dead? The door creaked open. He barely had enough strength to lift his head. "Soph?"

Just before he slipped out of consciousness, a welcoming voice replied, "My brave son. I knew you could do it."

"Hurry, she's close," whispered an unfamiliar voice from above.

Matt's body jostled like a sack of flour being carried to the kitchen. Two arms wrapped around him from under his legs and back. He forced his eyelids up to see fluorescent lights passing by and the face of a familiar-looking stranger with a dark complexion. His vision cleared.

The stranger was carrying him back up the hallway down which he'd just run. Two women led the way. One was short, with a complexion that matched Matt's handler. The other was tall and thin, with fluttering, blonde hair.

"Mom?"

The women stopped and turned to him. The tall woman reached out, placed a slender finger over his mouth, and whispered, "Yes, son. Shhhh."

It was Zoe. The mother Matt knew only from cryptic messages uploaded to his Neural. The mother who had died years ago, or, Matt realized, the mother who hadn't yet died. His pulse raced.

"Hello. Is anyone here?" whined a familiar voice from around the corner.

"Franny—quick, in here," whispered his handler.

The other woman opened a door, ushered them in, and clicked the door closed.

The man laid Matt on a couch next to the door.

His mother leaned down and, this time, placed an index finger over her own mouth.

Matt whispered, "What? It's Mrs. Pet—"

His mother's hand rushed to cover his mouth. Her reddening face was enough to silence him. Matt's eyes darted around to his three companions. Why were they hiding from the one adult who openly defied his father? The one adult who'd always been there for him.

The whiny voice grew closer until it was just outside the door.

Franny whispered, "Will, what are you doing?"

Will reached for the doorknob. "I'm going to knock her out before she sees us."

Matt bolted up, but his mother pressed him back to the couch.

Will began to turn the knob, when a sweet voice arose from the other side of the door. "Hello, Liz."

"Sue. What are you doing down here?" Liz asked.

"I suppose I could ask you the same thing."

"I've been sent to investigate who's been coming down here. You know it's off limits. I'll ask once more. Why are you here?"

"You know my daughter's been sick. I'm going to my old apartment to get something I left behind."

"What, medicine?"

"Not exactly."

"Well, what?"

"I don't think that's any of your business."

"Well, we'll just let our esteemed judge decide. Come on, let's go."

Footsteps echoed beyond the door, growing softer and softer.

Franny whispered, "That little...I'd like to show her what's her business."

Matt shot back up from the couch. "What are you talking about? Without her, I wouldn't have made it here."

Will's eyebrows furrowed. "That woman's pure evil. She's secretly working with your father. If she'd found us, we'd be finished."

The room began to spin. Matt collapsed back to the couch, his head smacking the wall. He looked around at the three faces in front of him. "Who are you? Where am I?"

"Sweetie," his mother said as she massaged his head, "the question isn't where. You never left RM City. The question is when. It's June 2021."

Matt withdrew from her. "The Storm already happened."

Franny said, "Yes, last year."

"What am I doing here...in 2021?"

Will stepped in front of Matt. "You've got some unfinished business before you can jump the Storm."

Matt stared back at his mother.

"Son, you've chosen your path." She placed a hand under his chin and lifted his head. "We'll follow you down it and finish the mission. I believe in you." She looked back at Will and Franny. "*We* believe in you."

Matt looked around at his half-smiling new teammates. Settling his gaze on his mother, Matt reached over his shoulder and into the pack. One touch of the picture of Sophie.

"Okay. Let's go."

Free Digital Copy of *Project RM: Genesis*

Thank you for buying *Project Renaissance Man*. To receive a free digital copy of *Project RM: Genesis* (the first serial of the Project RM origin series), early access to new content, and bonus content, become an RM at https://projectrm.com/become-an-rm/.

Review

If you enjoyed *Project Renaissance Man, Project RM: Genesis,* or any other stories in the Project RM series, I'd really appreciate a short review. Your help in spreading the word is greatly appreciated and reviews make a huge difference to helping new readers find the books.